An advocate of mental health awareness, Omar is among the few that challenged the topic by writing his first book tackling mental health in the region. Growing up in a region where mental illness is still considered a taboo subject, he went against the grain and wrote a book that reveals realities that happen within an individual, suffering from mental issues in the form of a fictional story. The story is not only personal but reflects some issues that Omar himself has seen occur within his own environment. Among Omar's various interests, writing is his passion. He has written multiple short stories during his younger years and finally published his first book, *The Fall Queen*, at the age of 16. Omar hopes to write multiple sequels to his novel with the support of those around him that have never stopped encouraging him and believing in his initiative.

I would like to dedicate this to my mother and father who loved and supported me through all the hardships. To my two sisters for helping me grow into who I am today. To my late grandfather, for passing on his passion for literature onto me.

Omar Malkawi

THE FALL QUEEN

AUSTIN MACAULEY PUBLISHERS™
LONDON • CAMBRIDGE • NEW YORK • SHARJAH

Copyright © Omar Malkawi (2020)

The right of Omar Malkawi to be identified as author of this work has been asserted by him in accordance with Federal Law No. (7) of UAE, Year 2002, Concerning Copyrights and Neighboring Rights.

All rights reserved. No part of this publication may be reproduced, stored in a retrieval system, or transmitted in any form or by any means; electronic, mechanical, photocopying, recording, or otherwise, without the prior permission of the publishers.

Any person who commits any unauthorized act in relation to this publication may be liable to legal prosecution and civil claims for damages.

This is a work of fiction. Names, characters, businesses, places, events, locales, and incidents are either the products of the author's imagination or used in a fictitious manner. Any resemblance to actual persons, living or dead, or actual events is purely coincidental.

ISBN – 9789948345893 – (Paperback)
ISBN – 9789948345886 – (E-Book)

Application Number: MC-10-01-8775422
Age Classification: 13+

The age category suitable for the books' contents has been classified and defined in accordance to the Age Classification System issued by the National Media Council.

Printer Name: iPrint Global Ltd
Printer Address: Witchford, England

First Published (2020)
AUSTIN MACAULEY PUBLISHERS FZE
Sharjah Publishing City
P.O Box [519201]
Sharjah, UAE
www.austinmacauley.ae
+971 655 95 202

Prologue
Another Time, Another World, a Different Me

Winter Wonderland, Cataville, February 16th, 1988

Heartbreak. A tiny stupid shred of hope that was crushed, crumbled, squashed, and ripped apart. Mildred stood in front of Morina's door, unsure whether she should knock. It was a choice she had to make in her quest to find an answer to why all the time and effort she had dedicated was absolutely useless. Should she hold on to that final glimmer of hope that it was still possible? "No!" Mildred shook herself back to reality. She recalled the events of the previous night, when she had finally mustered up the strength to confess her love to Samuel. It was so difficult for her, as she had been preparing for this for months. She would come to Morina's place to work on a love spell she cast on Samuel, thinking that it was her only shot at finding a normal life and someone to accept her. But no, that didn't happen. Instead, all she got was heartbreak. Over and over and for the millionth time; she was devastated.

There she was, standing in front of the door that would give her an answer to the relapse she had endured. She was so anxious to get an explanation for her broken heart. As soon as the light cracked through her window curtain, she got out of bed. She had a sleepless night since all she had thought about was getting here. She put on sweatpants, a jacket, and a cloak to cover her entirely; her appearance was the least of her worries at this point. She bought her ticket and boarded the train as soon as she heard the announcement. Throughout her journey to Morina's house, she couldn't help but reminisce about all the memories she had made with Samuel. Flashbacks from January, when she took him to the train station in order to go to that garden that overlooked all of Winter Wonderland. The train journey was one full of pain, pain that provided no gain. Nothing but traces of memories that were painted black and white.

Mildred arrived at the complex where she was to see Morina. In a nutshell, Mildred was enraged that Morina's magic was not strong enough to help her, the cortisol levels in her brain were of no help in regard to the emotional malnourishment she was in. The princess finally rang Morina's doorbell after moments of hesitation.

"Good morning, Morina," the princess said in a calm but angry tone as soon as Morina opened the door.

"Good day, Your Highness. Are you alright?" Morina replied, questioning Mildred's outburst.

"I'm doing the best I can," Mildred replied, her voice breaking. Morina took Mildred into the magic room.

"What happened, dear Princess?" Morina asked.

"The spell didn't work; I finally professed my love to him, and the magic didn't work on him!" Mildred said, her voice breaking completely, her eyes tearing up.

"What! How did this happen?" Morina gasped, just as surprised.

"There must be an explanation, come to the magic room with me," Morina said, panicking. Mildred sat on the chair in the magic room and cried a bit. Morina performed a couple of spells that would uncover any obstacles that would have prevented the love spell from working. Morina performed a scanning spell on Samuel himself from afar and performed a scanning spell on the Jerram mansion.

"There seems to be no reason why the love spells aren't working when I scan Samuel and his mansion," Morina told Mildred.

"Is there anything else you can scan?" Mildred asked the witch, begging for an answer.

"I'll scan your school," Morina responded. The witch was true to her word, a sympathetic look on her face.

"I have the results," Morina said feeling sad. Mildred looked up after the long suspense.

"It's your school, there's a spell around it. There's a protective spell around your school; whoever enters it cannot have a spell cast upon them. Also, if a person who is under a spell enters the school, that spell will be weaker the more they stay at school until it's finally gone," Morina explained.

"Our spell was working that first month, between semesters. Our spells were very strong, they managed to keep Samuel in love with you throughout January. However, his love for you has decreased during January because of the protective spells around your school. By February, the protective spells have taken effect on Samuel completely. Any extra magic we have performed since the beginning of February, regardless of the dose, was absolutely useless. I'm sorry, Mildred," Morina explained.

Afterwards, although she did not care one little bit, Mildred asked Morina to give her back all of the jewels she paid to perform the magic. Morina gave back the jewelry, and Mildred left feeling very disappointed. She thought her suffering will never end.

Chapter One
A New Type of Weather

Winter Wonderland, Cataville, January 2nd, 1974

In a dim light blue room, a blonde woman lay in a hospital room sleeping peacefully, a man sat on the couch right next to the bed. The room lit up as a doctor walked in. A nurse came in after the doctor, each had a bassinet with a baby girl inside.

"Good morning, Your Highnesses!" the doctor said with a smile on his face. The woman and her husband woke up, slowly but elegantly.

"Good morning…" the woman said to the doctor.

"Our children, we would like to see them," the man firmly told the doctor in somewhat of a rude tone.

"Right away, Prince Maximus, Queen Annabella," the doctor shook slightly as he shrugged, the nurse walked both the bassinets to the queen's bed, one on each side.

Annabella reached for the baby from the bassinet to her right, a spark in her eye as the baby settled into her lap. The queen studied her baby daughter in her arms. Her daughter was an adorable baby, with a few wisps of platinum blonde hair on her head; so light, they were almost white. Her eyes were bluer than the bluest ocean, just like her mother's. The prince walked over to his wife's other side, he moved the bassinet that had the other baby in it. Maximus examined his baby daughter with uncertainty.

"Wow! Do you know who she looks like?" the prince asked his wife with an ugly sneer.

"Eliana… my great-great-grandmother! She has her freckles!" Annabella answered her husband, a condescending look on her face. Both the prince and queen laughed hysterically, which caused the nurse to roll her eyes and the doctor to feel even more terrified.

"Would you prefer to spend this moment alone?" the doctor asked, causing both royals to look at him and nurse with utmost contempt.

"If you must…" the queen answered rudely.

The doctor and nurse walked out of the room, one in fear, the other in disgust.

"Get our other daughter," the queen ordered her husband. Maximus lifted the other baby from the bassinet, not enjoying it at all. Their other baby was much taller than her twin but otherwise they were identical. A few drops of snow appeared out of the first baby's hands.

"Look! She has the family gift!" Annabella told her husband with excitement, bordering on hysterics.

"I'm going to call you Alaska, my darling!" she then said as she touched baby Alaska's nose. Their other daughter began wailing. When the prince and queen saw their baby cry, their unhidden repulsion toward her appeared on their faces.

"Quick, call the nurse…" the queen told her husband. Maximus rang the call button next to him. The nurse quickly entered the room and Maximus handed her the crying baby.

"Take her and figure out what she wants! Then return her to us and try not to take forever!" Annabella rudely told the nurse, her head held high.

"Alright, Your Highnesses," the nurse replied as she took the princess.

A few hours later, the queen and her husband got both their babies back and were able to leave the hospital. Annabella and Maximus walked out of the hospital, their guards walking beside them. They handed their second daughter to the guards. A white carriage pulled by decorated white horses stood in the usual deep snow. Everyone was dressed very heavily as they headed toward the carriage. The royals entered their carriage and took their other daughter from the guards, the guards rode beside the chauffer. The horses galloped through the road between the hills, through the winter park, down the hills, and under the bridge between frozen rivers through the icy cold secret woods.

Suddenly, a high wall with a great gate opened so the carriage could pass. Soon, they were in front of their old family castle.

Winter Wonderland, Cataville, January 8th, 1974

It had been almost a week since the birth of Princess Alaska and her sister. Queen Annabella and Prince Maximus sat gracefully on their thrones inside the enormous throne room, Princess Alaska sleeping peacefully in her father's arms. The other princess, having remained unnamed, lay in a cot at the end of the throne room. The walls in the throne room were beautifully painted, covered in amazing abstract and realistic art that left those who entered the room in awe. The stone floors were covered with royal carpets bluer than ice, there was a chandelier that had a great number of candles and there were many decorations giving the castle a striking look. A man in a suit stood at attention facing the monarchs.

"So, all your orders for Princess Alaska's ball have been sent out and should be done before the time of the ball tonight, will that be fine, Your Grace?" the man asked the queen specifically.

"Yes. You can go. Don't disturb us until dinner, Charles," Annabella replied quickly, shooing him with her hands.

"Of course, Your Grace," Charles replied with the calmest and most proper attitude, then he bowed and quickly walked away. The queen and her husband rolled their eyes making sounds of disgust and annoyance.

"He is very annoying and unpleasant; I can't believe he refused to pay for anything over ten-thousand Cateos for the ball. Such an appalling steward!" Annabella told her husband in an angry tone.

"I know! Just get rid of him and all these low-lives he works with!" Maximus rudely yelled.

"Talk to me properly! Never ever speak to me like that ever again!" Annabella scolded her husband.

"Sorry my darling, never again," Maximus said with his head down.

A young female royal servant mopping the floor overheard their conversation; she got up, took her cleaning supplies, and attempted to quickly walk towards the kitchen. But the queen's eyes caught her quickly.

"Where are you going? The floor is still dirty! I want it spotless tonight!" The queen called out to her with annoyance.

"I just wanted to go get more soap and water so I can continue cleaning the floor, Your Majesties, nothing more," the girl replied, terrified.

"Alright then! Do it quickly, and continue working or else I'll cut your salary!" Annabella answered angrily.

"At once! Of course!" she responded fast then walked out of the throne room faster than lightning. Both monarchs raised their heads as they looked at the girl leaving the throne room. The girl left the room and went to servant quarters; she hugged every one of the servants in the room. She told the other servants, including Charles, everything the queen and the prince had talked about.

"They are so materialistic!" A chef said, exhausted.

"They are very disrespectful and humiliating!" an old maid said, her face wrinkling in distaste.

"How ungrateful! Of course I am not going to pay ten thousand Cateos for party decorations, especially if I have to pay them from my own salary the way they force me to! I have been the nicest, most polite person to them for years, yet they still call me annoying and disgraceful!" Charles said calmly then rolled his eyes.

The day passed very slowly for everyone. Then night finally came. The castle was decorated with beautiful lights showing off its beauty. All the guests arrived at the castle and went into the ballroom. Annabella conjured up more snow outside, all over Winter Wonderland, enhancing its beauty.

The orchestra played a waltz as some guests danced, while others sat at the tables enjoying food from the royal buffet. During the course of the evening, all the guests went up to the princesses and played with them, causing the royals' faces to revert to their usual expressions of disgust. The unnamed princess hated the attention she received from the guests, and so red smoke that appeared out of the baby's hand spread through the ballroom and wilted plants with red, yellow, orange leaves and spiky stems tangled all the guests to the floor and continued to do so as she cried more and more.

"Witch! Witch! Our baby daughter is a witch!" Annabella backed away screaming.

"MILDRED! MILDRED, STOP!" Annabella yelled. New plants stopped forming after the queen yelled. It suddenly started raining autumn leaves in the ballroom but that did not last long. Plants that had been created by the baby princess still covered all the guests' bodies, ruining their formal clothes. The monarchs ordered the guards to cut the plants off of the guests with their swords. The guests left the castle as soon as they were freed from the plants, angry and unhappy looks on their faces as they went. One good thing did happen at the ball. The queen finally gave a name to her second baby, Mildred.

Chapter Two
Maximus's Parents

Winter Wonderland, Cataville, September 18th, 1979

Life for the royal family changed significantly following the incident at the ball. Annabella and her husband hated everything about the peculiar power that their daughter Mildred acquired. There was also another trait of Mildred's that her mother did not like; the fact that she did not develop any snow powers. It had been almost six years and the queen had not yet let her daughters meet her husband's family.

In the royal castle, the elder toddler princess Alaska sat on the floor of her elegant sky-blue master suite, her short blonde hair braided. She showed great interest in her toys as her freckles shone bright. Mildred slept on the bed in her bedroom, dressed while her parents got ready. Mildred looked exactly like her sister, but she was a lot taller. On the other side of the castle, Annabella and Maximus stood in their room arguing.

"They're my parents, Annabella! Why have you never let Alaska meet them?" Maximus angrily told his wife.

"And let them see that not only did one of them not get the family gift, but she is also unusually tall and has the wrong powers! We will be the laughingstock of that entire empire."

"Don't you dare speak of Mildred's height! You know she got her height from me!" Maximus argued. Annabella rolled her eyes at her husband, then gave him a look that made him feel no better than a speck of dust.

"It is important that our daughters meet their family, Annabella. What do you have against my family anyway?" Maximus asked his wife.

"What do I have against your family? More like what do they have against me, they never liked me. Your parents always thought I looked like a vampire and have always viewed me as a spoiled brat!" she replied in a most vicious tone.

Annabella and Maximus argued for hours and took forever to get ready. Annabella and Maximus both walked out of their room with their heads snobbishly held high. They walked through the west wing passing all the guest bedrooms and the four-story library, down to the throne room, then to the enormous eight-story ballroom, then upstairs, past the secret garden housing with the most beautiful and expensive trees and plants. Walking the long way through the castle, the prince and queen reached their daughters' bedrooms. The queen called out orders to the servants to carry their five-year-old daughters to the carriage. After another long walk through the castle, everyone was in the carriage.

"Blue and Shire mansion," the queen spoke to the driver in hidden rage. The carriage took off with the royal family inside.

The way to Maximus's parents' house was a long one, the shape of the mountains changed as the carriage left the area of the castle. The town square was visible in all its wonderous light and snow, and all the facilities and entertainment it provided. The trees were decorated with snowflakes, transforming them into Christmas trees. Inside the carriage, the queen and her husband were talking.

"Isn't Winter Wonderland wonderful?" Maximus said, trying to calm his wife down.

"Yes, it's nice," she replied with no emotion.

"Except it will be for that monkey in front of you, to ruin it with her no-good powers," Annabella remarked in a tone that mirrored her true emotions. A tree with autumn red and orange leaves could be seen outside the carriage. The queen and the prince eyed their daughter Mildred with disapproval as she used her powers. The prince then patted his other daughter on the head to show his appreciation. Mildred lowered her head in sadness.

It had been hours for everyone in that carriage. The family had left Winter Wonderland and were now in the center of Cataville. Half an hour later, the carriage arrived at the mansion where Maximus's parents lived. Maximus and the little princesses got down from the carriage and walked through the garden that Maximus had not seen in years. Annabella then left the carriage with her head held high as usual. They all went through the front garden and up the stairs to the front door of the mansion.

"Why hello, Your Majesties!" a young housekeeper said in greeting as she opened the door, but they did not answer.

"Lolita, are my parents inside?" Maximus asked the housekeeper.

"Yes, Duchess Mona Beth and Duke Marcellus are both inside," the housekeeper replied in her French accent as she curtsied. The four of them went inside the castle and sat in the white grand living room. The room was filled with white, expensive, and formal forties furniture, but the effect of all the furniture was vulgar. Annabella looked disgustingly around the room.

"I see they still have horrible taste," Annabella told her husband spitefully. Maximus rolled his eyes. A few moments later, a majestic woman elegantly came down the stairs, a graceful fifty-six-year old. She wore a very expensive but outmoded green dress. Her wrinkled face met the eyes of Annabella, but her motherly emotions and actions met Maximus's. Maximus stood up and so did the two princesses. The woman continued down the stairs and walked toward the prince.

"Mother!" Maximus said in happiness, welcoming his mother with an open heart.

"Maxi, my darling!" the middle-aged woman said excitedly, kissing each other's cheeks.

"Annabella," the prince's mother said as she saw her daughter-in-law. Annabella rolled her eyes and held her head higher.

"Mona Beth," she replied in a very demeaning tone. The little girls went up to their grandmother and each gave her a hug, despite having never seen her before.

"Are these my beautiful granddaughters?" Mona Beth said in excitement.

"Yes, they are, Mother," Maximus replied. The duchess sat down on her grand chair, she asked to let the two princesses sit on her lap. Princess Alaska went to sit on her grandmother's left leg. But Mildred looked at her grandmother very shyly, then saw her mother eye her, as if mocking her height. Mildred walked to her grandmother and sat on her right leg.

"Your father is in bed, my dear. He is not feeling well," Mona Beth told her son.

"Then I must go to him," Maximus said. Everyone except Annabella went upstairs to see Maximus' father. Mona Beth, Maximus, Alaska, and Mildred went to the bedroom of the duke and duchess.

"Marcellus, dear, you have guests," Mona Beth told him. A very tired old man lay in bed. He had reading glasses on and was wearing a robe. The man looked very old, even though he couldn't have been more than sixty-four.

"Why hello, my dear son," Marcellus said. He tried to move but was far too weak to do so.

"Stay my dear father," Maximus said as walked to the bed, then kissed his father's forehead.

"How are you doing?" he asked as he sat on the bed next to his father. Mona Beth carried the two princesses and placed them next to her husband, on each side of the bed.

"Are these your daughters, Maxi darling?" Marcellus asked weakly.

"Yes, Father, the one closer to you is Alaska," Maximus answered proudly.

"And the tall one is Mildred," he then answered with no emotion.

"Oh, aren't they precious?" the old man stated with a smile, getting a smile in response from both girls. Marcellus slowly moved both his arms and tickled his granddaughters. Alaska giggled with happiness.

"Oh, Grampa stop… stop," Alaska said laughingly, not truly wanting him to. Mildred laughed as well, but no one really paid as much attention to her as they did to Alaska.

Marcellus and Mona Beth laughed with their granddaughters for hours and had great fun. Maximus left the room as his parents played with his daughters. Down the long grand T-shaped stairs to the grand living room, he found his wife dancing to the music being played by the small orchestra in that room. Out of nowhere, Maximus walked to his wife and tried dancing with her. To his surprise, his wife immediately stopped dancing, tilting her head up. She saw Mona Beth watching them from over the bannister of the upper floor. Annabella was immediately repelled by her mother-in-law and walked to the kitchen, with even more arrogance than usual. Mona Beth went down the stairs to her son and hugged him.

"I'm so sorry, Maxi darling, I don't know why she does this," Mona Beth said. A tear fell down Maximus's face.

An hour later, Annabella and Maximus were sitting in the informal living room. Maximus's parents and daughters walked into the room, Mona Beth carried both the little princesses in her arms, and Marcellus sat in a wheelchair that a servant was pushing. Mona Beth sat on the couch next to her son, and Marcellus stayed next to one of the loveseats. Alaska and Mildred ran excitedly to a pile of gifts by the fireplace.

"It's not a holiday, why do you have gifts by the fireplace?" Annabella mocked her in-laws.

"Come on, Annabella, it may not be a holiday, but we never met our granddaughters before today, we should have gifts for them," Marcellus and Mona Beth said together. Annabella tilted her head up again and Mona Beth rolled her eyes at her.

"Time to open your presents, Alaska, Mildred," the duke said.

"Alright, Grampa," Alaska said.

"Sure, Grampapa," Mildred then replied. Mona Beth and a servant went over to the gifts.

"My wife and I each picked out a gift for the girls," Marcellus said.

"Let's open Alaska's gifts first," Annabella replied, both Marcellus and Mona Beth rolled their eyes. Mona Beth chose two gifts labelled "Alaska"; she opened the first one. The box contained paper, paint, and several paint brushes. Mona Beth opened the second gift box, which was much bigger than the other one. The second gift box for Alaska contained a doll house that looked exactly like the castle she lived in.

"OK, let's start with the gifts we got for Mildred," Marcellus said with happiness. The servant in the room then opened Mildred's first gift, which turned out to be a blue teddy bear with beads for eyes. Mildred played a little with her blue teddy bear but accidently ripped its arm and one of its eyes fell off, she was sad and cried for a little bit.

"Oh god, I'm so sorry. Do not worry, Maximus, I'll sew it for her and give it back as quickly as I can," Mona Beth stated in an apologetic tone.

"Let's open her other gifts," Marcellus said very quickly. The servant opened Mildred's other gift, and that turned out to be a gothic style doll. Annabella screamed in anger.

"She is pretty!" Mildred told her grandparents.

"That does not look good," Annabella told her daughter.

"Oh Annabella, what is up with you today?" Maximus asked his wife.

"We can get her a new one, if you'd like that, Annabella?" Mona Beth told Annabella. Annabella snorted in a way that made everyone cringe. Mildred burst into tears.

Annabella and Mona Beth got into a very big fight that could be heard miles away. Mildred continued crying, creating a big ray of magic between her hands. Afterwards it rained outside very heavily as she continued crying. And with every scream Mildred let out, lighting struck and set something on fire, but every fire was then put out by the rain. One of the servants managed to calm Mildred down, causing the rain to stop. The duke and duchess tried to make amends with their daughter-in-law but failed.

By 9.00 p.m. that night, everyone was exhausted, both Annabella and Mona Beth ended up with messy hair, their dresses badly crumpled. Marcellus and Maximus's suits were also crumpled by then, Marcellus ended up sleeping in his wheelchair, and Maximus ended up falling over as he nodded off, getting a scar above his eye.

"We are finished here!" Annabella said in a very unladylike and nasty angry voice.

"Maximus! We are leaving this place immediately!" she then declared. Maximus went along against his will; he was too afraid to do anything else. The four of them left the mansion and headed home, with Annabella enraged and out of control, Maximus feeling very sad, and the girls sleeping a restless sleep.

Chapter Three
Childhood

Winter Wonderland, Cataville, October 11th, 1979

One month passed. The twins grew significantly, especially Mildred. Annabella's treatment of the girls had not changed, the twins now noticed the difference in the way their mother treated Alaska and the way she treated Mildred. Not a day passed without Annabella mocking Mildred's height or her powers; not a week went by without Annabella indirectly lowering Mildred's view of herself. Their father was too weak to defend his daughters or even object, it even looked as if Maximus was supportive of the whole thing. Alaska still lived in the castle like a princess, but Mildred was treated as if she was unlikeable.

"Mildred, wake up!" a voice terrifyingly shouted from the end of Mildred's bedroom. Mildred was startled and when she opened her eyes, she saw Annabella wearing a very large silk red dress, with her hair done up in the Victorian style. Annabella's face was very close to Mildred's, invading her personal space. Her eyes were very scary, they were blue, but it looked blood shot.

"Alright... Mother," Mildred said to her mother.

"OK, we have to take you and your sister to school..." Annabella replied in a suspiciously calm voice.

"Maid... get over here and get this handful ready for school!" Annabella rudely called out to the servant in the room. The servant obeyed and helped Mildred get ready.

"Weren't they supposed to start last month, Your Highness?" the humble servant asked.

"Students in the last year of kindergarten always start in October, the rest start in September. Now do as you are told!" Annabella yelled at the servant in contempt.

Later, Mildred entered the kitchen dressed in a thin dress the color of golden stardust. The little princess then watched as her mother yelled at the chefs and scolded them for not having finished preparing breakfast faster. Mildred walked past the kitchen and into the grand two-story dining room, where she saw Maximus and Alaska sitting on the royalty chairs of the massive elegant dining table. Maximus had a black eye and still had the scar over his eye, from when he fell down, trying to deal with the tension between Annabella and his mother, the last time he was at his parents'.

"Good day, Mildred," Alaska said to her sister sweetly.

"And to you," Mildred said after she respectfully curtsied to her. She sat on the chair at the front, where she was still able to hear her mother continuing to roar at the chefs.

A few minutes later the food was finally ready. Annabella finally walked into the dining room; everyone in the room could tell she looked exhausted, mainly after all the time she spent yelling at her chefs and giving them hell. Annabella sat down on her chair, dazed in a way that was prominently dramatic and petty. Pancakes covered in whipping cream and chocolate, with bananas and cherries on the top, made their way into the room on a gold tray and were handed to the princesses, in honor of their first school day. A small plate of sunny-side-up eggs followed for Mildred and Alaska got a plate of deliciously looking hard boiled eggs. Maximus received a huge plate with the biggest omelet with a large chicken steak, rich with spices, and another large plate of chicken sandwiches; his breakfast was basically chicken, chicken, and more chicken. The queen's breakfast consisted of a large plate of Caesar salad, a plate with five different types of sushi, a whole albeit small lobster, and a few beautifully garnished vanilla cupcakes.

The girls ate their food, their parents consumed theirs as well.

"CHARLES!" The queen screamed. Charles the castle steward came into the room.

"Charles! Take my daughters to the Academy of Royalty and Nobility… and do not take a long time to return," the queen ordered, glaring at him. The princesses walked with Charles and left for school. A royal waitress came into the dining room which the queen noticed immediately.

"Waitress! Tell those low-lives in the kitchen to make me and my husband each a plate of vegetable and a plate of fruit salad," Annabella calmly stated.

"But you just ate, Your Highness," she innocently replied.

"I SAID MAKE MY... I mean our... salads," the queen ordered angrily. The waitress bowed and ran out of the room and into the kitchen.

Alaska and Mildred reached the school in a little over fifteen minutes. Their school was a mansion reserved just for the royalty and the nobility. They disembarked from their bus along with the rest of the nobility, each of the children had a guardian. Alaska and Mildred had Charles, but it seemed that he was paying more attention to Alaska. The snow in that area was very light, so everyone managed to go through the school grounds and into the kindergarten section of the school. After a few minutes Charles and the girls were at the bulletin board which had papers stapled onto it. The papers mentioned what classrooms the children were in. Charles read these papers and found that the princesses were in different classrooms.

Soon the princesses were in their classrooms, Charles dropped Alaska off first. Charles and Mildred soon reached Mildred's classroom that was right next to Alaska's. Two dozen other children were in Mildred's classroom which Mildred found amusing, for she never got to see people her age. Her teacher was a woman in her late seventies, one that seemed very cheerful and seemed to act younger than her age.

"Hello, how are you, Your Highness?" the teacher asked in happiness.

"I'm fine... What's your name?" Mildred replied.

"Why I am Mrs. Beulah," the teacher said, shaking hands with the princess, then curtsied to her. Mrs. Beulah called attention to the students and introduced them to the princess. The teacher then walked Charles out of the classroom.

Mildred looked at her classmates, they were playing together in groups. Mildred went to join each of these groups, one group ignored her, and another rudely told her to go away, the third moved entirely when she came near. As she went to join the last group, they allowed her to play with them, but they still made her feel invisible. She spent the rest of the day reading and playing alone. Almost all her days in kindergarten were no different. It was also rougher for her as she saw Alaska with many different friends in both the classroom and at recess, and sometimes, even at the castle.

Winter Wonderland, Cataville, June 8th, 1982

Three years passed, and the princesses' days at kindergarten were over but things barely changed, even when they went through first and second grade. As the princesses were to go to third grade, life was about to change. Annabella and Maximus had organized a gift giving party for their daughter Alaska; many of her friends were invited, and so were all her maternal extended family. But little did Annabella know, Maximus had something else in mind.

The luxurious main suite where the queen and prince slept, had its fireplace lit, giving the room a cozy ambiance. The prince sat on the bed holding in his hands a yellow envelope that he had found in the closet. The calming sounds of the fire filled the room with tranquility. Maximus opened the envelope; a white letter was inside. Maximus took out the letter and read the following:

Dear Prince Maximus,
I regret to inform you that your father, Duke Marcellus of Center Cataville, has passed away due to natural causes. We couldn't invite you to his funeral because your wife, the queen, would cause trouble and she disrespected the late duke and also, she would never allow you to come alone. I am very sorry, my dear, I know you wanted to see him healthy and free of sickness. I know you wanted to see him one last time, and I see now that we should not have forced you to marry Annabella. I, however, did not know that Annabella is not the lovely person that would provide you with the greatest happiness as I thought eleven years ago. We made a mistake that time, our weakness caused you pain, I am very sorry, Maxi Darling.
Cordially,
Duchess Mona Beth

Maximus was horrified at this letter that he received from his mother, especially since his father died without him being able to see him or even say goodbye. He was even more dismayed as he saw what was written at the bottom of the letter, "Duchess Mona Beth, center Cataville, January 14th, 1982" the letter was not even recent, it must have had been delivered to the castle months ago. Maximus wanted to find out when the envelope was sent and when it had arrived at the castle. Maximus turned the paper over and found a blank page. He then looked inside the envelope and saw a small note from the Winter Wonderland mailing office. He took it out and read what was written in red in a Center Cataville pen, "Sent from Center Cataville to Winter Wonderland on January 19th, 1982". The prince looked at the bottom of the paper and saw writing in blue in a Winter Wonderland pen that said, "Arrived at the royal castle of Cataville on February 4th, 1982". At that moment, Maximus's heart raced, there was no reasonable explanation for these dates; because he never noticed the letter until today. He replaced the letter in the envelope and hid the envelope in the side table.

A few moments later, Annabella came into the room, a few servants following her. Each one was carrying three gift boxes and two gift bags. Annabella had so many gifts that each of them had a gift box on each of their arms, one on their heads and had to improvise on how to carry the gift bags.

"So, I bought many gifts for Alaska from the mall of Cataville and the outdoor stores!" Annabella exclaimed in excitement.

"JANICE! Open these gifts," she then ordered with her usual rude tone.

"It's Janet," the humble servant told the queen respectfully.

"Whatever... Just open the gifts," Annabella said while moving her arms as if shooing a fly.

Janet began opening the presents, but Maximus interrupted Annabella immediately.

"Excuse me, Annabella..." Maximus told her quietly, in the next moment he immediately took out the envelope he had on the end table and threw it in his wife's face.

Chapter Four
Childhood II

Winter Wonderland, Cataville, April 4th, 1984

On her throne Mildred sat. The huge throne room recently renovated, with new gold fabric covering the tables and chairs. Annabella stood right in front of her, talking to a royal guard. Mildred stood up; she was the tallest ten-year-old girl anyone had ever seen. She saw her sister Alaska sitting on her throne, Alaska was much shorter than her. Alaska was also wearing a silk blue dress along with Annabella, while Mildred was wearing an ugly 1930s green dress that had belonged to her deceased maternal grandmother Annelise when she was her age. It had been let out to fit Mildred. Annabella did not care enough to buy Mildred clothes as nice as Alaska's, Maximus had been missing for more than a year and a half by now, and declared dead. He had been the one that would've treated Mildred less harshly and bought her her own gown at least. Annabella stopped talking to the guard and came toward Alaska.

"Today your aunt Felicity and her children will come to the castle for a royal buffet." Annabella told Alaska. Immediately, Mildred was reminded of the many dinner parties her parents threw. As she looked at her mother, she noticed that Annabella had gained a significant amount of weight, and according to the latest, but not new, portrait of Maximus, so had he. She then came to realize that Alaska received most of the attention of her uncles, aunts, and cousins. For none of them did truly care about her; she felt very alone.

"Mildred! Go to your room and get ready for the buffet," Annabella ordered her daughter sternly.

Mildred got up from her throne and begun walking gracefully to her room.

"DO I MAKE MYSELF CLEAR?!" Annabella lashed out furiously, which made Mildred run like a bat out of hell.

As Mildred arrived at her room, she removed her hairpieces and threw them to the hard wood floor. She began to cry, because this was the way her mother treated her regularly. Nobody came to her room that day, she stayed alone till she was finally ready for the buffet.

Mildred left her room, looking beautiful despite wearing another one of her grandmother's unsightly dresses. A loud noise that sounded like a crowd with petty bickering came out from the lower floor. Mildred ran to the stairs and ran down. When the massive and high formal living room met her eyes, a woman with three teenagers and two younger children openly took in the sight of the young princess.

Mildred identified her mother's sister in a heartbeat. Her aunt was a short woman who looked quite old, wrinkles covered the skin around eyes and mouth, with even deeper wrinkles etched on her forehead. The blonde hair on her head seemed to have a great deal of gray in-between. Her eyes also seemed to have lost their twinkle. A twenty-year-old girl stood next to the queen's sister, she was Annabella's spitting image but in a much younger and less intimidating form. Mildred could tell that those were her cousins whom she had only seen in pictures. The person next to them was an average looking boy who looked to be in twelfth grade. She guessed him to be her cousin Windle. A few of her cousins were closer to Mildred's age, to whom she paid attention properly.

Mildred curtsied to her aunt and cousins, then sat on the lavish old-fashioned loveseat. Annabella went and sat on the throne seat on the opposite side of Mildred's loveseat, afterwards her sister sat on an identical chair right next to Annabella's chair. The cousins and Alaska sat comfortably on the very spacious sofa in front of Mildred. Annabella and Felicity chattered away. And even though Alaska had only just met her cousins, she seemed to be more talkative with them than the queen. Mildred sat bored and alone on the couch.

"I am very happy that you are going to allow me and your dear nephews and nieces to stay here," Felicity told the queen.

"Oh, it's my pleasure," the queen said in a happy voice that Mildred and Alaska knew was fake. Little by little, Mildred could see that the conversation between Annabella and her sister was heating up, but it did not seem to be directed at Felicity but at Mildred herself. She could hear Annabella and Felicity talk about her, but she could not hear what was exactly being said, especially with the room being enormous and them being rather far away. A musical instrument began playing in the room, classical music flowed through the room like the wind on a beach.

And just like that, all the tension in the room disappeared. The chattering between Alaska and the cousins quickly stopped. Felicity stopped talking and begun listening to the music, feeling relaxed. Annabella looked horrified that the music had interrupted her conversation with her sister, even Felicity herself was not that interested in what Annabella had to say. All of this was noticed by Mildred. Mildred got up slowly, she snuck toward the door then hastily ran out of the room. Her steps were very quick and loud that she did not hear the other footsteps behind her. By the time she reached the stairs, Mildred stumbled on the third step and noticed that a few of her young cousins had followed and started kicking her.

She then heard them laughing and sniggering at her pain. The sight of Alaska met her eyes, but she did not defend her; she was too selfish to do so. Mildred ran up the stairs not looking back and went to her room and hid.

When Mildred reached her room, she ordered ice packs for her knee and ankle which hurt the most. The ice cubes arrived and the maid left, and Mildred took care of herself. Very quickly she was beyond angry, in a moment later her anger was very intense. Thunder struck outside the castle for the first time in Winter Wonderland in years. And every time Mildred's rage surged thunder struck. She could see from her balcony the chaos that occurred outside, for those people had never seen thunder before. Annabella and everyone downstairs screamed in fright. Mildred noticed that she was doing that with her anger. Mildred intentionally felt her anger and focused on it very hard. Another bolt of lightning struck outside which led to more screaming from downstairs.

Annabella ran into the room, her face as pale as snow and looked as if she had just seen a ghost.

"Mildred! What on earth are you doing?!" Annabella said in extreme fear, Mildred then saw her cousins behind her squealing in fear; people in Winter Wonderland had never seen thunder or lighting before.

"I do not know, Mother! It just came out of nowhere!" Mildred lied sheepishly to her mother.

"It couldn't happen just like this, this place does not have any changing weather, only snow that I generate. But now I guess your eerie disgusting powers too!" Annabella stated viciously.

"Mother, what do you know about my powers?" Mildred exclaimed calmly. "You have no right to tell me my powers are disgusting," Mildred stated.

"Of course, I do! Your powers are completely disgusting and unproductive. This is Winter Wonderland, not whatever the hell this is you're causing!" Annabella then replied angrily, her eyes gleaming like a snake.

Annabella continued to yell, in great rage that could be heard from the other side of the planet. Within minutes, Annabella's yelling turned to screeching and Mildred's eyes welling up. When Annabella stopped yelling and breaking down, she went to Mildred and slapped her hard, leaving a bright red mark on her white cheek. Annabella begun to hyperventilate.

"I need to lie down, dear sister, take me to my bed… for I need to rest," Annabella said looking toward her sister with excessive drama. Felicity walked Annabella to her bedroom while Annabella continued to be dramatic. Alaska felt bad for her sister but didn't show her feelings. She decided to shake it off as her cousins did not show any emotion.

Mildred watched the rest of her family leave her room in peace. Her view of her mother was that she was nothing more than insane. Mildred looked to her right. Her uninviting plain bed sat there on its own. She ran hastily towards her bed and jumped hard, her highest jump ever, onto her bed. More tears came as she cried herself to sleep that night.

Chapter Five
Friendship

Winter Wonderland, Cataville, November 9th, 1984

More months passed, Mildred remained poised and strong. Her aunt and cousins lived with her for a few months but returned been back to their place in September. Mildred lay sleeping in peace, till the grandfather clock outside the castle struck seven. She slowly opened her eyes, and got up from her bed and went to the mirror. She examined her appearance as usual, her height was always what she first thing she studied, for all her family could see in her was her height and her powers. She measured her height with the measuring tape in her bathroom, Mildred realized that the tape said "160 centimeters" and felt bad.

Mildred started to get ready for yet another day of school. She dressed in a black dress, a 1920s version, more old clothing that once belonged to her grandmother Annelise. She tied her hair in a bun with a red headband. Mildred then gracefully walked to the main staircase. The queen was still sleeping, so she met her sister at the carriage. Mildred carried her backpack and followed Alaska to the carriage. As soon as she arrived at the carriage, the chauffer took the two princesses to the elementary school.

"Good morning, Mildred," Alaska greeted her sister as soon as the carriage started moving.

"Good day, dear sister," Mildred greeted Alaska, surprised that she had even noticed her. The princesses barely spoke two words to each other afterwards. Mildred looked out the window as usual without any emotions. She felt a weird sensation in her hand, within seconds the sensation got stronger, a few droplets of water fell from the sky outside. The sky continued to release droplets of water and the sensation in Mildred's hand continued to grow stronger.

"Goodness! Is that rain?" Alaska exclaimed in astonishment.

"I read about it in books, it is not supposed to exist here, only on Earth," Alaska stated.

"I'm doing it!" Mildred said in happiness. Alaska slapped Mildred's hand. The rain stopped and the sensation in Mildred's hands was gone.

"Alaska, what is wrong with you?" Mildred exclaimed in offense.

"Mildred, you cannot keep using your powers! And you cannot tell anybody at school about them either! Mother will definitely have a breakdown over this, and I cannot imagine what people would say," Alaska heatedly stated.

Mildred listened to her sister's words; sadly Alaska's words were true, her mother would kill her, and the people of Winter Wonderland would not approve. Snowdrops and snowflakes fell from the sky afterwards, and with that happening, Mildred realized that her mother had noticed what had happened. Her teeth began chattering as she shivered in fright. The carriage started moving faster and faster as the snow got stronger and stronger. It had been twenty-five minutes and the carriage finally arrived at school. The chauffer got out and opened the door for the princesses. Both Alaska and Mildred held the edges of their dresses up and descended the carriage.

Mildred walked till she reached her classroom. To Mildred it looked like the usual hell. She entered quietly, each of her classmates sitting at their desks patiently waiting for the teacher. A middle-aged man walked into the room, he was wearing a shirt with black jeans and looked quite intimidating.

"Good morning, class," the man said sweetly in Western Cataville, which sounded like an Argentinian accent.

"I am Mr. Gonzalez, I will be your homeroom teacher because Mrs. Bird will not be here anymore," the man said.

The teacher looked at Mildred out of the corner of his eye and drifted off in thought for a few moments.

"Who organized the seating chart?" Mr. Gonzalez asked ruefully.

One girl raised her hand in the air. Mr. Gonzalez gave her permission to speak.

"Mrs. Bird organized us this way," the girl replied confidently.

"I am going to make up a new seating chart, everyone please get out of your seats and come up to the front of the classroom," the teacher smugly ordered. Soon all the students were sitting in new seats according to the new seating chart. Mildred now sat alone at a faraway desk, where no one could bother her.

Mildred settled into her new desk now feeling much better than before. Mildred was able to enjoy her lessons in peace. Soon it was time for recess. Mildred went to the cafeteria just as she did every day. As she looked at the benches in the cafeteria, she noticed groups of students sitting at each of the benches, none were left for her to sit on her own. She then saw another girl her age. The girl wore glasses, had black curly hair, and wore a long black dress. She was standing alone next to the water fountain, crying.

Mildred walked towards the girl next to the water fountain.

"Hey, are you OK?" Mildred asked the girl.

"Yes, I'm alright," the girl stated as she dried her eyes with a tissue.

"What's going on?" Mildred replied afterwards.

"Those ladies keep making fun of me and my glasses, they also keep saying I look like a witch because of my hair and my dress," the girl said as she continuing crying.

Mildred let out a sigh and touched the girl's back.

"How rude of me, I'm lady Catania, daughter of Baron Coleman and Baroness Catalina," the girl said and curtsied.

"Princess Mildred, daughter of queen Annabella and the late prince Maximus," Mildred introduced herself to the girl. Mildred and Catania hugged, got some food, and sat together for the rest of recess. The pair chattered away. They did not share a classroom, but that day they spent time together every chance they got.

A few hours later, Mildred and Alaska were on their way home. This time, the carriage ride was not as tense as the one in the morning; Mildred did not care about her sister, nor her mother for the matter. As soon as they arrived, Mildred left the carriage and quickly ran to her room, she entered and slammed the door. She was very happy; for the first time ever she had finally found a friend. She let her hair down slowly then smiled. Mildred went to the radio and turned it to listen to late seventies pop music. She jumped on the bed to her heart's content. Soon the phone in her room rang. She ran and answered it and turned the radio off.

"Hello," Mildred told her caller.

"Hey, Mildred, it's me Catania!" the caller replied to Mildred. The princess was very excited, she didn't even ask Catania how she got her number. They talked for hours and the princess lay on her bed while they talked.

For the first time in her life, Mildred did not feel lonely and isolated. There was a new light in her life. She did not leave her room for the rest of that day.

Winter Wonderland, Cataville, December 31st, 1984

"Mildred! Mildred! Mildred!" a voice behind Mildred yelled, Mildred looked behind her and saw Alaska. Mildred wasn't happy to hear her sister's voice. Her sister's friends were coming over to celebrate New Year's Eve in the castle, but then Mildred came up with the idea of inviting Catania over with her parents to celebrate New Year's in the castle as well.

"Yes, Alaska?" Mildred replied.

"You have to get ready for New Year's. Did you invite anyone to spend today with us?" Alaska asked.

"Yes, I've invited my friend Catania," Mildred answered with a smile.

"That witch girl that you are always hanging out with?" Alaska rudely asked.

"How dare you speak of her that way?" Mildred lashed out at her sister. She immediately realized that Alaska was beginning to sound a lot like Annabella.

"Mildred! Do not speak to your sister that way!" Annabella said.

"But, Mother, she keeps making fun of my friend," Mildred emotionally replied to her mother.

"I do not care if she is your friend, you do not get to talk in this dreadful tone to your sister!" Annabella replied. Mildred stopped talking, got up, and went to her room. She called her friend to invite her over to celebrate the coming of the New Year.

A few hours later Catania and her parents were at the castle. Mildred was at the front gate; she was wearing a green dress and had her hair hanging down her back. Catania along with a man walked to the door of the castle. A woman was behind Catania, she looked exactly like her but older.

"Hello, Princess Mildred. I am Baroness Catalina, and I am very pleased to meet you," the woman said as they shook hands. Mildred and Catania hugged. The three women went inside the castle.

Annabella stood in the throne room, yelling at a servant as usual. Annabella looked over to her right and saw Mildred with the others. Annabella looked at them with hatred.

"Baroness Catalina," Annabella whispered in a vicious tone.

"Queen Annabella," the baroness whispered in the same vicious tone.

"What are you doing here?" Annabella said beginning to have a meltdown.

"Long time no see," Catalina said.

"Oh, how I wish I didn't have to see your face again!" Annabella replied.

"You two know each other?" Mildred asked her mother.

"Yes, we do, she used to bully me in middle school before she got married," Catalina stated.

"I was hoping never to see you again," the baroness then mentioned.

Annabella raised her head and walked away.

The baroness said goodbye to her daughter and told her that she will pick her up thirty minutes after midnight. The castle was filled with security guards so Catalina did not mind letting her daughter stay after midnight. Mildred and Catania played to their hearts' content, receiving no attention from Annabella, who did direct her attention toward Alaska and her friends.

Mildred and Catania confided a lot of things to each other that night, but they did not broach the topic of Mildred's powers. More snow kept falling that night, for Annabella was fervently using her powers that night since it was New Year's Eve.

Mildred and Catania stayed in the princess's bedroom. They played with blocks. They kept talking about themselves all the time while playing. Mildred finally lived like a true child, even if it was for a little while. They played with the dollhouse that Mildred created with her powers, and they played tag, they also played hide and seek, and watched a movie. Mildred saw Alaska and her friends participate in activities that Annabella had organized just for them for that occasion. Mildred felt sad for a moment that Annabella did not let her and Catania participate, but at the same time she felt that she did not require her mother's attention, at least for now.

Soon it was eleven forty-five in Winter Wonderland, the queen called everyone to the ballroom. Mildred and Catania felt tired after of all the running around and all the laughing. Mildred and her friend walked to the ballroom where everyone was gathered. As soon as they arrived, the queen stood in the middle of the room, Alaska and her friends were also there. Alaska went and sat on her throne, and her friends sat on grand chairs that were brought for them by the servants.

"Mildred, darling, and lady Catania, please take your seat on the red carpet," Annabella said with a fake sweet tone. Mildred and her friend did as they were told, sitting on the long red carpet provided for them.

"Lacey! Go prepare the fireworks!" Annabella ordered the servant beside her.

"It's Blair," the servant corrected innocently.

"I don't care, just prepare the stupid fireworks," Annabella rudely replied moving her hands dismissively. The servant complied. It was three minutes to midnight by now. Annabella sat on her throne, which was the grandest chair in the room, and made sure that everything was in place. Everyone waited patiently for the countdown to New Year to begin.

"Ten, nine, eight, seven, six, five, four, three, two, one," they counted happily.

"Happy New Year!" Everyone screamed, and with that it was 1985. Everyone cheered, and each princess had a group hug with her friends, with Annabella standing awkwardly in the middle of the room. The sky was lit with fireworks.

"Happy New Year" the fireworks spelled out.

Chapter Six
Friendship II

Winter Wonderland, Cataville, February 23rd, 1985

IT had been little over a month. The princesses' winter holiday was up. Mildred was excited to go back to school; she had not seen her friend since New Year's Eve, not even for her birthday. This made her feel lonely and isolated; especially since her life at home did not get better. Annabella hit Mildred regularly when she made a "mistake" or was deemed not good enough, which happened often. Alaska always received whatever she desired, a new gown, a new toy, more accessories, a day spent with her friends. But Mildred received none of that from Annabella, and there was still no word from Maximus.

The holidays had been a royal pain for Mildred, and she was glad when they were finally over. Mildred got ready and followed her usual routine before school. When she was ready, she checked her appearance. A couple of bruises appeared on her forehead from yesterday's slap, this reminded her of the scar in her heart from the recurrent negative comments of Annabella towards her appearance, which she noticed even Alaska found unreasonable.

Mildred was excited about seeing Catania every day once again, she did not feel like facing anyone from the castle, not the queen, not the servants, or the steward, and certainly not her sister. When Mildred left the castle premises, she noticed the snow, which drew her attention to the balcony of her mother's bedroom; where Annabella was magically creating snow as usual. However, today Alaska has joined Annabella in casting the incantations for the snow for a while. There was fire in

Mildred's head, so fierce as if dragons were creating them. Mildred ignored that sight and ran to the stables, looking about her wildly, as if looking for a specific horse.

Finally, she found it. A silver horse stood in front of her, its dark mane and tail shone bright in the sunlight. Its eyes met hers with pride and defiance. Then she saw its blue horn shining like a gem. This was the one, Alaska's unicorn, the horse that will take her to school very quickly. Mildred saddled the unicorn, but it resisted. Eventually Mildred was able to saddle him properly. The young princess mounted the horse and began galloping to school.

Mildred rode through the snowy land like the wind. The horse was difficult to tame. It kept resisting Mildred as its rider. The princess kept holding on, fighting the horse's attempts to throw her off. For such a young rider, she had accomplished discipline, agility, and grace. This went on for some time, but when Mildred saw the palace carriage with Alaska in it, she felt trapped, guilty, and stupid. This made her mind wander off for a few moments, and she was thrown off the majestic unicorn backwards, where she quickly and painfully hit the ground with her arms and legs, a force that gravity would not fail to recall.

Soon Mildred found herself in the castle, in her own bedroom once again, lying in bed, a pair of crutches beside her bed. Looking on she saw her bandaged left arm and right leg. The last thing she remembered was falling off the unicorn. Servants around her tended to her needs.

"Thank you, good madams," Mildred told the servants around her. She received no response from most of them while one rolled her eyes. Annabella then entered the room gracefully but looking scary.

In the presence of the queen, the servants left the room.

"Good day, Mildred," Annabella said as she went to stand next to her daughter's bed.

"And to you," Mildred replied fearfully.

"I am here to inquire about your disgraceful and improper business today," Annabella spoke as her agitation began to show.

"How did this happen?" the queen then asked as if insult had come to her own name. Without hesitation, the queen begun berating Mildred as usual without allowing her to explain herself.

"How could you steal your sister's beloved horse that your dear father Maximus paid for?" the queen began yelling.

"I do not care for any excuse you may provide, you little dumb twit!" Annabella yelled, unbefitting the image she sought to maintain.

"Mother, I am tired of you treating me badly all the time!" Mildred replied in defense. Annabella was offended, and she slapped Mildred again without thinking. No new marks appeared on Mildred's face, but it was still very painful.

"This is about that Baroness's daughter… Catania, isn't it?" Annabella said as she walked to the window deep in thought. Mildred did not answer the question, so the queen took that response as a yes.

"Oh, you foolish girl," Annabella stated with even more anger while cracking her knuckles.

"I can't believe you don't know," Annabella then said slowly.

"I don't follow," Mildred asked innocently.

"That girl was never your true friend, no one would willingly want to be friends with you," Annabella then said.

"Mother, please stop, you do not know her, and you don't even know what friendship is!" Mildred replied to her mother defensively.

"Mildred, daughter, your sister overheard that girl, she told the other girls that she and her mother were using you; so her mother can get her revenge from me," Annabella said slyly.

"Mother, Catania would never betray me like that, why do you and Alaska think everything is about you?!" Mildred burst into tears.

"Don't you dare talk to me this way!" Annabella continued scolding her daughter.

"This is not about us, Mildred, it's about that Baroness and her ego," Annabella said.

"I definitely made sure that the Baroness got a three-year sentence, effective immediately," Annabella continued speaking. Mildred's shock appeared on her young face, the tears in her eyes showing the betrayal she felt.

Annabella left the room, and Alaska entered afterwards.

"I'm sorry, Mildred, but it's true," Alaska said sweetly without looking Mildred in the eye.

"Then why didn't you say anything?!" Mildred screamed at her sister at the top of her voice.

"Mother wouldn't let me," Alaska said weakly, lowering her head. Mildred felt numb and weak and stopped talking. Usually these situations aren't left unanswered, but Mildred remained silent, which led Alaska to leave the room feeling sorry. Mildred then cried herself in bed but couldn't fall sleep, it was late at night by then. The polar nightingales in Winter Wonderland sung their song that night, making Mildred feel worse and worse.

Winter Wonderland, Cataville, March 7th, 1985

After another school break for Mildred due to her injury, she finally got to go back to school. She did not resist and just succumbed to going to school with Alaska in the carriage. Her injury was healed by then, and she had stopped using the crutches. Mildred made sure to ignore Alaska for the entire carriage ride, she had not forgiven her or Annabella for what they had done. Alaska showed guilt but couldn't really face her sister again.

Soon the princesses left the carriage, Mildred ran to her classroom, she managed to attend class and pay the proper attention required of her. She was attending the extra support sessions provided to her due to her injury. Mildred and Catania did not speak or even make eye contact for most of the day, which led Mildred to feeling increasingly anxious. When Catania finally looked at Mildred, she could tell that the princess was very anxious to see her, to which Catania replied with a snub.

Soon the school day ended, but Mildred did not leave school, she walked towards the ice playground where kids played. There, she found Catania speaking with the daughters of Dukes. Catania laughed with them and seemed to show more emotion towards them than she ever showed Mildred.

The attention of those girls was directed at Mildred which led everyone else, including boys, to look at her. Catania burst out laughing when she saw the princess, leading to everyone else doing the same. Catania then started pointing her fingers at Mildred and gave her a sly look that was hurtful. Mildred's eyes were brimming with tears, for she hadn't forgotten the betrayal.

Mildred ran out of there; she made sure to leave and walked more swiftly. Down that hill she was in front of the main school. The young princess ordered a carriage to take her home, she ended up staying for a while. She watched Catania and all the others leave before her carriage arrived. Seeing Catania happy with those other girls; what did Catania see in them that she did not see in her, that Mildred did not understand.

Soon the carriage arrived to take Mildred home. Mildred got into the carriage and sat, continuing to feel anxious and sad. She could not wait to arrive at home, she longed now for a true friend, one that wouldn't hurt her, one that would play with her and treat her well. But in her head she knew that wasn't going to happen. Dread then consumed her mind once more, for now she had to go back to dealing with her mother and sister.

Chapter Seven
An Eerie Incidence

Winter Wonderland, Cataville, May 5th, 1985

Even with the many days off that were provided by their school, Mildred never got enough time away from the environment in her school. This was another one of those days, by that time Annabella was almost never out of her room. Alaska was regularly taken out and was never home, leading to Mildred to live in peace and quiet for a little while, at least at home. Mildred performed the basic goals she had set for herself for every weekend, which included: studying, reading, and hanging around the castle. It was very boring and when Mildred had all those activities done, she would sit in her room and do nothing, as there was nothing to do in this enormous and boring but really beautiful castle.

Mildred had her breakfast, brushed her teeth, and got dressed. She then went and checked her study Gantt chart, which on that day included topics such as history, royalty, and language, those she had covered for sure. Mildred then read some of her favorite literature. The topics that she read were difficult for her age, but she managed to read them with full understanding. Since no one was home but the servants, Mildred ran around the castle and played, she continued to play and play till she was tired.

Mildred soon found herself bored out of her mind. A thought crossed her mind, one that she never thought she'd get. Mildred wanted to know what was going on with Annabella. She walked to the T-shaped stairs, which she knew led to Annabella's wing in the castle. The princess went up the stairs, and soon found herself in a dark and eerie hallway, this part of the castle seemed to have once been beautiful and well-decorated. However, it seemed to have been neglected with time. Mildred walked through the hallway past a few paintings, many of which were of Maximus. The portraits were either ripped apart or covered in cobwebs. One thing was certain, hatred was displayed in the treatment these paintings had received and Mildred saw it. Statues that also seemed to have been stunning once were also present. Mildred began quivering with fear, her teeth chattering. Mildred found that to be weird; while her mother was mean and weird, she was not unkempt, which made Mildred question her surroundings more and more. Especially since the element of hatred could be sensed strongly throughout the entire area.

Mildred was finally at the door of her mother's bedroom. The princess knocked a few times, but got no response. Mildred opened the door and went in. The inside of the room was not as eerie and hideous as the outer corridor, but it was undeniably not the same bedroom it had been in the 1970s. Mildred saw her mother at the far end of her bedroom, she was wearing a red dress that looked as if it were made out of blood. Her blonde hair unkempt, Annabella did not notice her daughter, giving Mildred time to hide. She hid in the walk-in closet. Annabella looked around the room lost in thought, insanity seemed to have consumed her mind. Annabella walked towards more portraits which were inside her bedroom, to one specific portrait. It was of Maximus; Mildred then watched her mother eye the portrait with a look of hate.

"Dear husband, I hate you. You cowardly selfish snake," Annabella exclaimed, talking to herself.

"I will hunt you down one day, I will never forgive you for what you've done," Annabella said while talking more, she seemed to be completely out of it. Mildred's teeth began chattering more and the fear in her heart grew. Mildred was smart not to make any sound, and let Annabella speak her crazy mind alone.

"It was you; you knew your parents have humiliated me a hundred times, you knew that my mother disgusted me for a thousand years. You knew that I was hurting for a million years," Annabella then said, as if she was in a dialogue with a ghost.

"You did this, you left this monster inside my head, for it to consume me," Annabella then said, but she did not seem to be talking to Maximus anymore. She tilted her head to another portrait. The portrait was of a middle-aged woman, she was blonde like Annabella and the princesses. The woman in the portrait also seemed to have a face like Annabella's, but did not look exactly like Annabella.

"Oh Mother, you placed me with him, it was not just him, it was more you," Annabella said to her mother Anneliese's portrait.

"I loathe you more than anyone else in this entire room," Annabella said, in a tone impersonal, like a computer; Annabella did not seem to be conscious, but seemed to be in a whole other world. Mildred knew that Annabella was acting weird, but she was too young to understand what exactly was wrong with her. Mildred ran through the room to escape, but Annabella noticed her, she was, however too deep in her own thoughts to be completely comprehend Mildred's presence, leading her to go back into her musings. Mildred flew through her mother's suite of rooms as if she was flying out of hell. Mildred immediately sought out Charles.

Charles stood in the middle of the servant quarters where Mildred knew she would find him. Mildred hugged Charles quickly, hanging on to him.

"What's the matter, Your Highness?" Charles asked the princess nicely.

"It's Mother, she's in her room, she needs your help," Mildred said to Charles. Even though Mildred did not love her mother, and she knew that Annabella was not a good person, she still had the heart to get her mother help.

The servants then went to check on Annabella, confirming that she was indeed going through an episode of mental instability. The servants immediately called for the doctor, others tried to console the queen, but Annabella kept resisting them. The servants together were stronger than her, and eventually were able to sedate Annabella and she fell asleep while they were waiting for the doctor. Mildred feeling panic and dread, and a bit of hatred, did not stay next to her mother but sat some distance away.

Winter Wonderland, Cataville, May 6th, 1985, 12:08 AM

The doctor that the servants called for the queen arrived after his journey from Center Cataville, it was a few minutes past midnight when he began tending to Annabella. She seemed to be on the verge of waking up when the servants greeted the doctor.

To Mildred, the doctor looked like a respectable professor. She couldn't remember much of the night though as she ended up sleeping only two hours. When Mildred woke up, she was still exhausted, but she was awake enough to see the doctor mention to Charles something about severe illness and medication, including injections. She heard Charles thank the doctor. Annabella went back to her regular temperament after being treated by the doctor. Mildred did not understand what occurred that night, but she had one wish. Mildred wished for a happy family life with her mother and sister. With the queen's mistreatment of Mildred appearing to be the result of mental illness, she hoped that her mother's treatment could give her the mother that she had always wanted.

Chapter Eight
Mildred's Average Life

Winter Wonderland, Cataville, September 19th, 1985

Life was a rollercoaster for the princess in the past months. After she took her pills and injections regularly, Annabella recovered well from the horrible mental state she had been in. Along with the medication were occasional doctor visits; to bring her back to her normal self. She returned to her old ways.

Alaska stopped going out very often and was usually at the castle. Mildred became sadder by the minute; she had recently started the sixth grade which had been hell. Every day Mildred woke up feeling more dread than the day before. It felt as if every day in her life was a rollercoaster repeatedly going through a loop. She sat at the dining table all alone, eating breakfast. It was early morning, the birds singing, and the sun was shining. Alaska was creating snow along with her mother. Alaska's snow felt even more hateful towards Mildred than Annabella's snow ever did.

Mildred stopped eating and left the room. Even though it was still early, Mildred went to the carriage that was supposed to take her to school. Mildred waited there for a long time reading her book. The weather kept getting worse and Mildred knew that Alaska's magic was getting out of control.

At the top of the highest tower of the castle, Alaska and Annabella stood casting the snow. A blizzard had started in Winter Wonderland, for Alaska's powers were getting stronger and it became harder for her to control them.

"Alaska! What on Cataville are you doing?!" Annabella yelled at Alaska.

"You're going to make us the laughingstock of the entire kingdom!" Annabella said while continuing to criticize Alaska.

"Mother, my powers are getting stronger! You cannot expect me to have complete control over my powers!" Alaska argued.

"Of course, I do! Alaska you are the heir to my throne, I cannot have Mildred as the heir to my throne!" Annabella stated as if she had been told something crazy.

"And why not? Isn't she the older twin?" Alaska asked Annabella.

"Because she's stupid, she's wasteful, just look at those powers, they don't fit the name of Winter Wonderland," Annabella said in a tone of disgust.

"Mother! You cannot call your daughter stupid or a wasteful, she's your daughter, and she's a princess of Winter Wonderland like me. Her powers aren't disgusting, they're beautiful and unique," Alaska said standing up to her mother.

"How dare you argue with me!" Annabella yelled, about to transform into a monster. Alaska was shocked; she hung her head down.

"I'm very sorry, Mother," Alaska replied while curtsying.

"You should be with all that nonsense you were saying," Annabella then told Alaska.

"One more time from the top," Annabella told Alaska and ordered her to go back to practicing her powers.

Back in the carriage Mildred had finished five chapters from the novel she was reading, she was supposed to be at school in fifteen minutes.

"Come on, where is she?!" Mildred whispered angrily. She left the carriage and found the driver. The princess then saw Charles entering the castle stables.

"Charles, please check to see that my sister comes to the carriage, we're supposed to be at school in fifteen minutes," Mildred told him. Charles obeyed her words without saying a word.

Charles came back with Alaska a few minutes later. Alaska went into the carriage, and they left for school. The carriage ride passed as usual, both girls said absolutely nothing to each other. However, Mildred was extremely dreading going to school. Mildred did not want the carriage ride to end, as a whole day in school for her was far worse than a million years in the carriage with Alaska. Mildred left the carriage as soon as they arrived at school.

There she went, she thought. Mildred begged God that the children not bully her today. Mildred sat at her remote desk in the classroom and waited for the teacher to arrive. A few girls of the nobility came up to Mildred's desk.

The girls began making fun of Mildred, to her face, as usual. One mocked Mildred's clothes for being all 1920s fashion, one ridiculed her grace and etiquette, while the last one taunted her on her height. After Mildred heard the words from the girl about her height, she wondered. Mildred was not ugly, but why does everyone make fun of her appearance? Mildred then noticed that all the comments that have to do with her appearance come from people with low levels of intelligence, such as Annabella.

Mildred tried to ignore the girls, but soon the attention of the entire classroom was caught up. A few boys then shot spitballs at her. More boys and girls kept laughing and laughing. It was like that every day for the princess, she thought about it being prohibited in Winter Wonderland to treat a princess this way, but Annabella's unfairness hampered and stopped that, she reported them one-hundred times but to no end. It went on like this for a while till Mildred got very annoyed. The princess lashed out at all the kids in anger, and even soaked some of them with rain using her powers.

Their fourth-grade teacher came in, she managed to temporarily stop the chaos in her classroom. Mildred was then able to attend this class in peace. During recess, Mildred ate alone as usual. Mildred would still see groups or pairs of boys or girls sitting together, either hanging out or playing. The girl did not understand the reason why everyone was horrible to her, or why she had nobody as a friend. It was like this every day at recess as well as in class. Sometimes, Mildred would also end up getting bullied at recess. By this time Mildred stopped crying over this, it still hurt her but with time she had forgotten friendship and what it felt like. The young princess tried her best to ignore everything. She tried to play in each of the indoor playgrounds, or in the school skating rink on her own, sometimes this would work and sometimes it wouldn't.

Class then began, and the bullying started once more. The school day felt so long to her and this one was no different; she did not believe it when she got to go home. Mildred left school and went home as usual in the carriage. As Mildred left the carriage, she got another lecture from Annabella.

"Mildred! I would like to speak with you," Annabella then told Mildred as she grabbed her arm and pulled her to a private area. Mildred's heart was pounded hard, and her face went pale; she was having an inner panic attack. Why did Annabella want to talk to her? These situations were never good. When Annabella finished pulling Mildred to the place where she wanted to talk, Mildred saw her mother's eyes red with anger. Annabella's head was about to burst, it seemed like she did not know where she needed to begin speaking.

"Mildred, daughter, you disappoint me!" Annabella stated sharply.

"Mother, what did I do this time?" Mildred then asked in fear.

"I'll tell you what you did you brat! I got a telephone call from your principal that you have been dozing off in class! Is this true?" Annabella asked as her head was burning up.

"He says that he gets complaints from the teacher that you lose your focus in the class, and that you are always very miserable," Annabella said like she was a demon. Mildred did nothing to defend herself and just let her mother treat her like she was nothing.

"You cannot show sadness in class; you are going to ruin my reputation! Do not show any emotions in school and forget about your horrible life just because you're a meaningless little nothing!" Annabella shouted so enraged that smoke could've been coming out of her ears.

"Now get out of my sight, you twerp!" Annabella exclaimed even more sharply, then pushed Mildred very hard if she was nothing. Mildred was in pain, making her run to her room as though she was flying. She started studying and set the radio to her favorite station and did not leave her room that day.

Mildred started reading books to help her escape. The books that Mildred read had gradually increased in difficulty and themes; she began reading children's books in the early eighties and now read huge novels, that's how much she hoped for a different life, a different her, a different now. This was how it was that day and had been for weeks and months, maybe even years. Mildred heard the door creak, she turned around and saw the main source for her misery, Alaska.

Mildred was feeling down, and she started to have a breakdown. How could everyone get away with doing terrible things, while she couldn't do anything? It made no sense at all. How was it that she got nothing, while bad people got everything? Why did Mildred get treated this way, but bullies and Annabella have everything they want? Mildred did not understand the answers to any questions that she had just asked herself. The young princess begged her life for mercy, and never received it.

Mildred looked at the grandfather clock at the very end of her room and saw that it was past 11 at night. She changed into her blue 1930s nightgown, it was also an old piece of clothing from her grandmother Anneliese, which was ripped at the bottom. But that was the least of her worries at this point. She looked at herself in the mirror and saw bags under her eyes, the exact same that Annabella had when she had her meltdowns. She went to her bed and lay there preparing for another escape from her reality.

Mildred slept restlessly that night, she kept tossing and turning, she also woke up several times with nightmares. After she woke up and went back to sleep, she finally had a good dream. Mildred was very happy in that dream; she forgot everything. The minutes that had the dream in them felt like years and an eternity of happiness and escape.

Winter Wonderland, Cataville, September 20th, 1985

Mildred awoke from her wonderful dreams where she could've been the child she was supposed to be. Mildred dreaded the fact that she woke up again, for she hoped she could stay in her slumber forever and ever. The princess knew that her feelings were very strong, and she had way too much anger for her age. She prepared herself for her school day, she was happy that it was a Friday, the last school day of the week.

The princess made sure not to encounter Annabella, she hardly spoke to her sister at breakfast because the tension was killing both of them. The two sisters couldn't wait to finish the food to go to the carriage so they could arrive at school and be separated. During the carriage ride, anxiety consumed her excessively. The anxiety helped Mildred ignore her sister, but it caused her pain over having to see and deal with her classmates and fellow noble students one more time.

The school day was the same as usual, however since it was a Friday, many students had planned to spend the day outside their homes, or with their friends. Mildred got none of that. The bullying kept going on throughout the day, and because it was a Friday, each member of the administration kept calling students to their offices; because of complaints about bullying as well as student wellbeing. Every Friday that went by without Mildred herself being called left her relieved. This time, however, she was called to the stage office.

Mildred was called to the stage office where she was asked questions that had to do with her student life. To her all the questions that they asked required long answers, which she was not able to give after her mother's lecture. Mildred lied in answer to every question she was asked, she could tell that the stage principal was more than willing to help her. However, Mildred's fear of Annabella was stronger than her will to answer any of these questions, what did not help her was that she was tied to time constraints.

The school bell rang as it was time to go home, many children played in the school playground or the school ice rink and ice park. Mildred saw them playing, waiting for their carriages to take them on their outings, some of them went to their friends' houses for play dates, others went out to a place where they could play, Alaska included. Mildred was constantly reminded and haunted by the thought of her having absolutely no friends or plans with friends.

Mildred left the school premises. And like every Friday, Alaska did not accompany her on the carriage ride, so the carriage ride was less tense. Mildred went to her room and changed her clothes into an ugly but warm dress, along with a very old coat. Mildred was tired of always being bored, and always being at the castle.

Mildred, however, was very anxious about discussing this with her mother. The princess went to Annabella who was in the basement of the castle, which was right next to the stables.

"Good afternoon, Mother," Mildred said with trepidation.

"Oh, Mildred," Annabella replied like she was talking to a rat. Annabella then raised her head, not wanting to speak to her daughter.

"Mother, I am going to the skating rink then to the mall," Mildred told her mother sharply.

"Yes, whatever, do whatever you want," Annabella stated with indifference. Charles came to where the queen and her daughter were.

"Charles, will you please be my chaperone for today?" Mildred asked Charles sweetly.

"I'll be by the car in the garage in five minutes, be sure to be there if you want to go out," Charles then said. Mildred was ready for her outing. She got to the car, Charles sat in the drivers' seat and promptly drove to the ice-skating rink.

By the time Mildred arrived at the ice-skating rink, she was glowing with happiness and peace. The snow was entrancing; Mildred found it to be beautiful and made her forget her pain. The rink was just a frozen pond, one of the things that Annabella froze so very much. Mildred saw Alaska with her friends at the rink skating happily. She was envious of Alaska but attempted to disregard the feeling.

Mildred went to the bulletin board hanging on the outer walls of the restroom building. On it hung several different reviews, many of them from parents of kids, teenagers, and others closer to Mildred's age. The young princess saw of photographs of kids having fun at this rink, which made her feel even more abandoned. She left the bulletin board to relieve herself and stop feeling envious. Charles paid for the princess to skate on the pond, where she stayed for an hour and a half. The place was safe, and nobody was too cold.

Mildred was actually having some fun skating, however, she saw many different children from her school together. The princess was feeling quite jealous. Mildred was then kicked and fell to the icy ground, which was luckily frozen solid from Annabella's magic, so there was little impact on the ice. She picked herself up and turned around, she found that boys from her school had kicked her and were laughing at her. Alaska's friends joined in. Mildred looked at Alaska and saw sympathy in her eyes, but she also saw weakness; she realized that Alaska was sorry, just not sorry enough. She angrily walked off the rink and went toward Charles.

"Come on, Charles, we're going to the mall!" Mildred said angrily, and she felt her anger still rising. Her bad mood, combined with depression, anger, and anxiety resulted in stormy rain. Not just any rain, but acid rain. After she realized what she was doing, she immediately stopped the magic. Many people at the rink were afraid and looked toward her as if she were a dangerous witch.

Mildred's eye filled with tears, she got into the car and left. She did not even want to go to the mall at that point, she just wanted to cry as usual then sleep. What just happened to her was very difficult. It was after all predictable, but Mildred had wanted to have a good time on a Friday for once.

"I'm very sorry, Your Highness," Charles said to the princess.

"Do you still want to go to the mall?" Charles then said trying to make her feel better.

"No, just take me home," Mildred said sadly.

Charles complied. Mildred looked out the window of the car, watching the snow slowly coming back down after the acid rain had fallen. Mildred looked at the mountains, she looked at the land. She took one last look at the city, where she begun daydreaming then ended up falling asleep.

Chapter Nine
A Decision of Insanity

Winter Wonderland, Cataville, March 5th, 1986

IT had been a while for the royal family of Winter Wonderland. Annabella continued to berate Mildred over the fact that she was not as "good" as Alaska, and for being "a giant," and other times over her powers. Alaska still got everything without asking, things that Mildred so dearly wanted. Mildred's life in school was no better, the bullying became extensive, one would think that the students would forget but they did not.

It was Wednesday, a school day. But Annabella had something else in mind. Both Alaska and Mildred were told to get ready for a special "workshop," instead of going to school that day. Mildred woke up that morning feeling anxious; a special workshop, especially if it was associated with Annabella, was never a good thing. She wore the outfit that was assigned to her, a big Victorian red ball gown along with red sandals and a crown. Mildred left her room, the young princess was breathing quickly as she walked, the exact same hallway that she walked through every day but it wasn't the same for her, the walk through it today felt too long. Strangely, the characters in the paintings seemed to be looking at her slyly and the room felt like it were spinning.

Mildred was very dizzy, but she left the hallway and ran down the stairs quickly, even though she was wearing uncomfortable shoes. Soon she arrived at the ballroom. Alaska was standing in the center of the room, her face appeared peaceful. Alaska was wearing an outfit identical to Mildred's, except it was silver and strangely, more glamorous. Annabella entered the room and appeared to be in a hurry.

"Come on, girls, we need to leave now, Charles! Fetch the carriage!" Annabella then said, as both ideas in her head intertwined into one breath.

"Mother, what is this workshop?" Alaska asked her mother shyly.

"They'll tell you when we get there," Annabella said dismissively.

"Who's they?" Alaska asked. Annabella ignored her.

"Come on," Annabella said when she saw the carriage outside. She walked swiftly out of the palace, Mildred and Alaska had to follow.

The queen sat inside the carriage along with her two daughters.

"International Winter Wonderland City Hall," Annabella told the driver. The carriage took off quickly, making everyone in the carriage anxious. Annabella took out a mirror to check her appearance. Alaska copied her. Mildred started chewing on her finger nails. She also bit her skin as stress consumed her and monsters took over her thoughts. Annabella turned her attention to Mildred and slapped her hand to make her stop.

"Mildred, I do not care how anxious you are! Do not chew your nails! You need to be at your best for this workshop!" Annabella yelled out anxiously. Mildred was annoyed that her mother would not leave her alone. Mildred thought that Annabella was too crazed to know what was good for her. As soon as Mildred had that thought, she took it back, and knew she was beginning to think like her teenage cousins; as she regularly had these thoughts towards adults lately.

Alaska was scared and Mildred felt even more so. The carriage ride went on like this for an hour, nervousness made it seem much longer. Annabella kept rearranging the inside of the carriage, and made it more "presentable." She did the same with her own appearance. She even read books about etiquette, even though she was the most graceful woman Mildred had ever known. Mildred could tell that Annabella was working hard to be at her "best," and because that was what Annabella was doing, Alaska was of course copying her. Mildred felt that it was important to prepare for whatever this event was.

The carriage ride kept going for another hour. The princesses and Annabella had had enough of the carriage ride, each one felt like the ride had gone on forever. It was eleven in the morning when they finally arrived, each of them in a hurry to get out of the carriage. As soon as they did, Alaska felt dizzy, Mildred was completely out of it, and Annabella tried to act normal even though she was the most exhausted.

"Come on, girls, let's go," Annabella calmly told her girls while holding her dress up to lift its edges off the ground. The three of them went inside the building, it looked like a castle, both from the inside and as well as the outside, but it was far smaller and less extravagant. The tension was mounting for the queen and Mildred. Alaska seemed to be the least worried at that point as they walked into the main corridor.

A tall and sophisticated woman walked toward the queen and her daughters. A middle-aged man followed her to meet the queen and her daughters.

"Greetings, Queen Annabella, and how do you do?" the woman said excitedly. The women greeted each other by kissing on the cheek.

"Greetings! Marchioness Gwendoline, we're doing fine, as good as we can be," Annabella said hopelessly. Marchioness Gwendoline looked at the queen's daughters happily.

"Are these our noble princesses?" Gwendoline asked Annabella excitedly.

"Gwendoline, dear, calm down, show respect to their highnesses," the man behind Gwendoline said. Mildred took one look at him and deduced that he was the marquees.

"It's alright dear, just take us to the room where the presentation will be," Annabella told Gwendoline calmly, very much unlike her usual self. Gwendoline and her husband led the three royal women to the central sitting room of city hall.

As Annabella and the princesses entered the room, they saw long and wide stairs that went downwards, with rows and rows of seats as they descended the stairs. Each of them went down the stairs holding their huge dress up. Annabella, Alaska, and Mildred sat at the bottom seats, where they had a complete view of the presentation.

Mildred looked around the huge area. She noticed the hundreds of people filling up the rows, including members of the nobility and the gentry. Each of these people had children her age with them. There was a drumroll to get everyone's attention. An elegant woman was on stage walking toward the podium. The woman was carrying a booklet with her. Mildred guessed the woman would be delivering a speech.

"Greetings your majesties, your highnesses, ladies, and gentlemen. I have a presentation for you." The woman began speaking in a monotonous tone, her voice sounding robotic through the microphone. Next, Annabella smiled and gave a weird look to Alaska, then cast a sad one toward Mildred.

"For many centuries, our planet has suffered from under-population, and it still does. Thankfully, the Great Queen Eliana found a solution in 1878 and most of our problems were solved. On the other hand, our population nowadays does not exceed fifty thousand, much better than the 350 in 1875, but it is still very low. We have gathered here today to introduce the new generation of 1974 to the solution that Eliana's daughter, Queen Adeline, had come up with for under population in 1911," the woman continued.

The wheels in Mildred's head began turning, what could this woman possibly be talking about? Mildred did not imagine anything good to be the "solution" that the woman was talking about. She looked at Alaska's face and saw that she was not a fan of this idea either. However, little did Mildred know, she was about to listen to the voice of true insanity discuss the most atrocious idea she had ever heard in her life.

"The solution that Queen Adeline suggested was…" the woman continued speaking as sweat poured from her head. Mildred could not bear to hear what this woman could possibly be saying, she was too nervous.

"Early marriage…" the woman at the podium finally stated. The tone was set for the rest of the speech. The children, especially Mildred, were not happy. Why on Cataville did early marriage still take place in Winter Wonderland in the eighties? That decision was from 1911. Mildred felt like she was about to faint as the woman continued.

"Our population rates have decreased significantly especially due to the late 1700s and early 1800s war in the entire planet. Marrying children early was the only way we were able to save not just Winter Wonderland, but Cataville. Since taking that decision in 1911, our population has gone from eleven hundred to fifty thousand. Marriage of children in their teens was the best solution that the royal family came up with in order to increase the population needed for Cataville. Royals and nobles have been marrying their children at the ages of 13, 14, and 15 for many years. According to studies, children in Winter Wonderland mature much faster than children on Earth and can fall in love at an early age. Prepare yourselves for this part of your life, especially if you want to save your planet," the woman said.

Misery took over Mildred's head, for the stupidity and the terrors of life in Winter Wonderland would never end. Mildred thought, *she could barely find friends, much less a good husband and prince in Winter Wonderland.* The woman continued saying more ridiculous things that made no sense.

"Oh, for the love of God!" Alaska yelled loudly as she stood up from her seat, interrupting the woman's speech.

"Mother, what on Cataville is she saying?" Alaska began screaming as she looked at Annabella.

"This is terrible, Mother! Do you have any idea what this lady is saying?" Alaska said as she continued to berate Annabella.

"Mother, you made us miss school, you woke us up early this morning, you made us wear these extremely uncomfortable exaggerated outfits, you took us on a two-hour carriage ride, only to hear that I, along with many other people my age, are expected to find love and be married before the age of fifteen!" Mildred roared at Annabella. She had never heard anything more insane, especially about such a serious matter.

"Mildred, behave and stop shouting, you are making us look bad," Annabella said in a whisper.

"Mother, I will not listen one more second to this horrible speech!" Alaska told Annabella angrily.

"Me too," Mildred said.

"What is wrong with the speech? It's a solution for underpopulation, it's alright. I've done it, your grandmother Anneliese has done it, your father has done it, your grandfather has done it, and the parents of your friends have done it! I do not understand what is wrong!" Annabella calmly replied. Mildred was shocked at her mother's response, she never imagined that her mother would be this irrational. Annabella officially had lost her mind.

"Behave, and listen to this lady's speech, I will not tolerate another word," Annabella said. The princesses complied with their mother's words, it was their responsibility to listen to this speech and obey. There was nothing they could do, which made Alaska angry and made Mildred fall apart on the inside.

"I am very sorry, dear, please continue with your speech," Annabella said apologetically to the woman. The woman went on with her speech. Mildred stopped listening and felt nauseous, it was like hearing loud drums which made her head pound.

After hours of listening to a very long speech, the three ladies finally left city hall. Mildred and Alaska sat in the carriage waiting for their mother. Suddenly, and out of nowhere, Alaska struck up a conversation with Mildred.

"God, can you believe Mother! She still believes in this horrible 1911 decision!" Alaska angrily said to her sister.

"It doesn't surprise me, Mother has always been irrational. I'm just worried about what this will do to me," Mildred calmly replied to Alaska.

Alaska and Mildred both sighed at the truth in Mildred's words.

"The woman giving the speech is also out of her mind, this was the most disturbing thing I have ever heard in my life!" Alaska yelled trying to get her sister on board, she knew Mildred agreed for sure.

"It was crazy, but I guess I have to obey Mother's orders," Mildred resignedly said.

"It's hopeless! We will never be normal!" Mildred angrily replied, bursting into tears. Annabella finished talking to people and got into the carriage.

"The castle," Annabella told the chauffer. The carriage started moving, Annabella angrily looked at Mildred.

"Your conduct was improper; you have humiliated me in front of the entire nobility and gentry!" Annabella angrily said to Mildred.

"This is not how a princess should act," Annabella haughtily added.

"Mother, did you really expect us to be quiet! It is the worst idea I have ever heard. You could not possibly believe in what this woman was saying!" Alaska said to her mother.

"Alaska, dear, don't you want riches? Don't you want to be in power? Don't you want to find love? Don't you want a family?" Annabella calmly replied to Alaska, trying to get her to accept.

"You could be happy, you could have a handsome husband, you could bear heirs, and you could have everything!" Annabella continued trying to get Alaska on board.

"Mother, it's not about power or a 'handsome husband' or heirs. It's about our life, we do not need any of this at this age, we are children, and we need to figure ourselves out first," Alaska continued arguing with Annabella.

"Don't act like this will be hard for you, Alaska, I'm not even worried about you, you'll do this very easily. It's Mildred who worries me," Annabella said condescendingly while tilting her head upwards.

Mildred sadly knew that Annabella's words were true, but it was still not what any of them wanted. Especially not Mildred herself.

"No matter how much we argue, this will always be required of you!" Annabella said desperately trying to calm down. The princesses both surrendered to Annabella's words and to the speech; there was no way out, and no way to convince Annabella otherwise.

Mildred felt as if she were drowning, there was nothing she could do. Mildred thought that she just needed to go along with everything that happened today. The carriage ride continued with everyone stressed out. As soon as they left the carriage, each of them went to a separate wing in the castle.

Chapter Ten
Abstract Thought

Winter Wonderland, Cataville, July 27th, 1986

The long break between the sixth and seventh grades was more than halfway done. Ever since the speech, Mildred had been haunted by the woman who had given it, but more so by its contents. Mildred woke up that morning, like every other morning, dreading waking up. She couldn't help feel empty, and this morning was no exception. Life was not exciting anymore, she would just wake up, put on a gown, and be criticized or even struck by Annabella.

Mildred hardly ever left the castle, and if she did, she would not be fully mindful of it, she would know she was out, but she would be too focused on what went on in her head. Sometimes she would stay in her room and cry. She wanted to be happy, but she couldn't, she tried to be brave and not feel anxious all the time, but she failed to do that either. It was like she was tired all the time, she was not physically tired, but she was weary. Every day at breakfast, lunch or dinner, she would hardly notice the food, or her surroundings, it was like she memorized her surroundings but did not understand them. It was the same with food, she realized that she had to eat, but she didn't pay attention to the flavor. She would just eat quickly and be done with it. The young princess would then go back to her room and sulk.

Whenever she spoke to Annabella, the queen was never nice to her. Mildred went back up to her room that morning, she was daydreaming as she walked through the hallway. The girl couldn't think about anything except very few things. Although she wanted to do so, it was as if she was not physically able to do it. It was difficult to live like this, but the princess had no choice, she had no solution to this absent-mindedness. Mildred couldn't imagine what would happen when school began. She lay on her bed and daydreamed some more.

The terrifying speech was on her mind once more. She couldn't be able to marry in her teens, it was something she thought about all day every day. Mildred gave up on happiness, she gave up on trying to help herself get better; it was not like there was anything in her life to get better for. No one liked her, it was like nobody wanted anything to do with her or her life. It was already very difficult to deal with Annabella, much less all her princess duties, her education, and all the stuff that she was meant to do.

The young princess was tired of this, she was desperately looking for an escape. Mildred looked through the window, she saw Alaska playing outside in the snow, and Annabella sitting outside watching her. Mildred sat in her room then lost focus again. What if she hadn't been this tall? What if she had acquired the snow powers her family had? Mildred looked in the mirror, there were many blemishes on her face, and her attention turned to the black circles around her eyes. Mildred realized that she looked quite mature for her age, as did Alaska. Mildred took out her calendar and looked through it. She held her pen and wrote down an appointment with her facial specialist for the first time.

Mildred picked up the phone in her room. Her attention was still inward and her actions were automatic as well as what she had to say.

"Hello…" Mildred spoke as she breathed into the phone, when the facial specialist answered the phone.

"How do you do?" Mildred asked the woman on the other end, after she greeted Mildred.

"I'm looking to book a session with you, maybe today at six?" Mildred said, because that's what she had decided she'd say.

"Oh, you have one with Alaska today at six?" Mildred said without emotion. She did not know what to say next, she was nervous until the woman replied.

"Alright that means tomorrow, seven o'clock," Mildred said, accepting the appointment the woman gave, then hung up.

Mildred felt very energetic, she walked toward the stereo, and pressed the on button. Pop music started playing, Mildred started dancing and floating into a whole other world. As she danced, she dreamt up scenarios of her speaking to people in different places about random topics. A habit she had picked up months ago, which she loved and did not feel the need to get rid of. The princess continued dancing for hours.

Loud sounds came from Mildred's room, they were so loud and strong, a lot like public parties that people such as Annabella found offensive. Charles went to the room.

"Mildred, are you OK?" Charles asked her, worried.

"Oh Charles, I'm fine," Mildred answered wildly.

"Alright…" Charles replied then left.

Mildred continued dancing and went back to her day dreaming and her unfocused mindset in just a few seconds and continued to dance for a further hour and a half. That is, until Annabella and Alaska entered the room.

"Mildred, what are you doing?!" Annabella angrily asked Mildred.

"We could hear you from the other end of the castle?" Annabella yelled at Mildred.

"The vibrations your music is creating are utterly unbearable, it's horrible!" Annabella continued yelling some more.

"God, your room smells horrible, this is not suitable for a princess!" Annabella remarked haughtily, gesturing wildly with her hands.

What did her mother want with her? Why did Annabella care about Mildred's dancing? All she did was spoil Alaska and criticize Mildred.

"I'm just having fun, Mother!" Mildred replied defensively.

"Fine… Rot in here for all I care," Annabella said with disinterest, and a few moments, she and Alaska left Mildred's room.

Mildred stopped dancing, she washed up after all the physical activity and the rollercoaster of her emotions. She then left her room. After wasting half the day, Mildred went outside.

She sat on the bench in the middle of the beautiful snow-covered courtyard, she stayed on her own outside, lost in thought. That was all she did with her life, and she could not bring herself to get out of that mindset. It got harder every day, week, and month. Except that here the air was a bit fresher, it made no difference whether she was inside or out. The princess's mood worsened after a few thoughts, she hated the way her life was. Mildred hated how hard having these thoughts was, but she hated the fact that there was nothing nice about her life that would motivate her to rescue herself from this way of thinking even more.

Snow continued falling to the ground, which drew her attention to Annabella and Alaska working their magic as usual. Mildred got up and turned around, she walked through the garden and walked and walked, till she reached the secret garden.

Mildred adored this new place; she felt her powers. Mildred decided to give her powers a try. It rained, but only in that small secret garden. The power in her hands became even stronger, and she enjoyed it. Trees with autumn leaves rose from the ground, and the leaves of trees already in this secret garden turned yellow, and all the snow fell off of them. Mildred was angry at the sight of snow. She raised the rain fall in that area and made sure that every last bit of snow in the secret garden melted.

Mildred enjoyed doing this, she soon perfected the routine, then returned to drifting off in her own thought. Mildred worried about how she would deal with focusing at school, after remembering that school was starting in only four weeks. She also couldn't use her powers there and enjoy them like she was doing now. Not long afterwards, the rain Mildred was creating turned into acid rain which made her stop her magic.

The princess then felt she needed to get out of that place, it was painful but necessary. It was soon night time, and Mildred ran out of the garden, through the snowy land, past the castle doors and into her room. Mildred put on her nightgown and couldn't wait to go to bed.

Winter Wonderland, Cataville, July 28th, 1986

Mildred woke up that morning again, just like every day, in her never-ending nightmare. It was to be yet another day of cruelty, another day of feeling tired all the time, another day of extensive loneliness, another day of extreme dread, and another day of being unable to focus. Mildred went to wash up in the bathroom, then she put on a gown as usual, her actions were automatic as she put on the dress. Mildred left her bedroom and went through the way that she had memorized.

The princess reached the area of the grand majestic front door. As she was going down the large staircase toward that area, she saw Annabella and Alaska standing in front of the castle doors and stopped, they looked to be dressed in their coat-gown clothing they wore when they went out in very heavy snowy. Annabella was also speaking to Charles about something.

"I ordered the limousine outside, Alaska and I will be shopping for new gowns in order to help find her a husband. If you need me, we'll be in 'Grandiene Mall,'" Annabella said to Charles.

"Very well, Your Majesty, would you like anything else?" Charles asked the queen respectfully.

"No, go, don't disturb us… unless it's vital," Annabella said while raising her nose and rolling her eyes. Annabella did not notice Mildred standing on the steps of the long staircase, and just raised her gown and gracefully went through the doors of the castle. Alaska looked at Mildred out of the corner of her eye, not with hatred but with empathy, as if she couldn't face Mildred and didn't have the heart to say or do anything. Alaska turned around and just walked away following her mother. The doors of the castle closed behind them, Mildred stood rooted to her spot; she would usually feel troubled by this type of scenario but this time felt nothing.

Mildred continued going down the stairs and went to have breakfast, seemingly unaffected by what had just happened. She went back to her usual dream world, that she did not notice anything that she was doing and performed all her daily tasks stuck inside her head. Mildred went to the castle screen TV that she couldn't use without receiving a few harsh words from Annabella.

Mildred placed the tape inside the video player. It was a tape of a show that had been on before she had been born. She watched the episodes of the show, each of the episodes talked about friendship. The show also showed scenes of innocent romance. It also featured themes such as parent-child relationships. She stopped watching after the eighth episode. She didn't feel anything towards what she had just watched, and just got on with her day. The sound of the castle doors opening reached her ears, making Mildred realize that her mother and sister were back. She ran to her bedroom through a shortcut using the back staircase in of the castle.

Mildred was immediately anxious as she entered her bedroom, for she dreaded having to deal with her mother and sister. Alaska came to Mildred's room carrying a pile of new clothes.

"Good afternoon, Mildred, would you like to see my new dresses?" Alaska asked.

"Sure, whatever," Mildred replied to Alaska, with resentment. Alaska went on to try on each of her dresses, come out of the bathroom and showing each them to Mildred. Mildred looked at all the beautiful gowns, and although she thought they were completely wonderful, she was envious.

"Are you OK, Mildred?" Alaska asked her sister at one point, when she saw the indifference and sadness in her eyes.

"Oh yes, I'm fine. Continue," Mildred answered her sister. After Alaska finished showing Mildred all twenty new dresses, Mildred was more depressed than ever; her feelings of sadness were consuming her on the inside, not caused by anything that happened, or anything that Alaska had said, rather a reaction she had towards her overall life.

Mildred spent a couple of hours inside her room, she just contemplated her life for there was nothing else to do. As it neared seven o'clock, she had to get ready for her appointment.

Mildred walked to the castle spa, until she got to a room that had a bed covered in towels that Mildred would lay on. A relaxing smell wafted from the room, and the ambiance gave one a feeling of serenity. Mildred's attention was drawn to a device that accurately measured height. Mildred then considered it with sadness, for she knew she was too tall, and that was ruining her life. Mildred was then curious and anxious to see how tall she really was. She stood where she was supposed to measure to her height. "172.5 centimeters," the machine read, Mildred's mood then sank further. She was only twelve, how could she be 172.5 centimeters already. It was believable though; for whoever saw her, realized she is in fact that tall, was astonishing.

The spa specialist entered the room, and saw Mildred looking out the window peacefully.

"Hello, Your Highness," the woman greeted Mildred. The princess then turned around slowly.

"Oh, hello! Shall we start with my facial," Mildred replied. The specialist obeyed the princess's request. Mildred lay on the bed, on top of the towels and the specialist covered her with a blanket and her hair with a towel. Steam was coming out of the steam machine onto Mildred's face. As the steam blew onto her face, she suddenly realized that she was the one who booked this, Annabella did not do this for her like she did for Alaska. Yet the reason she booked this treatment was to meet the expectations of her idiotic society, and her idiotic nasty scheming mother and her deranged ideas.

The specialist let the steam go on for ten minutes, while she was applying all sorts of masks and lotions onto Mildred's face. At the end of these minutes, she massaged Mildred's face to clean it. When the session ended, Mildred got up and felt light headed, but she did not give it much thought. She did not care about the fact that her face was clean either, she had bigger things to worry about. It was nine in the evening at that point, and she just thanked the facial specialist and went to her room to sleep.

Winter Wonderland, Cataville, September 29th, 1986, Morning

Mildred woke up one more time, she was getting sick of this. She had to endure daily emotional torture, it made her feel as if she wanted to die. Mildred took another look at her bed, she wished she could've slept forever. She had to wake up, but she wished that she did not have to. Mildred wasn't happy, but nobody knew that. She freshened up as usual, only to find the two people that she hated the most, were standing in the middle of her room. What could they possibly want now?

Chapter Eleven
Unusual Intensity

Winter Wonderland, Cataville, September 10th, 1986

More time passed, and it got more difficult to cope. Especially as Mildred started her first day of seventh grade. Mildred and Alaska were in the carriage going to school as usual, the snow stronger and heavier than usual. Mildred titled her face and looked at the snow, without really paying much attention to it. The young princess's heart beat very quickly, the tension almost palpable in the carriage, Mildred fanned herself vigorously with her red fan. The carriage moved even faster with even more tension, the snow getting heavier by the minute. She was wondering what would happen this year at school? Would people continue to bully her? Would she finally make friends?

"Hey, Mildred, are you excited to start school today?" Alaska asked smiling, trying to disperse the tension. Mildred gave Alaska her angriest and dirtiest looks and appeared to be about to slap Alaska; she already knew the answer to that question, and it was not a good one. The carriage kept moving faster and faster, and the bad mood in the carriage grew deeper.

The princesses arrived at school, heaven for Alaska, hell for Mildred, and they parted ways. Mildred went to the bulletin board, she examined it, looking for her name and classroom. Mildred found her name in a list of names she didn't recognize which made her happy. The princess held up her thin black gown, and walked gracefully up the stairs and through the hallways till she got to her new classroom. Mildred entered her classroom, and her teacher assigned her to a remote seat.

In a few minutes everyone was at their seats, the homeroom teacher had a special treat for them.

"Greetings, royals and nobles, I am Ms. Shirley. I am your homeroom teacher and I will be teaching you English," the teacher said, clasping her hands.

"In honor of our first day, we are going to be playing a game, now I will toss this ball to one of you randomly, and whoever receives this ball has to say their name, title, and a fact about themselves," Ms. Shirley stated with anxious enthusiasm. Ms. Shirley tossed the ball towards the middle of the classroom. It landed in the hands of a boy who stood up. He wore a dark blue sweater with a tie and long pants that were the same dark blue. Mildred turned her attention to his face, examining it. The boy was not handsome at all, wavy black hair covered his head, he wore glasses, he had a few moles on his face, his lips were very wide and so was his nose. He also had a hairy forehead.

"Hello, I am lil' Baron Samuel Jerram, and I love to read in my spare time," the boy said, then tossed the ball back to Ms. Shirley. The teacher tossed the ball to many other students and all did the same thing as Samuel. Twenty-five minutes passed; it was halfway through the first period. After a girl had her turn, the teacher's attention was on Mildred. The teacher threw the ball towards Mildred, who caught it. Mildred then walked to the front of the classroom.

Mildred was very anxious, and she had nothing to say about herself, she thought that she had no personality, or that she had one that she didn't want to share.

"Good morning, I am Princess Mildred of Winter Wonderland..." Mildred said then froze. Seconds passed by slowly and sweat poured down her head.

"Don't you have anything that you'd like to share with us, Mildred?" the teacher kindly asked.

"And I... I like to dance..." Mildred said hesitantly. She went back to her chair and the game continued. The teacher tossed the ball to more students, till she was done with nearly all of them. The teacher threw the ball to the final student, who was a boy. He wore a suit, it was not that fancy though, he had messy brown curly hair. Mildred then saw his face, he was good looking.

"Hey, I'm lil' Duke Alexi Taylor, and I play soccer all the time," he said, Mildred felt unusual intensity towards him, she didn't know what it was, but it was there, nonetheless. It was as if she hated him, but at the same time she wanted to be close to him. Mildred tried to ignore the feeling. The day continued normally, until recess.

Mildred left the classroom and put on her coat and went to recess. She was full of dread, what was her mind doing to her? She saw Alexi again, and looked at him with the unusual intensity that had a touch of fondness. Mildred ignored this and ate her food. Mildred then saw Samuel, walking near the boys who were playing basketball, she wondered why he was not playing with them.

The princess felt bad, the students had other children to play with. She was not responsible for Samuel, and she was not about to go there as she was in no state to get hurt again, she ignored him and spent that recess alone, but it didn't end there.

Winter Wonderland, Cataville, September 24th, 1986

Mildred got used to her average days of school, she had been in the seventh grade for more than a week. She was still inside her head, stuck with her ideas all the time. The princess entered the classroom that day, she had a bright smile on her face. She sat on her seat in anticipation, she was unusually excited to see her new classmates, as if she was looking for something else.

Suddenly, the sound of the door opening slowly came from the other side of the castle. It was Alexi, he walked to a few boys in class who were his friends. Class had not started yet, and Mildred continued to watch Alexi quietly. *Good Alexi, he was so good looking*, at least she thought so. The way he spoke to the boys, his voice was mesmerizing. She told herself to snap out of it, what on Cataville was happening?

Mildred wondered how she could think such a thing, or why she had this burning hatred for him and was so intrigued by him at the same time. The bell rang, and Mildred turned her attention away from him, as the lesson was about to begin. She made sure to focus in class, because with time it became harder for her to do so.

The young princess's attention in classroom was no longer about Annabella or Alaska or the bullying; it was all on Alexi. Mildred's attention kept wandering off from the material being taught in class to Alexi, she would consciously bring her attention back to class, but it would go back to Alexi. This went on like a tug of war.

Recess began and the princess went to the playground. She was met the same sights that she encountered regularly, with Samuel hanging out near the other boys who played basketball without joining them; he did not join anyone else either. Mildred was sad; she was unable to make friends and her not having any was nothing new. But that someone else who had potential to make friends didn't have any made her feel sad. Mildred was in no shape to get hurt again, and kept resisting the urge to speak to Samuel, but she succumbed in the end.

Mildred went up to Samuel.

"Greetings, Samuel, how are you doing?" Mildred said warmly, even though her voice was slightly high-pitched.

"Greetings, Your Highness, I'm doing fine, what about you?" Samuel replied in an even more squeaky voice.

"Please, call me Mildred," the princess said as they began walking together.

"Why do you spend your time alone?" Mildred asked calmly.

"I don't. I have these guys as friends," Samuel answered, pointing to the boys were playing in the basketball court. Mildred could tell he was lying, but she didn't question him over it.

"Then why don't you play basketball with them?" Mildred asked trying to be nice.

"I do… usually…" the boy replied sheepishly. Mildred then realized that he was lying, she couldn't blame him though; their society was very judgmental.

They talked on for the rest of recess, as they walked throughout all the places they could go outside, the snow kept falling, but they enjoyed it along with their conversation. Mildred and Samuel talked about everything that had to do with school, it was like she was a mother teaching a child how to protect himself. They discussed Alexi, but Mildred did not mention anything about the way she felt towards him. It was like Alexi was attracted to her thoughts and to her conversation with Samuel like a magnet. This went on for quite a while.

Winter Wonderland, Cataville, October 31st, 1986

Mildred went on with her life, trying to hold on as hard as she could. She regularly had bad moods; the bad moods wouldn't leave her. Mildred's mind was also always occupied by Alexi which frustrated her. Today was Halloween. This day also included a birthday party for a girl in her classroom. Mildred was not close to that girl, but as a classmate she was invited. The princess also had something in mind.

The boys and girls in the classroom were all invited to the party, Mildred thought Alexi would be coming as well. The young princess went shopping on her own that morning; her mother wouldn't buy her nice clothing, so she had to do this herself. Mildred wanted to look good for "the party." The princess was also on a diet; for she didn't want to "gain weight" and wanted to "stay beautiful." Mildred bought a thin yellow dress from the mall in Winter Wonderland.

As the princess arrived back to her room, she began styling her hair, then her eyebrows the way Annabella taught Alaska. Mildred thought that she and Alaska were still too young to worry this much about their appearance, but people in Winter Wonderland disagreed, and she thought that it didn't matter at that point; she had never had a normal childhood anyway. Mildred took out her facial cleanser from her dresser, when suddenly Alaska came in.

"Hello, Mildred, how are you doing?" Alaska asked, giggling. Alaska then took in Mildred's yellow gown, her styled hair, the facial cleanser on Mildred face and knew how Mildred was doing.

"Mildred, you don't need to do all of this just to impress some guy," Alaska said sweetly, forcing Mildred to put down the facial cleanser and drag her attention back to Alaska with an eyeroll.

"Since when do you care? You've been the respected heir and mother's brat since we were born! You never had to improve yourself! You had the ability to make people love you by doing nothing! I have to do this for my soul to know what happiness is!" Mildred replied angrily, and went on fixing her appearance.

Alaska let out a big sigh, she understood Mildred, and couldn't do anything. She left her sister to do her business. By the time Mildred had finished at the end of that morning she looked sixteen or seventeen rather than twelve. The princess left the castle and went to the party.

The party was at a pavilion, a pavilion that had golden cobblestone circular flooring, and peach colored columns that had plants encircling them top to bottom, the color of ceiling of the pavilion was also peach, and diamonds sparkled all over it. Mildred took it all in as she entered; she was one of the first people to get to the party. She sat and waited for people to arrive, and eventually they did. Noble girls and noble boys started arriving at the party, but not Alexi. Samuel eventually arrived and he and Mildred hung out. More time passed without Alexi showing up. This made Mildred more and more anxious. She tried to ignore this and have fun with Samuel. The party was lot of fun, better than being criticized or slapped by Annabella at home.

Eventually it was time for snacks and the cake. Mildred and Samuel joined in where everyone was singing "Happy Birthday" to the birthday girl. The princess sang along with them, but it was all without thinking, rather she was focused on nothing but Alexi, she was not even thinking about her friend Samuel, rather on Alexi, the boy in her class who did not usually speak to her. Mildred's attention was back on her surrounding, where everyone was clapping for the birthday girl. It was time to eat. The main course was fast food made by the restaurant "RFO," and the cake was, well… cake. Mildred considered the food and felt nauseated. They expected her to eat this cake full of fat? Or this unhealthy fast food meal also full of fat? She couldn't do it, especially not if she wanted people to notice her.

Everyone at the party ate the food, but Mildred only ate a plain salad she got from the castle. When everyone was done, she spent some more time with Samuel, and they had fun as usual. When the limousine arrived, she went home before the end of the party. The princess was disappointed as she left the party, but she thought she would have other chances to become Alexi's "friend." That was what she thought she wanted.

Chapter Twelve
Progress

Winter Wonderland, Cataville, November 6th, 1986

Only a week had gone by, yet so much had happened since, at least in Mildred's head. Mildred's hatred toward her life grew. *But there was one light in her life*, at least she thought so. Every day that went by, Mildred looked forward to seeing Alexi, even though they hardly ever spoke. Something surprising happened that day, and the princess was happy about it.

Mildred woke up that morning. By then she had been paying much more attention to the way she looked. Her face had nearly cleared up, her hair was always nicely styled; she always looked as though she was going to a royal ball. She went to school and sat there for the entire day and hoped he would notice her, but she ended up just hanging out with Samuel. That day, the teacher called the classroom's attention.

"Good morning class, how are you doing? Today I have a new seating chart for you..." their teacher nervously said.

"Ugh..." some children exclaimed.

"But we're happy in our places!" another student angrily shouted. Mildred, however, did not care much, for once she did not hate anyone in that class, and so she didn't really care where she sat.

The teacher rearranged the students' seats. This new arrangement was heaven and hell for Mildred. Her new seat was in a group with two others, one girl who was called Selma and the other was Alexi. Mildred was as happy as she was angry. He drove her crazy, but he also excited her. Mildred settled into her new seat and saw both Selma and Alexi sit at their new desks. At last, Mildred and Alexi began talking properly in class. They discussed many things, not that day of course, but during the time they sat together, ranging from their hobbies, their friends, to their activities and dreams, and ending with their "families."

Mildred felt like she was getting closer to Alexi day by day. She and Samuel talked on the phone every day. But Alexi only hung out with Mildred in class and did not spend any time with her outside; he spent most of his time with his other "popular" friends. The princess spent time with Samuel which she didn't mind, Samuel was very nice, intelligent, and very much into reading.

Winter Wonderland, Cataville, November 13th, 1986

The same thing kept on going with Mildred and Alexi for the whole week, they talked in class, and then they'd part to spend time with their friends. Today, however, the school was organizing a big movie night for the students. Mildred had no idea what movie they were going to watch, but she was going to enjoy the socializing with her fellow students that she never had before. School ended for that day, and Mildred went home directly to get ready, which meant spending hours getting ready in order to look suitable.

Mildred was finished getting ready, after putting in a great deal of effort, both on the inside and the outside. It was quarter-past six by then, twenty minutes before the movie night started. She knew she had to hurry to arrive on time. Another thought came to her, she needed to face Annabella again; to tell her about this.

The young princess left her room, when suddenly she saw the statues alive for a few seconds. She blinked and thought she must have had been dreaming. She kept walking, trying to practice controlling her fantasies and steadiness, which she had convinced herself she needed to do in order not to drive Alexi away. She was worried that if Alaska heard her, she'd criticize her for thinking this way. Suddenly Annabella appeared in front of her and she gasped, only to realize that it was Charles. But why had she seen Annabella?

"Are you alright, Your Highness?" Charles asked.

"Oh… yes," Mildred answered, dazed.

"Dear Charles, take me to my mother… please," Mildred requested from the castle steward, still dazed and now getting one of her regular anxiety attacks. Charles walked with Mildred to her mother, as they walked, the princess drifted off into her daydreams yet again. Thoughts came to Mildred's mind, such as what Annabella would say or do when she and Mildred would meet? Will she be able to get close to Alexi? She wanted to get close to Alexi, but why?

The princess and Charles reached the formal sitting room, where Annabella was sitting berating servants as usual. The poor servant walked away when she saw Mildred and left in peace after Annabella gave her hell.

"What on Cataville could you possibly want now?!" Annabella yelled at Mildred, sitting gracefully with one leg crossed over the other, which was uncomfortable due to her big red dress. Annabella got up and walked over to Mildred, angrily waiting for a response as she glided across the room.

"Talk, you pain!" Annabella yelled pettily.

"Your Majesty, did you forget your pills today?" Charles asked Annabella.

"Why… yes, I did…" Annabella replied as if she realized something important she forgot.

"Mother, can I go to the school's movie night?" Mildred asked as Annabella walked in a circle slowly around Mildred and Charles, making the entire room feel suspense.

"A movie night, I see, your hair done perfectly, I see you're wearing your favorite dress… Don't tell me you actually think something might happen with…" Annabella mocked, while doing a second turn around Charles and Mildred, until Alaska came in and interrupted by touching her back.

"Whatever… go! … Do whatever you want…" Annabella said without interest.

"Charles, will you please take me to the school in the limousine quickly?" Mildred sweetly asked Charles, and they both hurried to the car.

During the ride Mildred went back to drifting into her daydreams, she kept thinking about Alexi, she didn't know why but she did. Mildred arrived, and met up with Samuel as the movie was about to start. Mildred got her snacks to enjoy during the movie, she hadn't spotted Alexi yet, but she was very anxious for that moment. Mildred spent the first hour of the event laughing and talking to Samuel while watching the movie, Samuel spent the night talking about the movie; for it was the first part of a movie series that he adored and had watched many times.

The first hour went by quickly, and Mildred went to go get more food, where she finally saw Alexi. Even though Alexi was the son of a duke, he was not wearing anything nearly as glamorous as Mildred, and neither was anything else about the way he looked. Mildred still found him very good-looking that night, even though he wasn't that much. Alexi waved to her and smiled, and Mildred waved back. The princess then saw him go back to his friends which was expected but it still hurt. They had been regularly talking, they hadn't had enough time.

Mildred went back to Samuel, and she tried to have fun. She comforted herself by knowing that she was making progress with Alexi. The princess enjoyed the rest of the night with Samuel, her friend; she was really glad to have him.

The princess stopped eating, she was constantly afraid of putting on weight, especially since she was Alexi was finally noticing her. It was still early, and the mood of the entire school was a happy one, at least in Mildred's eyes. The princess kept eying Alexi and saw him with his friends every time.

The young princess did not understand what she felt that night, or what she regularly felt around that person, could it be a crush? She was not sure, she didn't think it could be. The night ended and all was well, and everything seemed to be according to "working order and plan" in Mildred's words. The princess hoped for more, and she thought that would eventually happen.

Winter Wonderland, Cataville, The Remainder of November 1986

As the days went by, the cycle of "progress" continued. Mildred thought she was getting closer to Alexi, and she was hoping if she couldn't get respect at home, then she could at least be one of the cool kids.

This part of her life was quick and exciting, and handling Annabella's anger had become a little bit easier for Mildred, for she had a light in her life. Mildred was regularly excited about seeing Alexi at school. They still weren't close though; he still hung out with his friends who bullied her sometimes. Mildred was happy with Samuel, but she was not happy enough. The princess thought being close to Alexi would make her have a more normal life than the one she had.

Mildred had negative encounters with Annabella on a regular basis, encounters that involved the same kind of suffering, insults, and physical abuse, ending in emotional torture that remained with Mildred. Alaska continued to be spoiled by her mother, most of which she rejected but still got anyway.

Annabella began to look for a husband for Alaska, but obviously not for Mildred. This was especially a strain for Mildred, for that part of her life she had some hope that she could control life herself. Her life went on, constant disrespect from her mother, endless discrimination between her and her sister, and wanting to get closer to Alexi.

"Progress…" Mildred hoped for, she thought she had it, at least for a little while.

The princess especially caught on love songs, wasn't sure whether what she felt was love or even a crush; she constantly felt empty and worried. She related to many of the romantic songs she listened to, she committed herself to be the "approachable" type.

Mildred acted in a way that her mother cringed at, it was not clear whether it was disgust consuming Annabella or just envy. This was new for Mildred, and she couldn't understand it properly; she had a lot to think about.

Mildred knew she was a good student, she studied whenever there was a quiz. She'd get distracted, but it was not enough to stop good grades. The princess tended to doze off in class, usually thinking about her relationship with Alexi progressing, her problems or just about different things.

The princess's powers got stronger every day, and sometimes she'd find something new about them. Mildred discovered how to manipulate the amount of rain she released, she learned how to control the creation of autumn trees and her ability to transform winter trees to autumn trees. As the princess became more experienced with her abilities and powers, she used them more regularly; which got her more criticism from

Annabella. But the more she used them, the more she stopped caring about the queen's reaction.

Mildred's life was still harder at the castle, her home, which she considered to be prison. Her opinion of school was no different. If anything, it was the same, if not worse.

When it came to the princess's problems or even questions about her life, she was alone and had nobody to talk with. This made her rely on research, from books and letters, being reliable or unreliable, it was all she had. Mildred kept going like this for the rest of November. It was tough, but she had to keep holding on.

Chapter Thirteen
More Failure

Winter Wonderland, Cataville, December 3rd, 1986

The past month had been the longest for the princess of Winter Wonderland, she was happy that it was finally over. It was finally a school day after a five-day break. Mildred, feeling more anxious about what Alexi thought of her, which was an endless cycle of excitement and disappointment. The princess went through her daily school morning routine, with the usual amount of anxiety.

Mildred was in her classroom, she was hoping to build a closer friendship with Alexi. She sat at her desk, and Alexi and other classmate sat as well. The teacher entered and changed the seating chart again. Mildred now sat with Samuel, and Alexi now sat at the very back. The princess took that as normal and did not think that it would have any negative consequences on their relationship, especially since she thought they had achieved an actual relationship.

Winter Wonderland, Cataville, December 10th, 1986

Some time had passed since Mildred and Alexi's seats were separated. Mildred seemed to be more affected by this then Alexi, for him it was just normal, but she didn't think Alexi would stop talking to her, just after the seating chart was modified. It was strange, what if Alexi didn't like her? What if he hated her? What did he think of her?

Mildred then began planning a way to find out. Who did everyone like? Who did everyone trust? Who could find out what Alexi's true opinion was of Mildred? The princess thought of

Alaska. Mildred waited till it was recess, and went to the cafeteria, where Alaska and her friends hung out.

Mildred saw Alaska, sitting with a group of five other girls and two boys. She walked towards them where the sound of their chattering was louder than ever.

"Alaska…" Mildred called out to her sister shyly, which got everyone of Alaska's friends to roll their eyes or snort.

"May I have a word with you?" Mildred nervously asked her sister.

"But of course," Alaska answered, making the kids even more displeased. Nonetheless, Alaska still went with her sister. The two princesses went to a private area in order for Alaska to hear what Mildred had to ask.

"I would like to ask you for a favor," Mildred anxiously said.

"What favor?" Alaska replied to Mildred, interested, a reaction that Mildred rarely got from anyone. Alexi walked by the area between buildings where Alaska and Mildred were standing.

"Does it have to do with him?" Alaska asked Mildred.

"Yes…" Mildred sheepishly replied.

"Spill your guts," Alaska said to Mildred, her bad feelings getting stronger.

"I need you to find out whether he likes me or not," Mildred nervously blurted out the words.

"And how do you suggest doing that?" Alaska asked Mildred with an eyeroll. Mildred looked at Alaska with a lost look in her eyes. Alaska realized that Mildred was clueless.

"Alright, I have an idea," Alaska replied to Mildred with a sigh that hinted that she did not want to do this.

"Thank you, Alaska," Mildred said. Alaska did not reply but took Mildred with her back to the cafeteria.

When the two princesses entered the cafeteria, there was only nine minutes left of recess.

"We need to act fast… Hide somewhere, Mildred, we can't let anyone see you," Alaska said. Alaska went back to her friends and got an object they could spin.

"We will be playing truth or dare!" Alaska told her friends excitedly. Alexi walked into the cafeteria at that moment giving Alaska the perfect chance to get on with her plan.

"Alexi! We are playing truth or dare, come join us!" Alaska shouted.

"It's alright," Alexi replied.

"No, we insist," Alaska said sweetly to Alexi. Alexi walked over to Alaska and her friends where the game began. Mildred hid where Alexi couldn't see her, but where she could hear everything.

"I brought this with me to spin, the two people toward whom the edges are directed ask and answer," Alaska informed the group. The game began, and many people other than Alaska and Alexi asked and answered. The clock was ticking, and recess was nearly over, Alaska and Mildred were becoming very impatient. Alaska raised her hand slightly without anyone noticing, and worked her magic making a little wind blow the spinner lightly till it was between Alaska and Alexi.

"So, I guess, I will be asking you now," Alaska said to Alexi.

"Truth or dare…" Alaska said then looked at him with an intimidating look that was very much like Annabella's.

"Truth…" Alexi replied to Alaska, a little scared of her.

"Um…" Alaska said like a good actress. Mildred strained her ears at what was happening, the suspense killing her.

"Who do you not like in your classroom? Who do you hate? Which classmate has insulted you?" Alaska asked in a manner just like Annabella's, making Mildred roll her eyes.

"I guess… Lil' Count Mufasaleous and Princess Mildred," Alexi replied, making Alaska angry, but she was able to hide it. Mildred quietly gasped, and her feelings of helplessness began to heavily consume her. To everyone's relief, the bell rang which ended the game. The group playing the game dispersed, and Alaska was able to go back to Mildred.

"I'm very sorry, Mildred," Alaska said, and Mildred cried a bit.

"He's not worth it, dear sister," Alaska tried to comfort Mildred as she had never done before.

"I know, but I wanted this in my life so badly… I don't understand," Mildred unhappily said, and Alaska ran to her class leaving Mildred alone. The princess wiped her tears with napkins from her bag. Mildred then walked to her classroom and drifted off into her thoughts.

He hated her, why wouldn't he hate her? Who didn't hate her? It's very unreasonable… yet so very true. Mildred felt like a true failure, and her feelings of helplessness took over. Mildred was already always feeling sad, but now felt like she had no use of this world. She wished she was never born, she hated her life, and she hated herself. It was like a demon inside kept following her to torture her forever. The princess couldn't control that beast, but it controlled her.

Mildred couldn't focus at all for the rest of the day. When the day ended, she locked herself in her room, and withdrew from everything for the next few days. It was difficult for the princess. Eventually, she got better, and began to hate Alexi like he hated her. The princess stopped caring about him, she just went on with her life as usual. Mildred was able to focus in her classroom again and did not have anyone to think about much and just spent her time with Samuel. Samuel was more than enough at that point.

The end of term exams began, and she was able to get through them like many other previous exams. Mildred was doing alright, at least during that time. The princess always felt down, but it was no longer because of Alexi; it was because of her luck. What is it with everyone in her life disliking her? And if they liked her, it wasn't enough, or they stopped liking her.

What is it that she felt towards Alexi? Why was she this affected by him hating her? The thought of it was very strange and it was something that Mildred did not understand, or did she? What if she did know what it was and kept denying it? Did she like him romantically? This was certainly a first. She couldn't, she didn't want to. The princess finally was able to conclude, or rather admit what had been going on with her in the past months.

Winter Wonderland, Cataville, December 27th, 1986

Mildred woke up that Saturday morning feeling terrible as usual. It was a loophole that she was stuck in and couldn't leave. Mildred felt tired as she woke up that morning, she had just slept, but it was tiresome that sleep did not treat. The princess took out a book that she could read that morning, where she heard the creak of a door bursting open.

"Mildred!" A voice sounded in anger. Mildred looked up and saw Annabella, with the same red hue in her blue eyes that she had seen many years ago.

"Yes, Mother..." Mildred said to Annabella in utmost fear.

"Why don't you ever get out? You look absolutely horrible," Annabella said to Mildred just to criticize her. Mildred understood that children locking themselves in their room was something parents worried about, but surely Annabella was just telling her this to insult her.

"What do you want, Mother?" Mildred rudely asked.

"Don't you dare talk back to me, you brat!" Annabella loudly yelled. Mildred hid the heat she felt inside. Annabella walked to the very end of the room, and stood in front of the window. The queen looked out the window peacefully, and Mildred watched her and wondered about her actions.

"This is about that Count Alexi," Annabella spoke in a disconnected voice.

"What about him?" Mildred asked, annoyed.

"You liked him," Annabella answered.

"What are you implying?" Mildred anxiously asked her mother.

"You actually thought he would like you!" Annabella said, laughing hysterically. Annabella turned around and gave her the usual threatening stare, looking scarier than ever.

"You will never get married, Mildred, you will never meet society's standards as a princess," Annabella stated softly.

"Mother, who told you about Alexi?" Mildred respectfully asked her mother.

"Oh... nobody..." Annabella replied innocently.

"Mother!" Mildred said pushing the queen to give her an answer.

"Ah... Now that, I found out myself..." Annabella said as she walked back toward Mildred.

"How? Mother, how?!" the princess begged the queen.

"Look at you! Begging?" Annabella mocked Mildred, then laughed hysterically again.

"I used to hear you talking about it in your bedroom," the queen said calmly, as she sat on the chair in front of Mildred's dresser.

"Why is that?" Mildred questioned the queen more. "Why is it that you are obsessed with giving me trouble?! Why is it that you are obsessed with hearing about my life then criticizing it? Why do you want to make me miserable so badly?" Mildred angrily lashed out at Annabella. Annabella stood up from her seat gracefully, and walked to stand right in front of Mildred, who looked at her in unhidden fear.

"Never speak to me like that!" Annabella angrily said, then slapped Mildred yet again, which left a scar under her eye. Annabella then left the room. Mildred was very happy that Annabella left the room and that she could now spend her time in peace. A few moments, the princess couldn't stop herself from crying as she slipped back into her absent mindset, where nobody could hurt her.

Chapter Fourteen
Mental Pain

Winter Wonderland, Cataville, January 12th, 1987

Mildred was finally on break from school, it was later than usual. She felt free from the building of troubles she went to daily; she was free from all the people there who treated her terribly, including Alexi. The break was good. Annabella and Alaska had gone on vacation together to Southern Cataville; and the duchess of highest rank was acting as queen till Annabella got back. The queen did not bring Mildred on that vacation, only Alaska.

The clock tower that was right next to the castle struck eleven, Mildred was woken from her deep slumber by its loud sound. The princess did not want to wake up, she wanted to sleep forever. Mildred tried so hard to go back to sleep but couldn't. Mildred slowly got up like it was a great burden. As she got ready, she was going through the motions she memorized but was unaware of. She was listening to the demons inside her head disturbing and overwhelming her. There was nothing specific that happened that day that caused her to have such thoughts, but it was something that happened every day. Mildred was constantly thinking about death, about how it would be better for everyone if she didn't exist. For Mildred, real monsters didn't lurk under her huge canopy bed, but they were living inside her head. The princess kept thinking; would she ever find happiness? No. Would she be free of all those troubles? No. Would she ever get what she wanted, or even what she needed? It was a battle that she was fighting all the time.

Mildred went through her morning routine like that, she didn't even focus on what she was doing, or even if she was doing it correctly. The princess went down the stairs, to see Duchess Dandelion tending to the kingdom. That duchess was not as cruel as Annabella, but Mildred found that she was very neglectful, not only of Mildred but of her entire duties, she would tend to them but would put very little effort to ensure the kingdom was secure. Mildred thought Annabella was a better ruler than her, and she thought Annabella was insane and did not deserve to be queen.

After the princess turned her attention away from the duchess, she tried to read, but that didn't cheer her up. She tried to listen to music, but it only depressed her more. She tried using her powers, but it kept upsetting her that they were the source of her misery. Why was her life like that? Why was she treated this way? But not Alaska. This was a cliff she had been pushed off of against her will.

Mildred decided to walk around the castle, she walked by many halls where she saw many paintings, antique artifacts, and statues. Mildred walked feeling nothing towards her surroundings, until she stood before one specific statue. That statue was a sculpture of a man, but not just any man; one Mildred once knew. The statue was very tall, and the face on the statue told Mildred that the man was handsome. Mildred saw writing engraved at the bottom of the statue. "Love, Annabella…" Mildred noticed an engraved heart next to those words. The princess was not surprised to see something else engraved on the other side of the statue, the statue had the date "1970" engraved on it. Mildred then looked at a painting which was right beside the statue, Mildred recognized the man in the painting and knew it was the same man as the statue. It was their father Maximus, she barely remembered him but was surprised to know that he and her mother had loved each other once.

Mildred pulled the painting toward her and saw a photo hidden at the back of the frame. The photo was of a bride and a groom, they seemed very young, both younger than eighteen, the photo was black and white, and it was of her parents on their wedding day. Mildred saw the date written on the back of the photo, "January 1971." Mildred could tell by the year that it was definitely her parents, Mildred was anxious because of what she saw. Annabella was very different, she looked like she wasn't even fifteen, she seemed very happy and in love, she seemed very sweet and very different from the woman that she had become, less than twenty years after the photo was taken. Mildred was very upset, what if she ended up like her mother? The thought of that disturbed her a lot. Mildred panicked and even started to shiver, she never noticed or even saw these things before, and they were quite scary. The princess ran out of the hall in fright.

Mildred was dazed, she was also very saddened by what she had seen. The princess thought of a way that she could alleviate her anxiety. She decided to watch a movie, the movie she chose was an old one filled with elements and events of which she was very much envious. Mildred wished that her life was like the characters in that movie, it was very difficult for her to deal with all these different emotions at once.

Mildred felt very weary as the sun was setting, she sat in her secret garden she had created a while back. It was now a beautiful garden, it was protected from the snow, but it maintained its beauty through the many colors of the leaves and her magic. She thought it a shame that the people of Winter Wonderland did not see what she saw. She saw a power that had nothing wrong with it, but to Annabella and the rest of the people her powers were a pack of unneeded rubbish.

It was a sad to see something that she worked so hard to maintain from creation till present be one of the most hated things by so many around her. Mildred hoped for a permanent escape, many thought she was lucky because she had plenty, but she disagreed. Mildred lay back on the bench she was sitting on, falling asleep for a few minutes in the cold. A few minutes later, she woke up feeling cold. She went back to the castle to relax and go to bed, for a long time. The day felt very long, and it had been one of the worst days of her life.

Mildred could not wait to go back into her deep slumber, she didn't even care about how boring the castle was; it was all about her mental pain and endless loneliness. Mildred wanted something, something different, something wonderful to change her life forever. Mildred lay in her bed and was asleep in less than half a minute.

Winter Wonderland, Cataville, January 1987

Mildred kept going that way for a while. Alaska and Annabella came back from their vacation. Mildred already felt terrible, and now Annabella's return added to those feelings. Mildred's life treated her that way all the time, she would be suffering and something worse would come and add to her suffering. As soon as her mother and sister were back, Mildred was used to spending time alone and sulking. It was very painful, but she coped, because she felt that she had to; she couldn't risk her family's reputation and she had to protect herself from her judgmental society, it wasn't as if she wanted to be something that her society thought less of, but it was forced upon her from the start.

Mildred also was stressed about what would happen to her once she got back to school. She was also stressing about how Annabella was going to treat her. Mildred read books, watched movies, and danced, but never left the castle. The feeling of unkindness and prejudice never left her, not even for a moment, not even a single moment. The month felt like a millennium, the weeks were distorted, and the days were like poison in Mildred's mind.

Winter Wonderland, Cataville, March 16th, 1987

Mildred had been back at school for a while, almost at the middle of the second semester. The princess did not experience any change in her life, it was all still the same. But a part that she suffered through four times every school year were the exams. This part of life was very stressful for the average student, but one would have to come up with a special word to describe what it felt like for Mildred. The following day was the day of her first midterm for that semester. She had previously been able to study well for her exams and receive good grades. The princess spent that day studying for her first exam, relying on the fact that she regularly received good grades anyway. She studied the material, but she couldn't focus.

Her attention was divided between her mind and her studies. She tried to study; she highlighted the important lines, wrote down notes, and tried to get herself to understand everything. But she couldn't focus properly; it was as if it was physically impossible for her to focus only on her studies or leave her abstract thought completely for a while.

The princess thought about her problems while she was studying. It was as if she was balancing revising for her exam and talking to herself and thinking about scenarios which she wished were true. No matter what she was doing, even studying, her subconscious found thinking about problems more important and forced her to do this no matter what. The princess trusted herself when it came to exams a little too well; she managed to go over the material that day. Mildred then continued to be distracted by everything around her and analyzing it and was too unstable to even think of revising or studying any more.

Winter Wonderland, Cataville, March 17th, 1987

Mildred woke up that morning feeling like her old self, even a bit smug. The princess went through her morning routine as usual, with the same anxiety, misery, and emptiness she constantly felt. Mildred and Alaska were soon at their school and they each walked to their classrooms. Alaska was scared and stressed and that could be seen even from far away, but Mildred walked to the classroom as usual as if exams were something that was very easy. When Mildred walked into class, the entire classroom was waiting anxiously for the exam and they were all revising or discussing the material. She went to talk and revise with Samuel, but her mind was daydreaming while Samuel was explaining something to her.

The exam papers were soon in front of the students. The princess began answering the question on the exam paper, she felt she knew the answers to all the questions. She wrote down the answer to every question as she remembered from class as well as what she studied, but there were some questions that she still couldn't answer. Mildred was done with her exam before everyone, she felt that she had answered everything correctly like she usually did because she always aced these exams.

The time for the exam was up, and it was time to submit the papers to the examiner; each of the students had their own examiner. Mildred went to her examiner and gave him her paper. The examiner read the answers to all the questions and began correcting as soon as she left the room. The princess did not feel any anxiety while waiting for the results, she was expecting a positive result. Fifteen minutes passed, and Mildred was still waiting for her first paper to be corrected and to receive a result, and soon the examiner called her to his desk.

"Greetings, Princess Mildred, here is your exam, please read my notes and comments, it would really help you," the examiner said to her in a way that showed he was not very happy.

The princess took her paper not understanding what had just happened, Mildred saw her grade at the top of her paper; "62%" was written in red. The princess was shocked at what she saw, she was sure she had studied. Mildred thought and analyzed how and why this had happened. She was determined to work harder for her next exam.

The princess went home, and was very sad for the entire day. She thought about dying more than usual, because if she didn't keep her former good grades, she would be ruined on top of the fact that she already was crumbling. Mildred went home and went straight to her room, determined to work harder. She began studying the material for her next exam paper, which was just as difficult as last time. Mildred focused harder on trying to prevent herself from drifting off into her other world, rather than concentrating on reality. While studying for the test, her attention kept drifting more between her scatterbrained state and focusing on something that was supposed to build her future.

Mildred still couldn't focus, and couldn't change what she was being forced to do. It was nearly midnight, and the princess was still trying to study but couldn't do it properly, once again it came to her that she was really losing her focus and her self-control.

Winter Wonderland, Cataville, March 18th, 1987

Mildred sat her second exam; the princess hadn't studied well for it, and it was an exam she found extremely difficult. Mildred found a lot of questions that she couldn't answer in the exam paper, her nervousness was a strong force that consumed her. Mildred desperately wanted a better result for this exam and did not want something that would contribute to her plummeting self-esteem. The clock was ticking and Mildred was trying to get as much done as she could. It was not easy, and she thought that she had done well enough at the end before she turned in her paper.

The princess turned in her exam to the examiner who greeted her happily.

"How good do you think you did?" the examiner asked the princess hoping for a positive answer.

"Well, I hope," Mildred replied.

"Did you understand my feedback and use it?" the examiner asked.

"I believe so," the princess sheepishly answered her examiner.

"Alright, please wait outside like yesterday," the examiner told her, and began doing his job as soon as Mildred left the room. Mildred waited, trembling in fear; she chewed her nails as the clock went tick tock. Thoughts of helplessness and death continued to haunt and consume Mildred till her examiner was done correcting her exam. She was then again called to the examiner's room.

"Did I do better?" Mildred asked her examiner as soon as she took the paper.

"Not so much," the examiner said in disappointment. Mildred looked at the result for this exam and felt an incredible amount of shame, she realized that she only got a result of 56% for this paper. The princess left the room and sank into her usual emotional torture. This went on for the entire group of exams. She kept receiving bad results that blackened her mood. This kept on going, and the disapproval that she recognized from her family was more than she could bear.

Chapter Fifteen
Ruin

Winter Wonderland, Cataville, April 16th, 1987

Life remained rough for Mildred for a while, she was falling deeper into the unstable state of mind she was in, and life in school was no better. The princess felt as she was being ruined slowly, she was lucky to have not failed any midterm exams, but lately all the results she received from quizzes, essays, and any sort of work were on the edge of failing. It was unusual; she was once a good student, she did not know what had happened. Everything was changing, and not for the better. The few final breaths of her potential happiness were disappearing slowly.

Mildred was stuck, and she tried to get out of what she was feeling inside every single day. The princess was pushing herself hard, putting in her heart and soul to change everything about herself. Her powers which were there for her every second of her life were her worst enemy and her best friend, they ruined her life but supported her through these rough times. This was an endless cycle that she couldn't stop thinking about. Mildred felt like she was becoming a machine, like all those around her were regular functioning human beings and she was a broken computer that was not being fixed.

Mildred was sitting in class that day, not focusing as usual. The information that the teachers gave in class was important, and had once been interesting to the princess, but nothing was stronger than the magnetic force pulling Mildred to her subconscious. Thoughts black as death filled every single unit of space inside her head, thoughts that disturbed her regularly, it was like there was no world outside of her head. No matter how much she tried she could not focus in class, or get good grades like she used to, that everybody did not fully understand.

"Study harder," people kept telling her.

"Spend more time studying," those around her kept saying.

"Keep trying!" she also heard, but these comments were only from the few positive people in her life.

"Get your idiotic mind to focus in class! I don't care how you do it! Just don't embarrass us!" was an example of things she heard more often, but what was more upsetting for Mildred when it came to exams was that no one did or was even able to give her a proper solution.

The class ended and Mildred was relieved that it had. It was a prison that caused emotional torture in her head, what with the bullying, the academic pressure, and the horrible state her mind was in. All the time at school, from class to recess to activities to individual work, all her thoughts were involuntarily focused on the abuse she endured all the time, the rejection of those around her, her failing grades, her loneliness, and the constant pressure of romance in her mind.

At home, Mildred was sulking. The princess sat at her desk, she imagined a group of people in front of her, and she began pretending to talk to them. Mildred's bedroom door was open, and Alaska peeked in and saw her talking to herself.

"Mildred... Who are you talking to?" Alaska asked Mildred.

"No one..." Mildred sheepishly replied.

"Mildred, you're always doing this!" Alaska worriedly told her sister.

"Doing what?" Mildred nervously asked her sister.

"Talking to yourself..." Alaska said, her eyes welling up.

"Just leave me alone!" Mildred begged her sister with all her heart.

Mildred continued talking to her imaginary friends, but soon she just imagined them in her head, and kept moving her lips and without making any sound. Alaska kept going back to look, sometimes she would talk to Mildred again, but more often she just watched her talk to herself and worried.

Alaska went downstairs and stepped into the servant quarters. The room was a dimly lit one, painted brown, and most of the servants sat there, some resting and others preparing their work things.

"Have any of you seen Charles?" Alaska asked in a serious but kind manner, so that everyone answered.

"He's in the ballroom, organizing the ball that the queen is having," one servant happily told her. Alaska went to the ballroom, where she saw the man she was looking for standing in the middle of the gigantic area, holding a clipboard.

"Charles!" Alaska called out.

"Yes, sweet Highness, Alaska," Charles answered, delighted to help her.

"It's Mildred, she keeps talking to herself," Alaska said then sighed in a way that hinted at her true sadness.

"I'm sure she's alright…" a voice came from behind Alaska. Alaska turned around and saw Annabella, looking cross.

"How could you say that, Mother?" Alaska said to her mother, unamused.

"Mildred has always been crazy and pulling these kinds of stunts," Annabella arrogantly said.

"Ignore it," Annabella replied smugly, even though she did not know, and did not care what went on with Mildred. Annabella walked away with no shame, showing no care for anything that was around her.

"Why is Mildred acting this way?" Alaska asked the castle steward in desperation.

"Poor child has become so lonely that this is how she copes," Charles answered in sympathy, and triggered his feeling of helplessness for being unable to do anything about it.

"In a way, she's like you, my child, you always feel the need to speak to someone, and you do that and don't stop. Well, she's like that, but with herself," Charles exclaimed.

"I'll look for a solution to this, dear, there has to be some kind of way we can help her," Charles said, trying to reassure that everything will be fine. Alaska left the room still worried. Charles sighed, and continued planning Annabella's ball because he was forced to deal with that first.

Meanwhile, Mildred sat in the room, she finished her pretend conversation and started doing her schoolwork. She only focused on completing her schoolwork rather than understanding it; because her mind forced her to do so and go back to drifting off into her agony. Mildred solved her math problems, without caring if they were done properly or even correctly. She tried to do her chemistry and biology problems which were due soon, but she either couldn't answer them or did them poorly. Mildred found the temptation to go back to the absent mindset very exhausting and wished nothing more than for it to be gone.

Winter Wonderland, Cataville, May 20th, 1987

"38%" Mildred saw, as she looked at the grade for the essay about etiquette that she had worked so hard on. Moments later, she was crying. It was difficult to deal with, because it could affect her entire reputation and future as a princess. This was becoming more predictable, it was very painful because there was such a huge emphasis on receiving good results at school. The fear of being ruined and shunned in Winter Wonderland as a princess was something that disturbed Mildred badly at this point, all these thoughts came to her every time she got the results of her school work.

Mildred came back to the castle that day from school with a couple of assignments in her bag. Mildred heard a woman's voice calling her. She was standing in the middle of the front courtyard trying to walk through the heavy snow.

"Mildred, daughter... May I speak to you in private?" the voice said in a deceptively soothing manner. Mildred turned around stiffly and without interest to see Annabella standing a short distance away. Annabella did not look pleased, but then this was Annabella, nothing that had to do with pleased her.

"Whatever do you want, Mother?" Mildred replied to her mother angrily, she was done dealing with her. Annabella and Mildred reached at the queen's chambers. The room that belonged to the queen that was once the most beautiful room in the castle now looked like it was part of a haunted mansion. All the fabrics were ripped along with all the wallpaper, the chandelier was dimmer than ever. Everything in the room looked just as damaged as the sight of Annabella to Mildred.

"I would like to inquire about your schoolwork," Annabella said calmly, as if she wanted to start yelling but hadn't started yet.

"What about my schoolwork?" Mildred asked guiltily with a fake smile.

"Your performance... It's terrible..." Annabella said with hesitation about which idea to mention.

"Why is that?" Annabella asked while looking at Mildred like a predator ready to attack its prey. Annabella stood up from next to Mildred and started pacing.

"You do realize if this gets out… we'll be the talk of the entire empire!" Annabella yelled, finally doing what she wanted to do.

"You will be ruined and shunned, and I will be looked down upon by the kingdom," the queen said, full of hate. Mildred remained quiet and tried to show that she agreed with her mother, even though she thought Annabella had no idea what she was talking about.

"You will work harder and you will get better grades and you will snap out of your craziness, because if you don't, I will be ruined and then I will ruin you!" Annabella yelled, lost in thought with a haunted look in her eye.

"Leave… before you do more damage…" Annabella said then placed her hand hopelessly on her forehead. Mildred stood up but stayed still, curiously looking at her mother.

"Didn't you hear me…? Leave my room!" Annabella shouted at the top of her lungs.

"Leave my room…" Annabella whispered loudly then started crying hysterically as soon as Mildred left the bedroom. Mildred felt very strange after what happened. Annabella was rude as usual, but it was weird how weak she appeared that day.

Mildred was disturbed by that conversation, but not very much. She felt hopeless, and idea of not being able to achieve the good grades she once was able to get consumed her. Yet it was not long before Mildred went back to drifting off into her thoughts again, that had become a natural reflex for her. Criticism affected Mildred severely by then, especially since it felt like she was not physically strong enough to obey commands that were given to her.

Winter Wonderland, Cataville, Early June 1987

The school year was finally over, and Mildred was going through her finals which was so difficult for her. With her mind constantly troubling her, along with the stress of understanding the material and studying, Mildred was tired and sad all the time. Mildred was crawling through the material, it was going slowly and painfully. The princess was trying very hard to understand the material, and to improve the skills she was meant to perfect.

Would Mildred finally get good grades? She was putting in all her effort to receive something that would stop what she feared very much. The stress that Annabella had been putting on Mildred was not easy either, it only made everything worse. Every time Mildred completed some material, it would be nearly one in the morning on the day of the exam, having studied for days.

Mildred would sit for an exam, get it corrected, and would go home directly to study for the next exam, she had an exam every few days. It was tedious, and she wanted so badly for it to end. The results she was receiving were slightly better, but still nowhere near something her society, and more importantly, she, would approve of. Her life was in an emotional turmoil on top of the emotional rollercoaster that it was already in.

It became very difficult, so difficult in fact that Mildred started thinking: why did it even matter how high her grades were? Why did she have to be ruined for not being able to get good grades? But more importantly, she asked: Why wasn't she good enough? Why was it that she worked hard but still got absolutely nothing? It was enough that she wasn't good enough for her society in every other way. Why did she have to be lacking here as well? The material was long and hard.

Mildred got through those exams, not failing anything but on the edge of doing so. This caused her self-esteem to drop. In the main subjects she got "56%," "54%," "60%" and "58%," highest at "64%" and the lowest at "50.5%." The princess couldn't help but remember the times when she got grades in the nineties. Mildred was relieved when she was done, and she wanted nothing more than to not go back to school ever. It was a feeling so strong that she did not want to start the eighth grade, but she vowed that it would be different, and she would get better, and figured out things about herself that she was desperate to find answers to. All in all, she wanted a solution to the state she was in, she felt like she was drowning and couldn't come up for air.

Chapter Sixteen
Desperation

Winter Wonderland, Cataville, July 7th, 1987

The long break between the seventh and the eighth grade was the hardest for Mildred. It wasn't anything that occurred during the break, or anything anyone did. It was because of her mind continuing to torture her. The anxiety of the prospect of marriage and being enough for her family and society followed her through her daily activities that day. The longing and desperation for freedom and happiness that Mildred felt while performing her morning routine, her royal duties, eating, drinking, doing her hobbies, and everything she did was only getting stronger and tougher for her.

Mildred walked by the ballroom, she saw Alaska and Annabella greeting different aristocratic men around their age. Mildred found out afterwards that Alaska was getting visits that had to do with courtship. The princess felt terrible that Alaska was getting this attention and she wasn't. Mildred thought that if she could just get married, since she was not heir to the throne, she could just move to her husband's home and be rid of Annabella, be finally homeschooled without any of the expectations of an unmarried princess. It would be a chance for her to recover from this mental state that came from this horrid environment.

"Mildred… Mildred… Are you alright?" Mildred heard Alaska worriedly calling out to her.

"I'm fine!" Mildred replied feeling envious and angry.

"Are you sure? You were staring hard," Alaska asked her sister in innocence.

"Why do you care? Let her envy you all she wants… she'll get her turn," Annabella told Alaska, trying hard to get her attention off Mildred, which many of the men, and Alaska herself, did not like, but had to stay silent in order to respect the queen because of her status.

Mildred left the room, and went to the castle cinema, which she had become addicted to using. It was a room a little smaller than the bedrooms, but it was bigger than the big rooms in an average mansion, it had four rows of seats, each containing six seats at most. Mildred grabbed her favorite romance movie "1942", a classic 1918 Winter Wonderland love story and Mildred dreamed of being in something similar. Mildred watched the movie, which kept her mind and self-torment about love going on and on.

Love in general, and how it was something that she wanted so badly, and was so hard for her, specifically to get was something that troubled her. Mildred went up to her room to spend time there.

"Mildred… Are you OK?" Mildred thought that echoed in her mind, but she tilted her head to the right only to see her sister standing next to her.

"Oh, will you and Mother please stop doing that?!" Mildred yelled.

"Sorry…" Alaska sheepishly said.

"What do you want?" Mildred said with disinterest.

"I wanted to check on you; are you alright after you saw me with the princes of other kingdoms of Cataville?" Alaska worriedly inquired.

"I'm as alright as I'll ever be," Mildred replied.

"You don't have to speak, I know how to comfort you anyway," Alaska said, trying to make the situation better.

"You do not need any prince to be happy, you are strong, powerful and independent as you are. You do not need a man!" Alaska said trying very hard to comfort her sister. Mildred stayed silent, Alaska saw that she was still as miserable as always and left the room. The wheels in Mildred's head began turning. Did Alaska really think that Mildred was depressed over love because she was doubting herself as a young woman? Of course not, it was not like that. It was about escaping, it was about life letting her feel one of its most beautiful emotions ever.

It was hard dealing with this every single second, of every single minute, of each hour, of every day, each and every day. It was hard for her to think about anything but her problems, and that mental state she found to be in involuntarily. It was like she lost her personality, her principles, and her opinion, everything about her that was once present and strong. Why had this changed? Why didn't she get anything the other kids seemed to get in their lives?

Mildred went on to have another one of her imaginary conversations, they were easier and happened more often than real ones. Charles checked in on her while she was having that conversation with herself, he was worried but then left. Mildred did not have fun during those imaginary conversations, but she not only had nothing else, but her mind also forced her to keep to them as well.

Mildred began dancing to loud music, something that resulted in her drifting off into the whole other world she wished she lived in. Mildred's dancing was not anything professional, it was just jumping maniacally and thinking about things that she wished would happen. Mildred was a dreamer, she wanted to do many things, but she couldn't and wished she could. All the time, Mildred couldn't do anything but dream.

Mildred was bored, and it was 2 a.m. The princess wanted to sleep; both metaphorically and literally, she didn't know why she was still up. Mildred put on her nightgown, she lay on her canopy bed and held on to a big teddy, for the first time in years. The princess was very tired of her life, the same daily routine of royal pain being repeated over and over again, she wanted it to end very badly, she thought, *if only I was dead*. She drifted off to sleep with her teddy bear between her arms.

Winter Wonderland, Cataville, August 11th, 1987

The eighth grade was getting close, the first serious school year. Mildred was dreading going back to school significantly, more than anyone, and she was not ready to face getting low grades or dealing with the kids, along with everything about school. Mildred was in a bad mood even more regularly. More princes and aristocrats were invited to court Alaska and that was something that upset Mildred. Annabella still treated her daughter terribly. Each time the princess woke up, she remembered all of that and these ideas consumed her throughout the day.

The sinister thoughts of death that Mildred had continued to disrupt her ability to do anything about her life. The princess had no choice but to live this way; because she kept fighting in order to find a solution and never did. Many of the things that Mildred so dearly loved left her, but the awful curse of misery on her life didn't leave.

Mildred was on the carriage, riding to the event where Annabella expected her to perform that day. She couldn't help but remember the one vital thing in her life, that she did not lose yet, was her faith in her potential happiness. It became hard for her to continue having that faith, she tried to keep it where it always was, in her heart, but she was losing it slowly. Mildred watched the snow outside the carriage and thought, *how can a world so beautiful be so cruel? Why is it that a place that looks so much like a dream, is so horrifying in reality?*

Mildred got to the central park of Winter Wonderland. She was expected to read a speech to the people of Winter Wonderland to start off her campaign. It was vital that she did so; in order for her people to have what they needed. Mildred was looking at a podium, like the one she stood behind at the beginning of the previous year. She walked up the stairs of the stage in front of her entire audience, took out a paper, got up to the podium. Mildred turned on the switch that turned on the microphone and began her speech.

"Greetings, women, men, lords, and ladies of Winter Wonderland. I have come to speak about a vital matter taking place in Winter Wonderland. Many of you have been complaining about queen Annabella being incompetent and careless about the real problems going on in the kingdom…" Mildred read her speech nervously, she knew that Annabella wrote the speech and saw that her audience were not pleased at what they were hearing.

"Your queen and I have heard your complaints about many things in our nation. I have come to address a few of them, the first one being the rule of child marriage…" As Mildred read through that speech, she neither liked not agreed with what she was about to say, but she had to do it so she kept going.

"The rule that our kingdom decrees that teenagers are to be married by their fifteenth birthday is a rule that was established by Queen Adeline in 1911. Many of you dislike that rule and want it changed, however, the queen states that this rule is to increase the population of Cataville to solve the problem of under-population, therefore we cannot get rid of it yet," Mildred read pushing through the speech.

"Sorry…" Mildred awkwardly told her people and continued her mother's speech.

"My mother has also been receiving grievances about the taxes being extremely high. The queen states that the taxes are not very high, and the people are just being unreasonable," Mildred read, horrified by the speech and its contents. Annabella was being very rude in her speech, and Mildred knew that the people were right to think that she did not care about her people.

"The queen also heard complaints about the limitations of the public-school education system in Winter Wonderland. I would like to say that the queen is doing the best she can in order to improve the state of the public-school education in Winter Wonderland," the princess said while looking at the paper in confusion, feeling the same displeasure that the people were feeling.

"Furthermore, the queen also states that as a nation we have enough job opportunities and decent income that do not need improving. Please stop complaining, we are doing fine. The socially acceptable age of marriage does not need raising, it is fine. The taxes do not need lowering, the public-school education is in the process of being improved and the work industry is OK. Regards, Queen Annabella," Mildred finished reading the speech. The disappointment of the people in the audience was extreme. Mildred began hearing a lot of booing and disruption during the campaign. Mildred placed a large container in the middle of the park grounds.

"This is the container for the campaign, the queen asks that you drop money in order to help solve problems in Winter Wonderland," Mildred said as she had been ordered to say, even though it was completely against what she believed. Soon, an egg was thrown onto Mildred, afterwards a tomato, then an onion. Mildred kept having vegetables thrown at her until she felt like a salad.

The princess heard several different insults specifically to her, she didn't know why that was happening; it was Annabella who wrote the speech and disappointed her people, not Mildred. Mildred's regular dark thoughts ate her up, it was very hard for her to deal with this in public when she already was in a horrible state of mind. Why did Annabella write a speech this disappointing? Annabella was deranged and out of her mind. Mildred thought a monarch must show more care towards their people. She hated that the people took this out on her.

The princess went back to the carriage and was drifting off into her thoughts, it was a never-ending nightmare. Mildred felt like she needed to consult Annabella about this speech. The journey back was a blur, and Mildred was covered in different foods which made her feel horrible, on top of the shame of the speech she had been forced to deliver, that she kept remembering.

When Mildred descended from the carriage after arriving, she was met with the sight of the queen standing in the courtyard. Annabella started laughing hysterically, Mildred was not upset but emotional weariness hit her hard. The princess couldn't stop, she went up to Annabella without hesitation.

"Mother, I would like to speak with you," Mildred told her mother sternly. Annabella laughed more and more, then she followed Mildred to her bedroom having surprisingly agreed to talk to her. Mildred and Annabella stepped inside the queen's chambers again, it looked the exact same way it did when Mildred had last been there.

"What would you like to discuss?" Annabella said childishly trying not to laugh.

"Mother, what on Cataville was with that campaign?" Mildred stated calmly.

"What's with it?" Annabella said as if there was nothing wrong.

"Good lord... Mother," Mildred said disappointed and slapped her own face.

"That speech was humiliating! It was very harsh to your subjects! How could you do this to your people?" Mildred said sternly and loudly, making her point at last.

"What do you mean, Mildred? I just stated clear facts," Annabella replied not taking anything seriously.

"Mother... I do not understand your actions, you basically just told your subjects that there is no problem with the way you are running the nation, while your kingdom is rotting!" Mildred angrily replied to her mother, leaving the queen with no option but to lash out. Annabella walked to Mildred and slapped her face more than once, leaving many bright marks on Mildred's face.

Mildred was very sad. The princess felt alone and deserted, she fought hard not to cry. Mildred saw a paper on her mother's dresser which had a crooked mirror. Mildred walked curiously to the dresser to look at the paper. When the princess saw the paper, she found that it was Alaska's speech for her campaign. Mildred read that speech and saw that it conveyed a different content than hers; its content was far less appalling than Mildred's speech because it addressed different matters.

"Mother," Mildred called out to her mother, in an airy voice, about to ask something.

"Whatever in the world do you want?" Annabella angrily replied, not wanting to hear anything else.

"Did you give me the horrible speech about economic matters while you gave Alaska the good one about entertainment and tourism on purpose?" Mildred asked in a tone that conveyed how hurt she was.

"So, what if I have?" Annabella answered Mildred with a sneer.

"But of course you do this, my beloved mother," Mildred said.

"Good day, Mother," Mildred said, having had enough. The princess left the queen's chambers in anger, covered in tomatoes and other vegetables. Feelings of hurt and discrimination filled Mildred's head for a while, she felt as if life was against her for some reason.

The princess couldn't deal with her mother anymore, she could not deal with Alaska anymore, and she couldn't deal with having powers that made everybody dislike her. Suddenly an idea came to Mildred's head. The princess thought long and hard about it, until she got back to her own bedroom.

Mildred wanted to be someone else so very badly; many say that everyone wants to be a different person at some point, but the difference between her and everyone else was the intensity of that feeling. It was incredibly painful to be this person that was depressed and wanted nothing more than for her life to end, but what if she was not that person anymore?

The princess remembered, that unlike Earth, Winter Wonderland was a place where magic existed. Mildred cleaned herself up and put on new a new dress. Mildred fixed everything wrong with her appearance from the food having been thrown at her, she later sat on the bed and waited. The sun set, and the princess still waited patiently, everything around her was more calm and serene, and all the tension outside the castle was now gone. It was finally time for Mildred to put her idea into action, she put on a long cloak and disguised herself.

The princess grabbed a rope from her closet, she tied its top to a big hook that was on the frame of her bedroom window. She threw the rest of the really long rope down her bedroom window till it was on the ground, and she began climbing down till she reached the ground. The princess was lucky that none of the guards noticed her, and that she did everything properly and safely. The princess walked to the castle gates, being that they are the only way out. This was one of the times where disguising herself in a long cloak that covered most of her and her face was a good idea.

"Who goes there?" A guard yelled from the guard tower over the high wall.

"A humble castle servant," Mildred told the guard disguising her voice. She was happy that the guard did not recognize her with her cloak.

"Why are you leaving at this hour? Your shift is nowhere near over," the guard sharply said.

"My son is very ill, I need to go take care of him," Mildred told the guard in the same voice, even though in her eyes she was the one that was very ill, mentally.

"Did you get the queen's permission to leave castle premises?" the guard replied, exhausted himself.

"Why… yes, I have," Mildred lied, but she knew she had to.

"Did you get a permission slip from the queen?" the guard asked trying his hardest to do his job.

"I have one from Princess Mildred," Mildred told the guard taking out the slip that she had made herself. Another guard came toward her and looked at the permission slip without looking at

Mildred herself. The guard beside Mildred gave the gate guard a positive signal.

"Very well, you may pass," the guard at the top of the tower nodded, the castle gate opened for Mildred and she was able to leave. Mildred ran and ran, it was like a monster was chasing her. There was a specific place that Mildred so badly wanted to go. The run there was very exciting, Mildred was happy that the place was not too far away or else she would be in trouble.

Mildred arrived in front of a store. The store looked like any other market; it was a small place with things for people to buy. Mildred entered the store and heard a very loud bell chime as she walked in. There were many things that she could buy, the store held normal things from food to cleaning supplies. Mildred walked deeper inside the store, until she reached an area filled with antiques.

Mildred looked hard for a certain product in this part of the store. Mildred saw different antique lamps, decorations, and paintings, and most importantly books. The princess looked hard for a specific book, it was tense looking and trying to find the exact one that she was looking for. Five minutes later, Mildred finally found the book. It was an aged brown color, covered in dust so she puffed it away with a long breath, and coughed at the dust that blew all around her. "Granpul spelleth booketh" Mildred read on top of the cover, it was what she was looking for; it was a sixteen-hundred spell book that had the same language that Earth writer Shakespeare utilized. The princess went to the cashier and paid for it, nobody questioned who she was, and everyone thought she was a civilian, otherwise it would have been a scandal if the princess of Winter Wonderland were to be seen buying a spell book.

However, there was something else that the princess needed to buy in order to sneak back into the castle. Mildred left the store and had to walk through to another place. Mildred pushed through the snow and walked against the wind that was pushing her back. The princess kept going for an hour, until she was at the town center of Winter Wonderland. There it was absolutely beautiful, the snow covering the cobblestone road along with the wooden roofs which had icicles dangling from their sides. There was a fountain from the eighteen-hundreds in the middle of the area, all the water in it was completely frozen. Mildred looked at the beautiful city, she wished she was someone else in it, someone with a better life. She continued with her journey. Mildred looked at an unkempt man, he appeared to be of middle class, he had a small store that wasn't in a building, and it was just a wooden shack with cloth covering it. She went over to that man because she knew he was the one she was looking for.

"Hello, kind sir," Mildred told the man in her fake airy voice from beneath her cloak.

"Good morrow fair maiden," the man replied to her kindly.

"I need a certain item of clothing," Mildred said.

"Why come in, my dear, take whatever you need," the man said to Mildred in a rough voice. Mildred went into the store through a crooked door, she looked through the shelves of different clothing. The clothing that Mildred looked at was inexpensive, she kept looking till she found what she was looking for. Mildred chose a thin long yellow dress that was not too extravagant or expensive, exactly what she needed to get back into the palace. Mildred went into the fitting room, put on her new dress, then put the cloak on and paid for it.

Mildred left the shop; she found a wooden carriage with no roof that was nothing like the castle carriages. A brown pony was pulling the carriage, he was bigger than your average pony but not big enough to be a regular horse. A woman was driving the carriage, Mildred went up to her.

"Excuse me, ma'am, but where are you going?" Mildred asked the woman driving the carriage.

"Why I am a driver, my job is to give people rides in my carriage," the woman answered Mildred with a smile.

"May I have a ride to the castle?" Mildred asked the woman innocently.

"Sure, my pet," the woman happily replied to Mildred, leaving the princess surprised that women were allowed to do that, but she didn't say anything about it. Mildred hopped into the carriage and it began moving. The pony was surprisingly fast, and she had a conversation with the woman driving the carriage, which helped her learn more about the true state of her kingdom.

Nearly fifteen minutes later Mildred started feeling really cold, she was surprised to see that the driver didn't seem cold. The carriage ride was short, but Mildred kept feeling weaker as time went by. It took them almost half an hour to reach the nearest point to the castle that the woman was allowed. Mildred paid the woman her fare of 6 Cateos, and got down from the carriage. The woman left with her carriage, which meant Mildred needed to walk a couple of blocks in order to reach the castle gates. The princess cut off the hood part of her cloak and threw the rest of it into the snow. Mildred ran to the castle doors, her yellow dress shone through the snow, but her face and head did not.

Mildred was at the castle gates. The same guard called out to her from the guard tower.

"Who goes there?" The guard asked.

"The royal messenger of Southern Cataville, I have a letter for queen Annabella from the queen of the south," Mildred told the guard in a new voice.

"What does the letter say?" the guard demanded an answer.

"The queen of Southern Cataville has a son who's asking for princess Alaska's hand, I have a letter about this matter for the queen," Mildred said in a fake voice, but not fake enough for anyone to notice.

"Another one asking for princess Alaska's hand," the guard said with envy and disappointment.

"Very well, come in," the guard replied. Mildred entered the premises of the castle and went back to her room to work on her idea. The princess took out the book she had bought, she skimmed through it till she found the correct spell. "Body swap spell," Mildred read, she read the instructions of how to perform the ritual, she was very desperate that she was going to do it.

Mildred changed into her nightgown, and she began preparing herself for the spell. The first step was to wait till ten p.m., this left her excited; she could finally recover and get rid of the demon torturing her. The time passed, and it was finally ten p.m. Mildred lay down on her bed and began reading out the spell.

"I wisheth yond a changeth wouldst occureth, yond I and Alaska of Wint'r Wond'rland wouldst switcheth bodies, I am h'r and the lady is me and yond I wouldst not rememb'r aught from me, f'r I wast at each moment h'r," Mildred chanted out one-hundred and ninety-five times.

The next step of the spell was to sleep, and it was vital that Mildred would be asleep before eleven for the enchantment to work. Mildred was very happy by then, she was extremely desperate for the magic to happen; that she endured insomnia, ended up not sleeping till three a.m. which made her anxious for the spell to work.

Mildred fell asleep, kneeling on her knees, pleading. The night went by very slowly, the time Mildred was asleep felt so long, that she thought she was dead.

Winter Wonderland, Cataville, August 12th, 1987

The princess woke up that morning, she saw that she was still Mildred and not Alaska and couldn't help but feel cheated, tired, and miserable. Mildred pushed through so hard for so long for this not to work. Her dark thoughts kept going on, till she broke down and released a monsoon of tears and excessive thoughts of death.

Chapter Seventeen
School and Scandals

Winter Wonderland, Cataville, August 25th, 1987

It was not that long till the eighth grade started, a school year that Mildred would never forget. This specific school year started earlier than usual. During the interval between this day and the day when Mildred tried the body swap spell for the first time, she continued to do the ritual every day desperate for something to change; especially before the eighth grade begun. The ritual continued failing miserably every day; Mildred ended up burning the spell book.

Mildred was nowhere near ready for this school year; every single minute was a distressed run from the painful fires of hell caused by her own mind. Mildred could not imagine what school, yet one more time, would add to that. No matter what was happening. Mildred woke up that morning at five-thirty, sweat rushing from her head, her teeth chattering fast, her heart pounding. The princess dreaded everything, from her inability to focus in class to receiving horrible exam and work results to dealing with the students.

Mildred began preparing herself for school, she made a promise to herself that she'd start studying after every lesson, that she would focus more and get good results, she hoped she could keep that promise to herself. Alaska was up at six-thirty, and Mildred was ready and battling many things inside her at that point. The princess made sure everything was fine, she hoped that the people there would leave her alone, and that she wouldn't have to deal with feelings towards anyone this year.

Mildred and Alaska were taken back to school in the carriage for the first time in a while, there she was trapped in her mind yet again, thinking about many different things without being able to stop. The failure of not being able to leave the body before this school year was a thought that troubled her throughout the entire ride.

As soon as Mildred arrived at the school, she was nervous over the fact that bullies would be in her classroom; but what she did not know was that this year it was those outside of the classroom that mattered. Mildred went to check the bulletin board to make sure that no bullies were in her classroom, unfortunately a few bullies were, but the numbers were decreasing significantly, that there were fewer classes and anywhere she went would cause her problems. One thing that seemed to be a good at the time was that she and Samuel shared a classroom again.

Mildred was in her classroom, she and Samuel sat at their desks. The rest of the aristocratic students sat at different desks. The teacher came in and began to explain the lesson, a little drama occurred between Mildred and the other students. But Mildred on the first day was not physically able to keep the promise she made to herself that she would focus in the classroom. Mildred couldn't help but think about the day she got married and left the castle and became homeschooled after becoming a married princess. A fight started in Mildred's head, and she ended up drifting off even though she didn't want to.

The lessons went by as slow as if a tortoise was in control of time. But when the class finally ended, she stayed with Samuel during recess because he was enough for her. During recess, Mildred convinced Samuel to study with her what they had taken during the past lessons; fearing low grades. It was a surprise that Samuel was even OK with it, but he was. The stress was consuming Mildred during all the time she studied or spent in class, with her on her knees begging for the school day to end. It did, and Mildred was wearier than usual. The darkest thoughts of death were in her mind.

Mildred spent the rest of the day in her room, trying her best to focus on studying that day's material. Samuel called her since school started and he regularly called. She now realized that at this point in life it turned out that Samuel meant more to her than she ever thought. Mildred rushed afterwards through her studies;

wanting to understand her school material better and get good marks and complete her studies quickly at the same time.

Winter Wonderland, Cataville, September 3rd, 1987

Some time had passed, still Mildred's school life in the new school year was less than perfect. However, something happened that day that affected the entire course of the eighth grade. Mildred freshened up and attended her classes as usual, soon they were in art class. Mildred was sitting on a stool at the table doing her art assignment. Her mind deep in her thoughts, her ability to think correctly weaker by the minute.

"Hey, are you singing?" a girl from Mildred's class asked her.

"Yes…" Mildred shyly replied.

"You have a really nice voice," the girl said with a smile.

"Thank you, Lilith," Mildred said to the girl, smiling back.

"You need to share it with the people here," Lilith said to Mildred.

"I don't know about that," Mildred replied, embarrassed. The conversation ended in peace, but Mildred was slightly happy that someone finally thought well of her that she found that extremely difficult to believe, she thought that Lilith just wanted to make fun of her so she did nothing.

More dreadful hours went by at school, Mildred just returned to class after the second recess to find a few noble classmates talking about her.

"Mildred, please sing for us," Lilith asked Mildred with a suspicious smile.

"Yes, Mildred, please sing," another student asked Mildred. After she heard a few more requests asking her to sing, Mildred felt betrayed. Lilith had told people, and not just any people but a few of the worst bullies in the school.

At first Mildred refused to sing, as time passed, more people kept asking her to sing. During the last two lessons that day, she was enduring the peer pressure and pushing through the regular torture she went through all the time. All while trying to focus in class and understand her lessons, which she was failing badly at it all. It was finally time to go home, everybody including

Samuel left the classroom while Mildred prepared her backpack and such. Only Lilith and Mildred were left in the room.

"Mildred, I would like to speak with you," Lilith told the princess. Mildred turned around, not willing to hear anything else feeling already more than annoyed.

"What could you possibly want now?" Mildred said angrily wanting nothing more than these people to leave her alone.

"I just want to say that I love your confidence, you have a lot of it, you need to put it to good use," Lilith calmly said. Mildred was still suspicious. The princess could not tell whether or not this Lil' Duchess was being sincere.

"Please sing for us tomorrow," Lilith said with the same smile from a few hours ago.

"I'll see," Mildred said, through the headache she constantly got. Mildred's mind left the school property. It began twisting and turning, as she walked to her carriage, then during her ride home and during her walk to her room. She thought about people's lack of respect for her, she wondered whether or not Lilith was being sincere or just needed something to make fun of. Mildred also kept daydreaming about the problems that she was not able to conquer.

Winter Wonderland, Cataville, September 6th, 1987

The spiral of the comments and requests for singing that reached Mildred during school kept going on and on. Mildred ignored them for a while but gradually started singing. Mildred began singing for her classmates only, they seemed to really like her singing which made her happy a little bit.

But it did not stop there, news about Mildred's "amazing" voice reached the popular noble kids, the boys and girls who were children of dukes. More pressure surrounded Mildred for her voice; at first, she stood her ground, she would not sing for bullies who would definitely make fun of her. But she ended up giving in to the peer pressure and agreed to sing only one time for everyone. After that, it was clear that everyone was just making fun of her, nobody liked her singing. It was embarrassing. It was weird, because Mildred really had a nice voice, but as she expected, they really just wanted to make fun of her.

The dark thoughts about death, the painful thoughts that terrorized and defeated her came into her mind. Mildred wanted to get married so badly; and leave the castle and finally be home-schooled and become a married princess in Winter Wonderland. If she could just get married as easily as Alaska could, she would leave the castle and leave the school. This was something else pressuring her.

"Mildred, this is a scandal, how could you be this stupid?" Samuel scolded her. Mildred received a lot of criticism from the very few people that supposedly "cared" about her. It was painful.

People made fun of her for it for a few weeks, until the story was nearly forgotten. Many people forgot about it, and those who asked her to sing again got a fiery rejection. Some people forgot and some never did. But this story caused the people who cared to hurt Mildred, for it was they who never truly forgot.

Chapter Eighteen
Wild Dreams

Winter Wonderland, Cataville, October 1st, 1987

Nothing much happened since the disappearance of the singing "scandal." The classmates made fun of Mildred for other things all the time as well. Both she and Samuel sat next to each other at a pair of desks. They talked almost all the time by then, they were always together. Mildred began finding him cute.

"So, I will write and decorate the poster, and you will come up with the ideas and do the research," Mildred told Samuel, to which he agreed. Mildred liked the smile that he gave her afterwards.

Samuel began to come up with the ideas, and Mildred just wrote because she was physically incapable of doing anything more because her mental state did not allow it. Samuel told Mildred what to write, but with her mind wandering, there were some things that she did not get.

"Darker..." Samuel told her to write in the paragraph.

"I don't follow," Mildred told Samuel.

"Darker, as in a darker color," Samuel told her, thinking she was utterly stupid.

"Just write darker..." Samuel asked her in a voice that Mildred found to be airy. Soon Samuel had had enough of Mildred's "stupidity" and just wrote the word himself. Mildred was not stupid, but something strange was going on in her mind; she would somehow "lose intellect," to a degree where she would not comprehend something as simple as "darker."

It began to disappoint Mildred whenever her mental state made her seem stupid in front of Samuel. The princess wanted nothing more than to get better and change, because there was a small chance, she could leave the rut she was living in. Mildred got through the English class and it was finally recess. Mildred had made plans with Samuel so he would tutor her in math, because she was having problems understanding during class; she didn't tell Samuel that, however. They walked to the library.

Mildred sat on a chair at one of the many tables in the library, and Samuel sat on the one next to it. Samuel began to teach Mildred how to apply the skills that she was supposed to learn, from the last few math lessons. Mildred began having thoughts about Samuel that she had been having lately. Mildred thought that it was so nice and adorable of him to do this for her. Mildred attempted to focus, managing to retain a decent amount of information.

The princess listened to Samuel with interest, she was interested because the words were coming from him; because she thought he was the only person who cared about her. It was difficult for the princess to admit that she began getting a crush on him, but she finally admitted it to herself. She did not know how it happened, but it did. This could cause problems for her because she thought he would never feel the same way.

As soon as Mildred got home, she started taking care of her appearance, making sure to rid herself of all the pimples, zits, and blackheads she could find. Next, she applied her facial cleanser. Then, she began planning how she was going on a diet to stay in shape. Mildred also did a couple dozen of sit-ups; in order to rid herself of belly fat that had been giving her grief. This was a ritual that she planned on doing every day, and because she was a perfectionist, she followed the ritual perfectly. Naturally, she performed this ritual while drifting off into her mind, thinking about many different scenarios that couldn't really happen in reality; as she was not able to properly pay attention to what she was doing.

Mildred left the bathroom after freshening up after working out, she caught sight of Alaska standing in the middle of her bedroom.

"Alaska... What on Cataville!" Mildred said hesitantly, not approving of Alaska's appearance in her bedroom.

"Oh… Mildred," Alaska turned around moving her arms like Annabella did, and replied with the same hesitant voice Mildred had used.

"Why are you in my chambers?" Mildred asked with disapproval that came from all the hurt and suffering.

"No reason…" Alaska said blushing, caring but not wanting Mildred to notice.

"Talk to me, have you been snooping in here?" Mildred asked concerned.

"Have you got feelings for someone?" Alaska questioned her sister with curiosity.

"No! Absolutely not," Mildred firmly responded, trying to keep Samuel a secret.

"It seems to me that you do," Alaska said.

"What makes you say that?" Mildred asked still trying to cover this up, but she was scared to death inside.

"You worked out, you're dieting, you are caring much more about your appearance," Alaska asked.

"So, what," Mildred said angrily, desperate for Alaska to just leave her alone.

"So… Is there someone?" Alaska inquired further.

"Alaska, no, there is no one! Please leave me in peace," Mildred said angrily trying hard to conceal her pain.

"Have it your way, however, I will repeat the same thing I told you last time," Alaska soothingly said.

"You do not need to do any of this, just for a man. You are enough as you are as a woman. You are a princess of Winter Wonderland!" Alaska said in the same soothing voice.

"Whatever, please leave!" Mildred wearily asked, completely done dealing with her sister.

Alaska left Mildred's bedroom, leaving her to drift off into the dark shadows lurking inside, what was once her happy place. Mildred thought about Samuel, she thought about death, she had moments where she was begging life for freedom and happiness. It was hard having to deal with a mind that was consistently talking, controlling you, and draining you. It was difficult having to handle being disliked and disrespected by everyone, not meeting the standards of society as a princess. The worst was drowning inside the consistent feeling of numbness and fighting the demons torturing every bit of Mildred's emotions.

Mildred went on to dream, she dreamt about many different solutions to her problems with her family, her royal duties, and those around her that never left. She could try harder to fall in love so she could get married soon as society expected her to; in order for her to leave the castle and school. Mildred thought that she could run away and legally disappear from Winter Wonderland. However, both of these solutions were incredibly difficult and most probably impossible to go through with. Nobody liked her, and Mildred was Mildred, who would want to marry her? She was convinced she couldn't run away and disappear; where would she go and what if she was found?

On and on Mildred went. Alaska kept making the argument that the actions she did for boys she liked were anti-feminist. But in Mildred's head, none of this was about her views towards women. If anything, she wished she didn't need to put in that much effort for a man. It was not about her being a woman and needing a man to be happy. It was about increasing the likelihood and attempting to escape from this nightmare of a life, along with living in a better area where she wouldn't be this much of an outcast.

Winter Wonderland, Cataville, October 18th, 1987

Life had gotten harder for Mildred recently. For now, she had another burden to carry; Samuel. Mildred finally gave in completely to the fact that she liked Samuel, she had for more than a month, however, now it was official to herself. Mildred lost a bit of the belly fat that had annoyed her. But the concept of beauty was something that Mildred had become addicted to. From her point of view, it was vital that absolutely nothing was ever wrong with the way she looked, the rituals she had started became more regular. Mildred's dieting became stronger and more serious, at first it was very difficult to stay away from comfort food, but the pain and longing for a happy ending was stronger than that challenge.

Mildred and Samuel were almost always together. The princess felt happy around him, he was the one good thing in her life. During the day, Samuel helped Mildred study. They worked on the projects assigned to them together, they hung out on their own during recess. When they went home, they would call each other's phones. Annabella's appalling treatment towards Mildred never stopped, but Samuel was an escape.

Mildred's mind kept switching between death wishes and Samuel, and sometimes she thought about both at once. She wanted to just perish, but at the same time she wanted to stay, in case she left the sorrow she was rotting inside of.

Winter Wonderland, Cataville, November 8th, 1987

Time kept going by very slowly. It became even harder to deal with everything, from Samuel to the continuing pressure from all those around her to Annabella, along with the judgmental society. It was a constant fight that would exhaust anyone and it never stopped. Especially with the feelings Mildred had been having toward Samuel that had gotten stronger. It was not just a simple crush, or just thinking about Samuel all the time, it was like magic, a feeling that could not be really explained. It became painful, because she understood her circumstances as a non-heir princess, being extremely tall, in addition to the powers that the entire kingdom seemed to deride.

Mildred went to school that day, she became excited to see Samuel each time she went to the school. Just as before, the pair spent all their time together, but the other nobles of the school began to slightly affect the relationship between Mildred and Samuel. Samuel started to hear rumors about Mildred, which he kept discussing with her.

"Mildred…" Samuel called her name; wanting to speak with her during recess.

"Yes, Samuel," Mildred said with complete interest in what he was about to say.

"You need to stop saying certain things. You keep drawing attention to yourself, and people keep making fun of you," Samuel told her, Mildred felt that Samuel cared about her wellbeing and safety. But this was not the only thing happening, Samuel discussing her actions.

"Stop talking to yourself, and swinging on your chair with your back, other students keep calling you mentally ill," Samuel warned her. Whenever anything similar to this happened, with her falling mental capabilities inability to think properly, she assumed that Samuel had good intentions.

Mildred used to obey and try her hardest not to do these things, but she couldn't do it, it was physically and mentally impossible for her. Yet she put in her head that he said these things because he was a good friend to her. The more time they spent together, the more she saw nothing but an image of the best friend she ever had.

As soon as Mildred was home, she did all her things to make sure she looked good. Annabella walked into Mildred's bedroom the exact minute Mildred was done.

"Look at you!" Annabella screamed from behind, startling her.

"What do you want, Mother?" Mildred responded emotionless, not expecting anything good to occur from this encounter.

"I see a boy is looking to court you, surprisingly…" Annabella said in disgust, then rolled her eyes.

"Or maybe, you're looking to court this boy, but he's never going to take one look at that idea," Annabella said with prejudice, while walking around Mildred in an intimidating manner.

"Mother, if you've come to cause me grief then please leave my room," Mildred angrily replied but in a low voice.

"Personally, I just hope you do get married, that's all," Annabella said while twirling in her gown and looking manic. Annabella left the room, leaving Mildred relieved that her mother was no longer there to threaten her possible joy.

Mildred still thought that the Winter Wonderland idea of early marriage was a sickening and backward idea; however, it was something that was expected by society from her as a princess. Mildred knew she was not ready for any of the things she was expected to do. The princess used to think that life did not want her to be happy.

Winter Wonderland, Cataville, November 22nd, 1987

More time went by as Mildred's problems got deeper and deeper. Her feelings were getting stronger, and her mental state was weakening even further than before. Mildred could no longer focus in class at all; she could no longer understand basic things well. All the princess knew that her life was now only in her mind, which kept her thinking about specific things that had to do with the outer world.

Mildred knew she was slowly falling in love with Samuel, she remembered how adults thought of young teenagers who implied that they're "in love," but Mildred knew in her heart that what she was going through was not like that. The princess wished she could change many things about that part of her life, especially since she knew that falling in love was not just a crush. She may be able to get over of a crush easily, but she knew it may take her months or even years to fall out of love. What she was about to enter was a really dark place, that didn't have an exit for millions of miles. But she could not just stop being friends with Samuel to protect herself from entering that loop; because if she did, she would have no friends and she was not just anyone, she couldn't just make new friends.

The thoughts of death were getting even closer to the central part of Mildred's life. There was not a moment where thoughts of death and hopelessness were not present.

Mildred also kept having negative exchanges with her peers in school. They constantly asked her personal questions that embarrassed her and gave them other things to bully her and make fun of her. Samuel started criticizing her over the way she handled these people, and by then both Samuel and Mildred hated everyone else. This made Mildred feel safe, but at the same time it gave her a lot of anxiety. She constantly worried about how to keep people from making fun of her, but that was only to please Samuel. Mildred herself did not care about the people making fun of her, they could rot in hell for all she cared. But Samuel seemed to want her to have peace. Mildred hated the action but was in love with the intention. The tension about that topic wasn't something that disrupted Mildred's friendship with Samuel that much.

Chapter Nineteen
Wilder Dreams

Winter Wonderland, Cataville, December 6Th, 1987

The first semester of the eighth grade was coming to an end. By then it was the beginning of a new era. Mildred was going through her midterm exams, the results from of these exams were less than satisfactory. This part of her life, December 1987, was especially difficult. Mildred got through the exams with some of the challenges that were normal to her at that point. The feelings that she had for Samuel were now wilder than before. Mildred now considered herself in love with him, and she was. It may be hard to believe, or comprehend, and one can easily ridicule the idea, but it was love, whether one would believe it or not.

In addition to Mildred already having emotions that were hard to handle at that age, her mental state had taken one of its biggest blows. Her mind had become so unstable, so weak, and so unable to focus or comprehend anything that she was nearly insane. Mildred knew that at the level of psychological weariness that she had reached, she would most probably end up in an asylum in a few months. Her circumstances which were challenging in addition to the fact that things had been going on for so long, caused her mind to begin the process of mental failure.

By then Mildred had been battling her love for her best friend Samuel, which she assumed was most probably unrequited, in a crumbling area. It was very difficult, because she had become extremely desperate for a rescue. The princess tried to rescue herself many times, with no solution. Mildred had just left the school building after sitting for her last exam. She was extremely weak-minded, that she didn't notice her surroundings, the snow with the decorated sky.

Mildred got to her bedroom, she lay on her bed, isolated as usual. This was something she did every day, and it was harder to do each day. That day, it got incredibly difficult that Mildred thought of a desperate way out. She had to research how to go through with that plan. The princess was aiming to try to get Samuel to reciprocate her feelings, but to her it seemed impossible. Still, Mildred was getting desperate for a way out of the turmoil inside her mind. If only she could get married, leave the castle, leave the school, and be homeschooled, like all princesses in her kingdom do as soon as they are married.

There was no way she could do this easily, not like her sister, not like her mother, not like the other noble girls at the school. Mildred needed some sort of extraordinary help, something like professional magic which one had access to in her world. The princess also thought she needed to put an extra effort into her diet, her face, and her workouts. In short, the princess had a lot of things on her list.

The sun set and Mildred had done all her daily rituals, but there was one more thing she had left to do. She needed to go visit a certain witch. Mildred planned a way to visit the witch in order to create the proper effects on Samuel that she had been hoping for, and so she needed to leave the castle without getting caught. Her head was spinning and her mind was filled with many different visualizations at once.

Another hour had passed, and Mildred was ready; this time she did not need to disguise herself in a cloak, especially since she no longer had one. Mildred went through the hallways and castle rooms she needed to go through until she was at the grand entrance of the castle. To everyone else it was like a normal walk through the castle. But she left from the area inside the castle and was now outdoors. Mildred walked through the courtyard and reached the castle gate. The guards asked her a few questions to ensure her safety, then she was able to go through. She took off in a carriage with a driver to a point she had planned.

Mildred kept admiring her surroundings through the window, especially when she passed the touristic and well-known places in Winter Wonderland. The snow was falling hard, a little stronger than usual, it became harder for the carriage to move. However, to Mildred's luck, she wasn't going the entire journey in the carriage; she had almost arrived at the "Winter Wonderland International Train Station." In less than five minutes, Mildred got down. She held her heavy red gown and walked toward the booth in order to buy a ticket to the northern west area in Winter Wonderland.

Mildred was at the booth, and a ticket attendant was there to tend to her.

"Where to?" the ticket attendant asked the princess, with the same bored tone that showed lack of interest. Mildred knew that the attendant had a tone as such; because hers was a redundant job that she repeated many times.

"Northern West Winter Wonderland," Mildred replied to the ticket attendant in a graceful manner.

"There is a train at seven and one at eight-thirty, which one would you like, Your Highness?" The ticket attendant replied in the same bored tone, but this time it seemed as if she was trying to be respectful to the princess.

"I'll take the one at seven," Mildred said; she wanted to get there as fast as she could.

"That will be 6 Cateos and 81 cents, including your 20 percent discount for being royalty," the attendant said to Mildred. The princess paid the money to the ticket attendant and she gave her visa in order for the attendant to check it.

"Here is your ticket and your visa, enjoy the trip, Your Highness," the ticket attendant said, giving her the ticket and her visa back, then bowed her head.

Mildred went inside the train station, it was a white area, and it was covered with many paintings, souvenirs, and decorations to illustrate parts of Winter Wonderland. The princess sat down where various other people were sitting. Mildred was bored but it was important that she stayed in order to get what she needed. Time spent waiting also included dark and depressive thoughts.

Soon, but not soon enough, the train was ready. Mildred got on the train and took one of the seats in the back of the train cart by the window. The train began moving. The princess kept looking through the window and drifted off into the depth of utter darkness. The thoughts kept haunting and taunting Mildred. Will this magic work? Could she really get Samuel to reciprocate her feelings? Would she be able to do this to save herself and maybe even feel happiness and love?

Fifty minutes went by, and these kinds of thoughts kept forcing themselves on Mildred. The train ride finally finished and she had reached her destination. She disembarked from the train and left the train station. The princess looked around this part of Winter Wonderland, which she had never seen before. It contained more thin ice than it did snow, the icicles covered each and every roof. This area seemed to be much poorer than the area Mildred lived and attended school in.

Mildred ran to the witch's cove using her map to guide her. Ten minutes later, she had arrived at an apartment building that looked abandoned. This was definitely the correct place. Mildred went up the stairs till she reached the door of the witch's apartment. She knocked on the door a couple times, until the door suddenly opened, as if a sudden gust of wind had opened it.

A normal looking woman stood in front of Mildred as soon as the door opened. The woman had her brown hair tied in a Victorian style and wore a regular red shirt with a big jacket along with a very long skirt. The woman did not resemble a witch at all in Mildred's eyes. Mildred went inside and saw a boy her age, then she saw a little girl playing in the living room, she assumed both of them were the witch's children, both looking completely human. The apartment did not look like a witch's apartment either, Mildred began to wonder if she got the right place.

"Greetings, Your Highness, I am Morina Sanderson, gracious witch of Winter Wonderland. These are my two children, Fabian and Fiona," the woman greeted Mildred with a curtsy, causing her kids to curtsey to Mildred as well.

"I have been expecting you, Princess Mildred," the witch said in an eerie voice.

"Come with me to the balcony," Morina said to Mildred, leading to Mildred obeying and following the witch to the balcony. The two stood in the middle of the balcony, Morina moved her arms and hands where dust surrounded the area around them. The balcony area was now a closed area, Morina closed the balcony door as well.

"Sit on this chair," Morina said in a manner that could have easily been mistaken for boredom. Mildred sat on the chair, then Morina turned the chair into a lounge chair.

"You want me to get a certain boy… Samuel Jerram… to return your feelings of love, or at least build the emotional foundation to what you want from his side," Morina sat on her chair then said, making Mildred really scared.

"Relax, Your Highness, my magic tells me information about people who seek me, and they seek me, this is how I expected you and knew what you wanted," Morina told the princess so she could comfort her. Mildred now felt more comfortable with what she was doing.

"First I am going to give you this potion, for this week be sure to drink 10 milliliters of it twice a day," Morina said as she put the potion and a syringe into a plastic bag, which she then gave to Mildred.

"Now we begin the ritual," Morina said. Mildred then impatiently nodded her head, however, Morina did not pay the slightest attention to that. Mildred relaxed in the chair some more, and Morina put her arms in position and kept moving them like a wave. Magic came out of Morina's hands and flew right into Mildred's head; the magic coming from Morina's hands looked like lightning, even though it wasn't.

Morina kept doing this for a while. Mildred, under the spell, began to think about Samuel. All Mildred heard was the boring sound of waves entering her head, however, these boring waves triggered the feeling of optimism towards Samuel in Mildred's heart. The spell made her more focused on her task, which she saw as an important part of her mission that could help her escape.

Getting through this ritual was a terribly boring task, and getting through it was like walking against a strong wind pushing. But Samuel and her mental state were something that was more important. The pain she constantly felt was something that was stronger than any boredom that she may feel.

As the clock ticked with moments of peace and moments of mental anguish, Mildred felt her body becoming weaker, her eyes tearing up, her head hurting, and in general being in a weak, dizzy state but in a relaxing way. Mildred made Morina continue performing the ritual for the same reason she resisted her boredom. More than half an hour passed and Morina had completed the ritual three times.

Mildred's session with the witch was over, but then the subject of payment came up.

"How much do you need, Morina?" Mildred kindly asked the witch.

"I do not take cateos, Your Highness," Morina replied, looking at her spell book like she was not focusing, but she understood everything around her.

"Then what do you take?" Mildred asked the witch, feeling weird.

"I know you have nothing on you right now, however, for the next session tomorrow, bring me two pieces of silver jewelry. One for each session," Morina answered the princess's question.

"You have to come, every single day; for a session, until you get the result you desire," Morina told the princess, then asked her to leave. Mildred left the witch's apartment and went through the same journey she went through to get here. The second journey was another rut through the outside world, and another spiral through abstract thoughts. But Mildred actually had hopeful thoughts; she felt as if this way she could actually get what she wanted, or at this point, what she needed. Mildred went to the castle, and for the first time in many, many months, the princess got proper sleep.

The princess slept that night in peace. But she now found herself in a land without snow, a city with skyscrapers, in front of a sunrise. Mildred saw a grown man in front of her, a man that looked a lot like Samuel, and she looked at herself to see that she now was a full-grown woman.

"Mildred... Are you happy?" Samuel asked the princess, Mildred then looked at him with a smile and replied.

"Yes Samuel, I'm happy," was Mildred's answer. The two held each other's hands with their wedding rings on their fingers. Nothing mattered, they were together, the feelings could not be imagined by those who hadn't experienced them. Mildred was feeling as if she was flying over the heavens. They then stood up and went on a scavenger hunt adventure. Soon they were at a suburban area with regular villas outside of the city. Apparently, it was where they lived. In that area Mildred was now at peace, she had herself together, not just for Samuel, but she had what made her happy. No more royal pain or royal worries. However, Mildred woke up the next morning, back at her bedroom in the Winter Wonderland palace, to realize that the life she was having with Samuel was nothing more than a dream.

Winter Wonderland, Cataville, December 13th, 1987

About a week had passed. That morning Mildred went to Morina for the ritual. Mildred got a potion prescription from Morina but a higher dose. Mildred made sure to take the potion like Morina told her, and she was obsessed with the way she looked by then. It was vital that she showered very often, took care of her facial cleanliness, and worked on everything that could be wrong with the way she looked. Mildred was taking zero chances, she had to ensure that she got the happy ending she wanted with Samuel. But more importantly, get rid of her society, everyone at the castle, the school, and everyone that was possibly ruining her life. Mildred also could be with the one she loved, as the princess wife of a baron, maybe not in a city or a suburb like in the dream, but at least in Samuel's isolated mansion. No royal or high noble standards, home education as a married princess, which Winter Wonderland society respected.

Alaska always tried to cheer Mildred up into thinking that she was so much more than to just keep obsessing over the way she looked and work herself so much just for a man to want to marry her. Alaska tried hard to show Mildred how her actions showed a lack of value. However, to Mildred, what was happening to her was not because she thought she was not enough without Samuel; but because of the escape plan and exciting feelings, it took Mildred away from the despair she always endured. She continued following the witch's orders, and working on herself more and more, every single day without failing.

Mildred's mental health was failing significantly. It was a struggle to try and control her mind, especially when she had almost lost it completely. Mildred's concentration was failing. Focus was a state that Mildred found almost impossible to get by then, she was living in her head, living in a world inside of her. This was one of the main issues that Mildred had wanted to tackle with the permanent change of her environment.

It became almost impossible to cope with the mental pain Mildred was going through. She had to continuously convince herself that the happy ending she might actually get with Samuel was something she had to live for.

Winter Wonderland, Cataville, December 23rd, 1987

Time passed by very slowly. Mildred followed the witch's orders; she began to get dizzy more often and now slept earlier. But she saw that it was worth it, especially since the spell had convinced her that he definitely liked her back by now. Mildred thought that because she was using real magic it did its job, and it was comforting for her.

Mildred's feelings were getting deeper, even though they weren't speaking during the school break, but it was as if the spell was connecting them together. Mildred also began noticing a difference in the way she looked. She finally achieved the flat belly she had wanted so badly. The princess's face was also cleaner, free of acne or anything.

Mildred felt more ready to face Samuel; she was thinking about it more than anything else. Visiting the witch had become a daily routine, the witch's ritual and potions had become therapeutic drugs to Mildred. It was still difficult dealing with the suspense of whether or not the magic was working on Samuel. It was definitely not easy to endure the mental strain that Mildred was going through. Still as blue as ever, the princess still longed for and wanted nothing more, absolutely nothing more, than to escape and be with the one she loved, away from those who always hurt her.

The princess went to the witch that day in the middle of the noon. Mildred went through the ritual that weakened her body as usual, the princess went through fifty minutes of the ritual, and she ended up with higher raised hopes for the happy ending she had been longing for. The day went by, and the more Mildred convinced herself to be patient for Samuel, the more she felt so happy that she could die. The feelings of happiness were of course accompanied with black thoughts of Mildred's death and destruction.

As soon as Mildred was home, she went to her own heart. The princess could not help but sing a terrible song she wrote for Samuel.

"A dream beyond the tower's highest beam,

A feeling that is so magical,

Through the storm and beyond the rain,

An adorable baron waiting for me." Mildred sung in low tones, she stayed silent for a few moments.

"Will you come to me?

Will you rescue me?

I need you now,

Will we officially be happy together?" Mildred continued singing, starting off suddenly with a high pitch.

"It is vital that you come,

It is vital that I come,

It is vital that we meet,

Can we please meet?" Mildred harmonized, in a voice filled with love, with eyes begging for mercy.

"We will meet down there,

You will know the magic I feel with you,

I hope you'll feel it too,

When will our time come?" Mildred sung like she was performing a concert.

"We'll be awed by paradise,

We'll have it all,

We will never ever bawl!

Please make it happen," Mildred sung in her high-pitched voice while walking towards the column in her room, holding it. Lowering her voice at the end of the verse.

"Please make this happen…

For the love of god, let this happen…

Cope with me….

I am begging you please, make this happen…" Mildred finished her song, with each stanza her voice lowered, and her desperation increased.

The princess snapped out of her song, still feeling as weak as ever, she just hoped that she could potentially be able to push through the days, weeks, and months she needed to endure in order to get her escape.

Winter Wonderland, Cataville, December 31ˢᵗ, 1987

Mildred woke up that morning feeling impatient, she had waited the entire month, and Samuel did not even ring her. The mental state Mildred was living in was still falling to its doom, the princess did a few daily activities to get over her boredom. Mildred dealt with Annabella that day as usual. The princess went through her daily ritual and visited the witch.

The princess also wanted to have lunch outside the castle, so she went to her favorite restaurant "Estate of Pancakes and Waffles." Mildred ate her favorite food there, chocolate chip pancakes. As she ate her food, she looked at the view outside the window. It was of the whole town square of Winter Wonderland, she only wished Samuel were here with her. It was a whole other dream, as adults she and Samuel would come here for coffee every day and enjoy their happiness.

The princess daydreamed about this idea of hers, until her new cell phone rang. Mildred saw the number that was calling her, it was Samuel.

"Greetings, Samuel, how are you doing dear friend?" Mildred excitedly said.

"Greetings, Mildred, I'm doing alright," Samuel replied to her happily.

"What is going on? I missed you dearly," Mildred told Samuel with a smile.

"I am having my birthday party in five days; would you like to come?" Samuel asked Mildred.

"I'd love to," Mildred responded happily.

"There is a catch, however, all of the people coming are not from our school, and they're all boys," Samuel warned Mildred. Usually Mildred would reject the outing after hearing something like that, but this was Samuel, and she would not ruin a chance to spend time with him just because silly boys were there, it also made her feel more special because she was the only girl.

"It's alright, it doesn't matter, I can still come," Mildred happily replied. The two then said goodbye and ended the call. Mildred was over the moon, she would finally see him, it was very exciting. But she needed to plan this perfectly. The princess finished her lunch, then left for the castle. She made sure that in these few days she would stick even harder to her diet and workouts. The princess worked hard to ensure she had a perfect appearance; she also needed a very extravagant outfit that would make her look better than everyone.

Alaska as usual voiced disapproval about how this type of behavior was not just demeaning to Mildred as a woman, but also about how unrealistic Mildred's view of love and her problems were. She did not and could not listen. The princess had to continuously remind her sister of how it was not about herself as a woman and more about escaping and rescuing herself from the monsters she fought every day. Alaska then tried to convince Mildred that marriage was not how she would save herself.

"What do you know, Alaska? You've had it all since day one," Mildred began criticizing Alaska.

"Mildred, I am only trying to help you!" Alaska worriedly said.

"Alaska, I do not need your help! You do not know how much this will help me!" Mildred lashed out at Alaska; as she saw that Alaska was the last person who could be right about this. Alaska saw that Mildred was not listening, she could tell how terrible Mildred was doing psychologically and she couldn't help crying. Alaska's crying got to Mildred. Mildred still was going to work hard to achieve the medieval dream of "happily ever after," but Alaska's reaction made her feel guilty.

It was almost midnight, the New Year was close to beginning. Mildred began wishing that Samuel was there with her, she hoped that by the subsequent New Year's Eve for 1989, she would have him by her side. But for the 1988 New Year's Eve, she needed to spend it alone in the castle, this may be the year where she would achieve what she had worked so hard for. Mildred felt a romantic atmosphere come from the entire kingdom while everyone in the kingdom was at the square near their houses.

Mildred watched the clock tick the last minute of 1987. 1988 began. An important year in Mildred's life, a year where many good things happened, yet so many terrible things also did. One of the most magical years for Mildred, and a traumatic one, had just begun. When she saw the new date, January 1st, 1988, she worked to make this the most romantic and best year of her life, after the long and hard year of 1987.

The fireworks were so bright, they were shining through the snowing sky as everybody cheered on. Mildred thought that a new day had finally come.

Chapter Twenty
Wildest Dreams

Winter Wonderland, Cataville, January 2nd, 1988

Mildred was woken up that morning very early, at 7 a.m. It was still difficult dealing with the task of taking care of herself and getting Samuel to like her. It was her fourteenth birthday, she was also depressed; last time she spoke to Samuel on the phone, he showed no emotion as he spoke to her. Mildred worried extremely that the ritual was not working. When Mildred went to the witch that day, she made sure that the witch gave her a higher dose of potion and a stronger ritual.

The princess went all around Winter Wonderland, from her hometown to the witch's hometown, every single mall in every single area of Winter Wonderland. She made sure to buy only the most expensive gowns and the most expensive accessories and shoes. By the end of the day she was tired. The princess was back at the castle at eight p.m., she entered and saw a huge gathering.

The ballroom was filled with their relatives, Alaska's friends. There was a twelve-tier cake standing on the table in the middle of the ballroom. Beautiful music was playing in the ballroom. Alaska danced the waltz with her mother, relatives, and friends. They seemed to be having great fun. It was a birthday party for Alaska only. Mildred watched for a little while and left for her bedroom. As soon as the princess was on the way to her chambers, she was as usual, unhappy with how she was always treated, by her family and those outside of it. She kept reminding herself that in a short time she would be out of the castle and living at the Jerram mansion, so she stayed strong.

The birthday party for Samuel was in two days, and she had to begin preparing herself early. The princess was done and wanted nothing more than to sleep. Which she did.

Winter Wonderland, Cataville, January 4th, 1988

It was the day of Samuel's birthday party. The princess had thought about many things since she went shopping. It was vital that she had nothing wrong with her appearance as usual and wore her absolute best outfit. The princess had spent about four hours in the bathroom. Once she was finished with everything she wanted to do, it was ten-thirty a.m. The princess had to come up with a whole new plan to spend time with Samuel, before the other boys arrived.

Mildred thought that Samuel had not spent any time with the boys for quite a while, therefore she should not be surprised if he focused on them. She planned to arrive at the party an hour early. She left the castle immediately, planning to arrive as early as possible. The ride in the limousine to central Winter Wonderland was a trip strained by anxiety. The princess obsessed over the way she looked. In addition to how much weight she had lost to better her appearance in the past month.

She was finally at the party. Nobody else was there, not even Samuel and his family. The princess waited half an hour for Samuel to arrive. By then it was nearly time for the party. The princess saw Samuel and his younger brother standing at the other side of the room by the entrance. Mildred walked to them in slow motion, she made sure that they saw her beforehand. The princess's hard work was shining through the light, she was much thinner and fitter than she was the last time he saw her, her hair done more magnificently than ever, her skin shining beautifully, her gown bigger and more glamorous than anything she had ever worn before. Any fancier than that, she would be dressed for her own wedding.

The princess went over to Samuel. Mildred greeted both of them, happy to see Samuel. She walked with both of them, they spoke a bit. The princess was very unhappy that Samuel barely talked to her and said absolutely nothing about the way she looked. If anything, it was Samuel's brother, Abraham, who focused on Mildred. The disappointment that day did not end there though. Just a few moments later, the first of the boys began arriving. Samuel began talking with the boys and talked more with them during the entire time when they were alone.

Mildred was devastated that Samuel, the one she loved and her only friend, did not say more than two words to her during the time when they were alone. He was supposed to like her back, Mildred was performing a ritual and killed herself over this every day. How was it that it ended up like that? Would she not get the happy ending that would help her recover? Soon, all the guests had arrived, and it was time to go watch the movie.

Mildred could not concentrate on the movie at all, she was not able to follow the storyline; she did not care. The movie felt so long, and the more she got through it the more she wanted it to end badly. Soon, but not soon enough, the movie ended. It was now time for food, cake, and celebrations.

Mildred had stayed silent the whole time, the monsters in her head kept torturing her during the entire party, the princess couldn't help but eat the whole burger and ruin her diet. Mildred ate the burger like a monster, which was what Samuel saw.

"And of course, Mildred goes like a monster for the food, as usual," Samuel jokingly said, not intentionally and directly meant to hurt Mildred. The princess stayed silent, too sad to say anything. When it was time for cake, Samuel's mother, Baroness Michelle of Winter Wonderland, wanted to take a picture of the entire group in front of the cake of all the boys, and being the only girl, Mildred looked better than everyone else in the picture, except for the fact that she was feeling depressed and it showed on camera. Mildred barely had any cake, and soon the boys began to leave. It was only Samuel, Abraham, Baroness Michelle, and Mildred herself at the place of the party. The princess's carriage was on the way, Michelle talked to Mildred for a bit until she finally left the party.

Winter Wonderland, Cataville, January 5th–6th, 1988

Mildred barely slept the night before January 5th, probably only two hours, for she felt nothing but her regular mental problems and heartbreak. Mildred had just spent that entire day being tortured by her own mind, nothing new. After the princess was up almost all night, she was also up all day, she just kept singing manically about her wild dreams, her wilder dreams, and then her wildest dreams.

She just spent the day bored and alone, locked in her bedroom the entire day. Then when everyone was asleep, she was up all night again. Insomnia had spent this entire interval of time making Mildred suffer, and her mental problems were not helping.

She barely opened her mouth those two days, during which she also spent almost all of January 6th awake. But ended up sleeping at 8 p.m. after 50 hours of non-stop pain and no sleeping.

Winter Wonderland, Cataville, January 7th, 1988

Mildred woke up when it was nearly afternoon, she felt sweaty and dirty, but she did not care. The princess did not shower that morning, which shocked everyone. For the past few days she had put no effort into her appearance. She just stayed in bed, put on music, and kept still. Her entire mood was completely changed, when something peculiar occurred.

Out of nowhere the phone next to Mildred in her room rang. Mildred did not even want to answer it. But she managed to get a peek at the number that had rang her. It was Samuel. The princess got extremely excited. She felt extremely anxious then picked up the phone.

"Hello, Samuel!" Mildred flirtatiously said.

"Greetings, Mildred," Samuel replied with a smile.

"How are you doing?" Mildred continued talking in the same manner as before, trying to cover up her over-excitement.

"I'm alright, what about you?" Samuel responded to her question with the same happiness as before.

"I'm great!" Mildred answered, continuing in the same tone.

"Would you like to come over to my house?" Samuel happily asked the princess. Mildred felt like he had just proposed to her, she got very excited. She wanted to reply with 'Yes! Yes! A thousand times yes!' But, she could not say that yet.

"Of course, Sammy!" Mildred said, even more flirtatiously.

"Awesome, when could you come?" he replied back.

"How about after tomorrow?" Samuel said.

"Excellent," Mildred responded. The two made plans, then they hung up their phones. Mildred was happier than ever. She jumped out of her bed and went to shower and do all the things she had been doing regularly before Samuel's birthday party.

Winter Wonderland, Cataville, January 9th, 1988

Mildred woke up very early from her slumber that day, she spent hours in the bathroom getting ready. The princess was expected to be at the Jerram mansion in two hours by the time she was done. The princess needed to hurry up, in one hour, she did everything she could possibly do to her appearance, and making sure she looked flawless. The princess couldn't think about anything else in a long time, she hoped this was a chance to change that.

It was not long till the princess was in the limousine that would take her to the Jerram mansion. The ride to the Jerram mansion was filled with suspense but at the same time it wasn't. The princess had high hopes; as the effects of the magic ritual were back. Mildred was about to experience real happiness today, but she did not know that.

Mildred enjoyed every single view she saw through the window, until she finally arrived. The Jerram mansion was big, nearly a quarter the size of the palace, it was built with beige bricks and its roof was covered in icicles and ice just like ice skating rinks. The princess found it to be a more serene place than her castle. Mildred took out her cell phone and called Samuel.

"Greetings Sammy, I'm in front of your house," Mildred said in an airy voice.

"Alright, here, I'm coming down to get you," Samuel replied in a way that she found adorable. He was out of the house in a few moments. Samuel and Mildred went into the house and went to their part of the mansion. The main hallway in their house was green, it had two archways, one leading to the dining room and one leading to the living area next to the main doorway.

Mildred was then greeted by Abraham. They both kept talking to her, and it made her glad. She played a board game with them. Samuel paid attention to her that day, the attention she wanted from him the day of the birthday party. But she no longer cared about what had happened at the birthday party. What she cared about was that day, and that day only. Then they played on a console some people would consider old. Samuel and Abraham played a game with guns and killings. Then they asked Mildred to play with them, typically Mildred would not have been interested in this kind of game, however, Mildred loved Samuel and she was willing to do this for him.

So Mildred played this 1980s game and actually had fun. They played a little, until baroness Michelle returned to the house. The baroness came into the corridor and saw Mildred.

"Greetings, Your Highness," the baroness said to Mildred.

"Greetings to you, Baroness Jerram," Mildred replied to Michelle.

"How are you?" Michelle asked Mildred with a smile of comfort.

"I'm great, how about you?" Mildred answered the baroness, over the moon to say otherwise. Michelle then complimented Mildred on her height. She was very happy and this changed her mood. She secretly did not like that; because her height was one of the main sources of her never-ending misery, but she knew that Michelle meant well.

"Thank you, Baroness Jerram," Mildred responded to Michelle with a smile. For a few minutes, Mildred asked about her height, was she really that tall? She had measured her height yesterday, the result was 184 centimeters, and it was definitely very tall.

Michelle went to the kitchen, then Mildred and the boys went to the living room. Samuel and Abraham began showing Mildred the Legos structures they had put together.

"You guys are talented," Mildred told them, having absolutely no thought of something proper to say.

"It's not talent, it is skill," Samuel told her, leaving Mildred impressed, even though she was living in her head. Samuel and his brother took Mildred to watch a movie. They set up the video with the movie they wanted. It was a movie about time travelling, it was pretty long, and she enjoyed watching it with Samuel. During the early parts of the movie. Mildred was laying on the floor, resting her head on the legs of the chair. Samuel looked at her and out of nowhere, their eyes met. Mildred saw love in his eyes, he kept looking at her with that same look for a few moments. Mildred loved that, with that she gathered that the magic ritual had not gone to waste. They ate and hung out, Mildred eating normally and forgot about her diet for the one day.

They spent a lot of time together and had loads of fun. The three of them played a board game, and Baroness Michelle also joined them for a little while. Mildred did not know how to play the game, and they ended up having to teach her, her mental health problems and weakness were also hindering her focus. Mildred was going crazy by then, as she realized that Michelle had become very fond of her, she sensed that if she knew the truth about Mildred's mental health and powers, the baroness's opinion would change.

Abraham tried to cheat at the game using Mildred. Samuel started an argument with him because of that. Mildred also found it cute that Samuel stood up for her like that, but she wanted him to be happy with his brother and stop arguing.

The three spent more time together and watched another movie and played the video game again. As they were playing the video game again, Mildred succeeded at a 'kill' in the video game so Samuel applauded her with pride.

It was soon past sunset, and Samuel's father, Baron Alexander, came back from his job at the council. Mildred was with Samuel and Abraham when they greeted him. Alexander Jerram, like his wife, were also very fond of the princess. That day was also Alexander's birthday, everyone including Mildred wished him a happy birthday.

Mildred and the family all went downstairs, to the part of the mansion where Samuel's grandparents lived. When everyone got downstairs, Samuel's grandmother opened the door. Mildred being a princess, both of Samuel's grandparents immediately recognized Mildred. Samuel's grandparents took kindly to Mildred. Everyone had some food, they all celebrated Alexander's birthday. Michelle asked Mildred to take a picture of their family. It looked good. And even though Mildred was not a good photographer, the family portrait she took in that 1986 camera still looked excellent.

The princess enjoyed the time with Samuel's family, and she could see that Samuel liked her. Mildred also ate a lot here, leaving her feeling terrible about her diet. Mildred, Samuel, and

Abraham went back up to the upper part of the mansion. They continued watching the movie, until Mildred received a phone call.

"Mildred, I am coming to get you, I'll be here at eight-thirty," Charles said.

"Alright, Charles," Mildred said sadly, not wanting to leave or for this day to end. Mildred went back to the living room where Samuel and Abraham were sitting.

"So, I just received a call from the castle steward, he said he'll be here at eight-thirty," she told Samuel.

"Mildred, will you please call and ask him to let you stay for an extra hour, we're still watching the movie," Samuel replied with a sad look. Mildred saw the 'love' in his eyes and saw how sad he was that she was leaving.

The princess called Charles back, and asked for that extra hour, which she got. So they continued watching the movie and playing games until it was nine-thirty.

The royal limousine was now in front of the Jerram mansion again. Mildred went to the window in the front of the house from the back side. That was when she saw the castle transportation. Mildred and the boys then went downstairs to go outside.

Mildred saw Michelle and Alexander once more, Michelle badly wanted to meet the queen, and she knew Annabella was in the car. Mildred went inside the limousine, where she saw Charles in the driver's seat and Annabella in the back seat. Michelle was at the window of the backseat, waiting to speak to the queen.

"Mother, Samuel's mother wants to speak with you," Mildred whispered to her mother. Annabella then turned her head and saw Michelle, making her open the window.

"Greetings, Queen Annabella," Michelle said to the queen, then curtsied.

"I am Baroness Michelle, Samuel's mother," Michelle continued.

"I hope you are doing well, dear," Annabella replied to Michelle.

"Very well! Princess Mildred is wonderful, Your highness," Michelle happily replied to Annabella leaving them both smiling at each another.

"Glad to hear that dear," Annabella said with a small sign of happiness.

"Definitely, she is more proper than my children. Best wishes to the both of you," Michelle said to the queen, then smiled at both of them. The queen and baroness then did the Winter Wonderland gesture of kissing each other's cheeks. They all said goodbye to one another. That beautiful day ended in peace.

Winter Wonderland, Cataville, January 13th, 1988

It was three days till the end of the mid-year vacation. Mildred was not excited at all. The princess continued doing her beauty and magic rituals in order for her plan to work. Mildred also increased the dose of the potion and the rituals with Morina to make sure that the spells worked.

The important thing about that day was that she also had a romantic meeting in mind for Samuel, but he didn't know that yet. Mildred called him that afternoon. She asked him to meet at a café, which he and his family accepted. Mildred made sure she looked like she was going to a ball. The princess had to pick him up from his house. After doing her beauty rituals, she curled her hair, put on a cream colored ballgown, by the time she was done getting ready, she looked like an angel.

The princess left the castle and went to the Jerram mansion in a carriage. She called Samuel as soon as she arrived, and they went to the café in the carriage. The two spent some time at the café, but Mildred wanted to do more.

"Sammy, come, I have a surprise for you!" Mildred happily said.

"What is it, Mildred?" Samuel ran after her. The two ran for a minute, they were at the train station.

"What are we doing here? Where are you taking me?" Samuel asked Mildred curious as to where they were going.

"Just wait and see," Mildred said as she took him by the hand, then went into the train station. Mildred took him on the train that was in Mid-Center Cataville, an area outside of Winter Wonderland and snow.

The two of them were on the train in less than fifteen minutes, the romantic atmosphere was felt through the entire train. Mildred was so happy, especially since she kept seeing signs that Samuel returned her feelings. Mildred had always wanted to go on the train with Samuel, and it finally happened. The most important thing to her was that they were together.

The train took off, and they chatted and enjoyed themselves until they had arrived an hour later. They had a lot of fun, Mildred was very happy she could have fainted or died happily. It was the type of feeling she never imagined experiencing.

The train arrived in Mid-Center Cataville, the two of them disembarked. In Mid-Center Cataville there was no snow, icicles, or ice. It was just pure greenery. Mildred took Samuel's hand again and ran towards the place she wanted to take him. It was hard to run with her choice of clothes and shoes, but it was worth it, and she did not ruin them.

Soon, the two were at a garden at the top of a hill. The area they reached was much higher than Winter Wonderland, the two saw what Winter Wonderland looked like from the garden which overlooked it. There was the grand winter paradise they lived in, the town square, the palace even, the red mall, all the antiques and beautiful historical iconic buildings. The view was absolutely breathtaking, with her curled blonde hair, beautiful cream gown, the enchanting smile on her face. Still Samuel said nothing about her appearance. Mildred enjoyed the romantic atmosphere, the lovely garden and with wonderful feelings, she hoped they would never ever end, ever. They talked, they laughed together, went through the maze in the garden, Samuel asked her about herself and her hobbies. Mildred then asked herself whether or not this was a sign that he could possibly like her back. Mildred went on believing that the magic ritual was doing its job. The princess spent time with Samuel in that gorgeous garden for what felt like minutes, and had one of the best times of her life.

Winter Wonderland, Cataville, January 16th, 1988

Today the princess was to return back to school; she woke up that morning feeling dizzy from the increased dose of the love potion she used on herself for Samuel. Mildred was now feeling more anxious than ever, because life at school was something she did not miss at all. The people there would continue to make fun of her. She knew that semester was going to be bad, but it was nothing compared to what she actually experienced.

Mildred had many worries while getting ready, and all the efforts she had made to improve her mental health for Samuel also had been completely worthless during the time between waking up and going to school. The princess ended up going to school which eased the anxiety she was feeling, even though after going through that semester, she realized she shouldn't have let her anxiety decrease.

One important note about this day was that she wanted to go out with Samuel again. There was this ice-skating place she had practically grown up at, with another amazing ambiance that she would love to experience with Samuel. The princess still struggled with anxiety, severe battles with depression, and constant thoughts of death.

Winter Wonderland, Cataville, January 18th, 1988

This was the day Mildred took Samuel ice skating. Mildred went to school, pushed through it a million times harder than other people. What was hard was that Samuel kept talking to other girls. Mildred felt jealousy every time he talked to another girl. She asked what was it that these girls had that she didn't. Was it beauty? Since her height made her ugly according to the standards of the society. Samuel talked to other girls so much and in a manner that he never spoke with her, that was painful especially since she was putting a lot effort into getting Samuel to return her feelings.

By the end of the school day, Mildred was having extreme suicidal thoughts over this. Not because she was in love with him in a tragic way, but because she was already living in hell, she needed to leave it with this happy ending. Her feelings for him were also of no help, and just made it much worse. But when the outing started, Mildred's thoughts were totally different.

Mildred took the carriage to the Jerram mansion to pick Samuel up; there were a lot of negative thoughts, until she reached the Jerram mansion. Samuel entered the carriage and sat on the seat next to Mildred. The princess loved how he looked in his sweater and pants, even though it was nowhere near as fancy as her coat and pants. The carriage then took them to the most romantic lake-park in Winter Wonderland.

Mildred and Samuel left the carriage and into that park. It had a huge frozen lake for skating and had trees surrounding the entire park. Decorations were covering many of the trees around the park. The area was completely private, there was nobody but Mildred and Samuel, the ticket attendant was also at the very end of the park playing music.

"Sammy," Mildred said happily.

"Yes, Mildred," Samuel replied with a smile.

"You did bring skating boots, right?" Mildred asked excitedly. Samuel nodded, then they both walked to the bench and put on their skates. She walked him to the pond, as he was not used to skates or ice skating. When they reached the pond, Samuel almost lost his balance a few times. Mildred stopped, holding on to him so he could learn to skate properly. It took him a while to get used to skating, but Mildred made sure she was never far away from him. Mildred and Samuel bumped into each other and fell. No one was injured and they ended up laughing. When they stood up, the song that Mildred always sung about Samuel in private began playing.

She was very excited; they both looked into each other's eyes and were smiling. The princess felt so happy she could fly. The two skated together, until their time was up.

The pair walked together through that entire area of Winter Wonderland, and they kept talking like before. Samuel talked about the kids in school for a little bit.

"People talk about you all the time, everyone bullies you," Samuel jokingly said. Mildred hated that, but she just brushed it off, she thought most of the things he said were for her benefit.

"Well, I don't care, they can say whatever they want," Mildred expressed what she truly felt, for only Samuel mattered at that point.

"Yeah, please just try to act more normal in class and during the breaks," Samuel asked of the princess. Mildred wanted to obey, for her own sake, for her own happiness, for her own opportunity to escape. The two continued talking, Samuel found out more about Mildred's past, still they hadn't gotten to very personal things. Mildred was very happy and had a lot fun. The princess felt that she was again receiving signals that he could actually like her back.

It was after 9 p.m., and they had to go back home, especially since last time they returned to their homes late after spending an amazing time together. Samuel was also very happy, Mildred hoped that Samuel's happiness was also because the one he was spending time with was her, and not just because the place they went to was glorious and fun.

Winter Wonderland, Cataville, January 24th, 1988

The last of wonderful adventures Mildred had with Samuel was on this day. A royal ball was taking place then, because Alaska was getting engaged. Annabella was happier about it than anyone else. Mildred invited Samuel to keep her occupied during the party. For one, she did not feel jealous; because she thought that she may have this for herself very soon, not just for her sister who always got everything.

The princess went to school, had her daily share of mental torture, and then went home to focus on Samuel. It was for a ball, so she needed to look better than usual. The princess visited the witch quickly and did the ritual a few times, went home quickly, and began getting ready.

By the time Mildred was done getting ready, she looked like an angel in red. Mildred did her hair into a Victorian hairstyle, wore a red gown, and a tiara. The princess was more than happy waiting for the ball to start. She went to see Alaska. Alaska was also as dressed up as Mildred was, wearing a blue gown slightly thinner than Mildred's, her skin shining bright. Alaska was standing on a chair in front of a dresser with a mirror, applying a few extra touches.

"Congratulations, dear Alaska!" Mildred said seeming happy on the outside, but dying with envy on the inside.

"Thank you, sweetheart," Alaska stood holding her dress up. Mildred hoped that would be her very soon. Alaska looked in her eyes and gave her a hug. She couldn't hug her sister back but did not reject Alaska's embrace. A man came into the room, he was two years older than Mildred and Alaska. The man looked better than Samuel, he had the physique of a warrior and was very tall, a little shorter than Mildred, his hair was golden and more mature and tidy than Samuel's, he had sea green eyes that were nicer than Samuel's, and like all royals he also had freckles from the sun. He looked a lot like Mildred and Alaska's late father Maximus. The man went and hugged Alaska, then bowed to Mildred.

"Hello, Princess Mildred, we never properly met, I am prince Malcom of Eastern Cataville, Alaska's fiancée," the man said with a smile. Leaving a mild cringe on Mildred's face. The princess couldn't but curtsy and leave the room. She bumped into her mother, leaving her with a look of fear on her face.

"Congratulations, Mother, I see you married Alaska off to the man of her dreams. Or is it a man of your dreams?" Mildred asked, leaving Annabella to turn her head left and right.

"What are you implying?" Annabella asked feeling threatened but still with a fake tone.

"Oh nothing," Mildred then said with complete disrespect as she noticed that Annabella understood exactly what she had meant before.

"Show some respect when talking to me! It's not my fault nobody will marry you," Annabella yelled harder than before. Annabella raised her hand, wanting to hit Mildred again, but she couldn't; because the ball was starting very soon. Mildred walked away, not wanting to deal with how narrow-minded her mother really was. This was another reason aside from her feelings why she was dying to leave and have Samuel return her feelings.

The princess felt depressed for a little while, until she, Annabella, Alaska, and Prince Malcom stood by the huge entrance door of the castle. Guests began entering, other random royals came in, with every guest giving them a royal courtesy and a kiss on both cheeks. Nobles entered and did the same. Mildred saw Samuel and his parents entering the ballroom, receiving a greeting from them as with everyone.

Their maternal family members came afterwards and greeted each of them. However, when there was no one else to greet, a woman in her mid-sixties came into the castle. She was a person that Mildred hardly remembered. The woman had gray hair that was tied in a bun in a style older than the Victorian style and was wearing an ugly blue dress.

"Mona Beth…" Annabella said trying to conceal her anger.

"Grandmother," Alaska and Mildred said as they took in her appearance. They hadn't seen her in nearly ten years, and they had been very young by then.

"Hello, dear princesses," Mona Beth said smiling at the two girls, giving each of them hugs and kisses.

"Do you remember me, girls? Last time I saw you, you two were this big," Mona Beth kept talking with excitement, lowering her two hands to show the height they had been.

"Congratulations, dear Alaska, I missed you so much," Mona Beth kept talking, giving Alaska more kisses. Mildred went to spend time with Samuel. Even though she looked beautiful, he still said nothing about it. They spent time and had fun. Mildred began flirting with Samuel in a way that was very direct. He seemed to have a positive response, which made her happy.

Soon it was time for the waltz. Everyone went to the dance floor, everyone started waltzing with their partners as the orchestra was beautifully playing. Alaska and Malcom waltzed in the center of the ballroom, with Annabella watching from the edge with pride. Mona Beth sat at one of the tables also watching Alaska. Mildred grabbed Samuel's arm without hesitation and walked towards the dance floor. The princess and Samuel began waltzing. With Mildred being taller and larger than Samuel, she was twirling and carrying him for the whole dance. The magic feelings she felt, the happiness, the hope. It was as if they were the only two in the world, dancing in heaven.

Mildred and Samuel snuck to the balcony next to Mildred's room. They continued talking, the more time they spent together, the more Mildred felt drawn to him. The night was shining just like all the other nights she spent like this, the stars in the sky were twinkling as they looked at them. Samuel told Mildred many stories, and so did she. She felt as if she was getting a positive response from all of this, if only this night would never end. If it were to end, she hoped at least with a positive result.

They kept talking and Mildred kept tolerating feelings of magic. She was begging for the ritual to do its job. She wanted so much better than to be at the palace, abused and oppressed all day every day. After all the times they spent together; Mildred's mind was at peace.

Chapter Twenty-One
I Love You

Winter Wonderland, Cataville, February 6th, 1988

For a month now, the princess had been having the most magical time of her life. She now felt as if it was over. Today was the day of the school party. Mildred looked perfect for these occasions. By then, Samuel was listening to kids who kept making fun and bringing Mildred down. Many of these were kids from another class but had to join Mildred's in English class. They had been saying a lot of things to her by then. What hurt the most though was that Samuel kept listening to them.

"Don't embarrass yourself," "You embarrassed yourself," or "When will you stop embarrassing yourself?" was something that she heard a lot of times from Samuel. That day as well Samuel kept talking about other girls and spent time with other girls and forgot about Mildred. The princess was angry about that, and kept having suicidal thoughts all day, more with people making fun of her, and with Samuel continuing to spend time with other girls all the time, when she had worked so hard to the level of strong magic. It made no sense whatsoever, and Mildred kept increasing the dose of magic every day. The princess now took four bottles of the potion Morina gave her, and Morina had to repeat the ritual more than twelve times. Samuel kept listening to those kids that she hated, and he kept blowing her off for different girls.

During the party she received a lot of negative comments from Samuel about different things that were being said about her. The problem was many of the things that she was being made fun of over were not her fault. The princess spent the entire party in pain. Mildred was seriously considered slipping away by then.

Winter Wonderland, Cataville, February 8th, 1988

Mildred was still dieting, and she was doing too much. The princess looked at herself in the mirror, she noticed that she was getting wrinkles under her eyes, she didn't know why, she did many things to get rid of them for a whole month. She was also becoming too thin, it was not healthy, and she had already lost five more kilograms on top of the weight she had lost the previous December. The stress from the castle and school were not helping either. Mildred was trying her best to get out of the dark place with Samuel and getting back to where they had been in January.

It got harder, and it got more tiring. Especially when she got to school that morning. She walked into class to see Samuel spending time with and smiling at another girl. Her name was Lil' Countess Serena. He never paid Mildred that type of attention; it was terrible. Mildred couldn't help but feel depressed. Samuel went back to his desk and he sat next to her.

"So, are you available at the end of the school week?" Mildred asked Samuel.

"Probably yes," Samuel replied.

"So, do you want to hang out at the Winter Wonderland mall, it's a lot of fun, there's a lot of activities there," Mildred asked.

"Eh, sure," Samuel replied, hesitating a little.

"Come on, it'll be fun," Mildred said encouraging him.

"Can we please go ice skating at that park again?" Samuel asked Mildred with a smile.

"Alright," Mildred agreed, they had already gone there which made her feel discontent, but she loved Samuel more, and trying to get Samuel to reciprocate her feelings was much more important.

Winter Wonderland, Cataville, February 10th, 1988

Five days were left till Mildred and Samuel were to go on the outing that would change her view of life forever. That morning Mildred woke up early, it was a weekend, and she had not seen Samuel for a few days. That was what had been regularly happening, Mildred's view of Samuel's feelings toward her kept changing according to his actions, and Samuel's actions upset Mildred more often.

The day passed by, Mildred went beyond with the magic ritual, Morina had to repeat the ritual fourteen times that day because of the many bad results Mildred was getting. The fact that Mildred was becoming pessimistic on this topic made the magic work less. That day Mildred was going be positive and she was going to believe that Samuel liked her back, that she would get the freedom she had waited so hard and so long for.

Mildred was doing the best she could, it was hard. Mildred stopped following her beauty rituals regularly and instead performed them every few days when she saw Samuel outside of school. By then the princess was begging life to relieve her, to tell her that she was not wasting her time.

Winter Wonderland, Cataville, February 11th, 1988

The school week had started, Mildred entered her classroom to find Samuel talking again to Countess Serena, in the same special way he never used with her. Whenever that happened, Mildred made sure to be there the whole time. Until.

"Mildred, can you please not follow me?" Samuel calmly asked Mildred.

"OK," Mildred replied without feeling, what happened then made her very angry, she just sat at her desk and was sad for a very long while. Even when he sat next to her, she remained very sad.

Mildred had P.E. afterwards; the teachers took her and her classmates to the field. The princess remained sad and stayed alone. Samuel saw Mildred sitting alone on a bench, miserable, and he came up to her.

"Mildred, why are you sad?" Samuel gently asked Mildred.

"I'm fine, it's not like you care!" Mildred weakly answered, and she walked away.

"Of course, I care, please tell me," Samuel replied in a warm voice. Mildred continued walking away sadly.

"Fine, suit yourself," Samuel answered as Mildred remained mad at him. The princess walked back to him with a smile, she was happy that he cared about her. She had to take it as a positive sign. Nothing else happened that day. Mildred took a high dose of potion that day and had a very long magical ritual session with Morina.

Winter Wonderland, Cataville, February 12th, 1988

As soon as English class started, more drama began. The kids from the other class came to join the class as usual. One boy who continuously joked about Mildred made his regular joke about her. Samuel had recently begun to find that joke funny. Even though he was just as unhappy with those kids joining at the beginning, later he began liking them and providing them with the support to make fun of Mildred, letting them bully her.

The princess was depressed as usual, with suicidal thoughts from these people and the already present emotional turmoil. Mildred wished she was dead, and more emotional torture followed.

"Eew, you have wrinkles," Samuel told her with a sly smile on his baby face.

Not that that wasn't enough, Mildred's self-esteem fell severely when Samuel talked to other girls during the day, and did not say, much less show, love towards her the entire day.

Winter Wonderland, Cataville, February 13th, 1988

Another day of suffering in school had gone by, and Mildred's life was nothing but Samuel, she got even more desperate. It was exactly the same as the previous day, Mildred went all out that day with the magic. Morina repeated the ritual for her nineteen times, which meant that Mildred spent more than three hours weak under a spell that involved being hypnotized. She also took a high dose of potion, an overdose. It was potion so it did not have physically damaging effects like medicine, but it made her sleep for the rest of the day.

The princess badly wanted her suffering to end, it was nearly time to come clean with the truth to Samuel. There was no going back, and it was depressing how Samuel kept blowing her off. She hoped that she would get a good result from today's session as she slept.

Winter Wonderland, Cataville, February 14th, 1988

It was valentine's day, Mildred wanted to receive good results from the ritual, it was all she ever thought about. Mildred woke up that morning at 4 am, she wanted the ritual to be done even more; to get the result she needed. It was crazy that she woke up at 4 a.m. for it, but by the time she would arrive at Morina's place it would be past six.

That part of her day went according to plan, she was there at 6 am. Morina, to Mildred's luck, was not only awake but open for business. Morina did the ritual for Mildred ten times that morning, the princess was also coming back after school for Morina to do the ritual a few more times. The princess rushed to school afterwards, taking the train to her school, and ended up arriving on time.

Winter Wonderland, Cataville, February 15th, 1988

That day Mildred's life changed forever. When Mildred arrived at school, she saw that Samuel was back with her, she saw that he badly wanted to go out with her, and she accepted. The princess tried to convince herself that he definitely liked her back. That day could end in despair or ecstasy. The princess had positive thoughts for the whole day.

The day went by very slow, and Mildred held on as much as she could. She was excited for the rainbow, but at the same time she was scared. It was like she could "see the light at the end of the tunnel" but could not. The old cherished memories Mildred had with Samuel kept her going, she waited for the day with great impatience. By the time school ended, and Mildred had gone through the week, she took the fastest limousine to the castle.

The princess ran to her room as soon as she was in the castle. She showered and performed her beauty rituals. By the time she was done with this it was nearly 5 p.m., she was getting late. Mildred put on a beautiful dark blue gown that was not too thin nor too big. She had looked better before with Samuel, however, her appearance that day had effort put into it. Mildred had to go quickly to the Jerram mansion, the princess took a car and her chauffer, and it was faster than the limousine and the carriage. She was more than twenty minutes late when she arrived at the Jerram mansion. As soon as she was there, her phone rang.

"Greetings, Samuel, I am at your house," Mildred said and Samuel assured her he will be out in one minute. He got into the car as quickly as possible and it took off to the skating park where Samuel wanted to go. When they arrived, things got complicated.

"You wanted to tell me something, spill," Samuel told Mildred as soon as they entered the park. Mildred became nervous, her heart beating a lot faster than usual, she was not ready to say anything just yet.

"Can we do it after our skating session?" Mildred replied nervously. Samuel nodded, and as they got to the area before the skating pond, Samuel began telling her stories until they were at the pond. They skated for the allotted time; Samuel did not fall as much as the previous time, and it wasn't nearly as romantic as when they were there in January. Their time at the rink went by quickly, there was nothing special about the skating part of that day.

Mildred and Samuel got off the pond, both of them kept walking. Samuel lead Mildred on till they reached an area that was somewhat isolated.

"Okay, talk!" Samuel said in a way that was neither rude nor friendly. The princess found it very hard to speak, she did not know where or how to begin. The seconds went by, and the more they did, the more Samuel pressured Mildred harder to "spill."

Mildred wanted to speak, to just say it, she couldn't. The princess was now in grave need for a positive answer, for she knew this was a loop with many difficulties around which she would not be over for months if the result was not positive. After a while, Samuel gave up, and they went back to hanging out. Mildred wanted to tell him, she waited for an opportunity to do it.

The pair walked to the food court at the park; Samuel just kept going on with stories. He kept asking Mildred about the meaning of inappropriate sentences said by kids in their school, which he did not understand. The princess felt embarrassed that she had to explain that to him, she soon realized that his mother's positive view of her would be completely shattered if she explained to Samuel what he was asking her to explain. They soon got to the topic of crushes, in which Mildred immediately realized she had an opportunity to speak.

"See, that's the thing, I want to tell you something, let's just go somewhere with less people," Mildred sheepishly said, she waited for Samuel to finish his food, especially since she had ordered nothing for herself; living in fear of gaining weight. Mildred and Samuel took off as soon as he was finished eating. The two walked downwards to a completely secluded area of Mildred's choice.

By then Mildred was more than ready to finally spit it out. Samuel also pressured her to speak. This time, Mildred failed to tell him only four times and repeated the scenario each time until.

"Three, two, one…" Mildred said.

Chapter Twenty-Two
Friends?

Winter Wonderland, Cataville, February 18th, 1988

Mildred woke up that morning in the castle, feeling absolutely worse than she had ever felt in the past fourteen years. Mildred had to go back to school, she guessed she would have to get used to Samuel as only a friend now. It was a shower in the fires of hell, having finally heard that all her hard work, all the nights of starvation, all the days of suffering, her dying every single day waiting for the prince on his white horse to come rescue her. She knew the way she was thinking was extremely demeaning towards her as a woman, but she consistently reminded herself that is wasn't because she thought she needed a man to be happy, but because it would have been an escape from a life that was awful. She needed to deal with the heartache on top of the life she was living at school and the castle.

Mildred went to school in the carriage that morning, blue as ever, her heart as broken as could possibly be. The princess arrived at the school, by the time she was at the classroom Samuel was obviously speaking to Serena, with Mildred too shattered to say anything. A shock came to Mildred afterwards, Samuel was ignoring her. In time it got worse, he kept showing her he hated her, she felt so much worse. Then it was as if he had a gun and shot her in the heart, and her heart bleeding all over. Things went from horrible to a complete hell.

The princess couldn't eat or drink at all that day. It was hard, she didn't have it in her to eat or drink, it especially became difficult when breakfast, lunch, or dinner were served, and she barely ate anything. Mildred developed lots of problems with her eating habits. Both heartbroken and depressed, the princess focused on nothing but death, both while at school, which she deemed a dungeon and it was the same exact thing for Mildred at the castle as well.

That day and many following it, Mildred attended school just to suffer, not to get an education. The princess felt nothing but pain, failure, and heartbreak.

Winter Wonderland, Cataville, March 15th, 1988

It had been a month since Samuel left her, Mildred felt miserable because of that, watching Annabella handle Alaska's wedding preparations was a strain, especially when it could have been hers as well, if only she hadn't been so extremely tall and had winter powers like the rest of her family.

By then Mildred was even deeper into her terrible psychological state. The pressure by those around her because of the Winter Wonderland traditions had become unbearable. Annabella criticized Mildred for her uselessness according to the Winter Wonderland standards, and continuously mocked her over Samuel and how she secretly knew that Mildred had feelings for Samuel.

When it came to her eating habits, telling or even ordering Mildred to eat was the equivalent of telling someone incapable of walking to "just walk." The princess had lost more than five extra kilos since Samuel ended his friendship with her, the physical sight of her made some break down in tears. If Mildred was forced to eat, it was utterly expected that she would vomit what she had eaten. She was always dizzy, every time she stood up, she would get dizzy. Along with her lack of eating, her relationship with water was just as bad, it had become typical of her to drink half a glass of water every twenty-four hours.

Like all days in late February and March, Mildred continued going on with very severe heartache. Every second she missed Samuel, every second she wished for a way out. Every moment she begged life for mercy. She cried very often; it became hard to stop. It was terrible, she barely slept. For the rest of March, she was completely drained of any sort of energy she had once had.

Winter Wonderland, Cataville, April 9th, 1988

The princess woke up that morning, there was no school that day, leaving her feeling a little better. But by then she had nothing for her, there was nothing to stay for. Thoughts of death stayed with her, and the loneliness consumed every part of her brain. She barely said any words these days, as she had nobody to say two words to. Mildred was plotting hard to perish; she had no hope.

Charles, the castle steward, entered the room, he saw Mildred staring out of her big window. The princess was singing a very sad lullaby, a love lullaby, her eyes watery, a full lake was inside them. To Charles it was apparent that she had lost more than fifteen kilos since he stopped hearing about Samuel, and five more since February started. She looked like she was done, her body and face looking weaker and bonier than ever. He knew it meant two things.

"Come," Mildred said bluntly, quickly noticing his presence.

"Do you require anything?" Mildred said, turning around.

"No dear, please follow me into my chambers, I have something for you," Charles said. Mildred had nothing better to do, nothing would change the fact that she was miserable and had nothing else to say. They walked through the bedroom hallway, down the main staircase, and into the servant quarters. The servant quarters were full of happy servants and miserable servants, some were sitting on chairs crying, some were sick, and some were happy, the rest were working. Charles went deeper into the servant quarters, into a private room.

The private room had a separate staircase only accessible through the servant quarters. Charles took Mildred up the staircase, it was a long climb. When the staircase ended, Mildred and Charles were at the top of the castle's tallest tower. There was a block that was a lot like a massage table.

"Please lay on this surface Mildred, I need to get the spell book," Charles said then walked toward the end of the room. He took hold of the spell book he was talking about and returned to her. She was already lying on the table.

"I know you're really burned out, Your Highness, I'm going to try to help you the best way I can," Charles told her in a sweet voice.

"Go ahead," Mildred responded with no emotion or care in the world.

"I know a spell that will help significantly heal your heartbreak, you'll be in a lot less pain," Charles told the princess, doing his best to comfort her. Charles moved his arms sideways then lowered them just over the princess.

"With this ritual I endeth thy loneliness, f'r thy happiness, alloweth the wounds lurking in thy mind and thy heart healeth themselves. F'r ev'rything yond knave hast done thee, thee wouldst feeleth bett'r. Th're is nothing thee can doth f'r that gent to beest with thee, but thee shall beest good now. Just waiteth, just waiteth. F'r thy loneliness and heartache shall dropeth to a v'ry high extent," Charles chanted fifty times in 1600s Shakespearean English.

Chapter Twenty-Three
Spinster at Heart

Winter Wonderland, Cataville, December 24th, 1988

The months went by, and Charles's spell had worked like it should. Mildred was now for the most part over Samuel, she recovered from her issues with eating and was now back to her average weight. Mildred was no longer heartbroken but there was still a flicker of hurt and betrayal left in her. For the most part she was back to her normal depression without heartbreak and eating problems. Unfortunately, there was no spell that could get Mildred out of her cycle of misery, and Annabella would not think about taking Mildred to the doctor.

On the other hand, Alaska's wedding was coming up soon. Annabella had booked them to go to the "Grande Lavish Pavilion" in Northern Winter Wonderland on December 31St; for Alaska's proper final wedding. Everything that Annabella had to do for Alaska, she did. But, there was one thing Annabella dreaded and wanted to do as quickly as possible.

"Mildred, get dressed, we need to go shopping for you," Annabella exclaimed in a manner that demonstrated a lack of interest.

"Why? I could just go alone, you know," Mildred also responded with a similar lack of interest.

"Just do it you deranged girl!" Annabella replied with anger and impatience.

"Whatever," Mildred said with intentional disrespect. Mildred got dressed in one of her least fancy clothes, which to regular standards was very fancy on many levels. Mildred met up with Annabella in front of the main staircase just before the main door of the castle.

The two went to a random store in the town square of Winter Wonderland, and the store Annabella took Mildred to was a vulgar place, and most of the clothes for sale there were very old and out of date. Some gowns at that store were from the seventeen and early eighteen hundreds. Mildred did not like most of the dresses there, however, it made perfect sense for Annabella to limit Mildred to old and out of fashion party clothes.

"Choose any of these gowns, we have an antique theme for your sister's wedding so choose wisely," Annabella said.

Mildred found it hard to believe that Annabella would take her there because the theme was antique Winter Wonderland. It was the theme Mildred wanted for her own wedding. Mildred took out a very full sea green gown from the 1870s, a decade where fashion was at its best in Winter Wonderland. She showed the gown to Annabella, getting a shocked expression on the queen's face, envy was visible in her eyes. Mildred was also feeling jealous of how Alaska got herself a wedding, but not her.

Annabella angrily went to the cash register and bought the gown. They both got into the carriage and went on their way to the castle. Not one of them said a letter to one another, Annabella sat on the right side of the carriage feeling threatened for herself and Alaska, while Mildred sat on the left side of the carriage in a poor frame of mind.

Winter Wonderland, Cataville, December 31st, 1988

Mildred woke up that morning at the castle, she freshened up, and then realized that it was the day of her sister's wedding.

"Ugh!" Mildred lashed out in jealous resentment and fury. However, none of this negative frame of mind was anything compared to what Mildred actually felt at the wedding. She got ready, fixed her appearance without will and out of habit, she knew her mother and sister were waiting for her downstairs. Mildred put on her new gown and did not put on any accessories.

The princess left her bedroom and went down to the dining hall. Mildred had her breakfast with Alaska and Annabella, being extremely proper eaters; they still looked the same before and after eating. Alaska was wearing comfortable shirt and sweatpants, she was going to wait till she arrived at the wedding pavilion to look bridal. That fact left Mildred and Annabella slightly envious, as they both were ready. The queen and her daughters went to their carriage, and got in.

"You know, we can just take the train, we'll arrive sooner," Mildred said. Annabella cringed, she looked like she was about to vomit. Alaska glared at Mildred as if she had just heard something stupid. Mildred didn't get why they hated the idea so much, the pavilion was very far, she always took the train to far places. Did they think they were too posh to take the train? The thought of that left Mildred cringing herself.

They continued on their journey to Northern Winter Wonderland, which took five and a half hours in the carriage. The three of them quickly got very bored, there was a radiator inside the carriage, which Annabella tampered with. Annabella and the princesses quickly had to deal with being hot as the carriage became very warm as it heated up. The three of them desperately tried to lower the temperature of the carriage but the heating system was faulty, it either got too hot or too cold, which made them redundantly switch it up. By the time the five and a half hours were up, Annabella and Mildred were done and they looked messed up.

There were three more hours left until the groom and his family would arrive, and four until the wedding would start. Annabella and Mildred had to freshen up, and Alaska had to start getting ready for her wedding in the large indoor reception next to the actual pavilion.

The four hours went by and everybody was at the wedding area. The pavilion was exotic, columns were connected to the roof of the pavilion. It had a historical theme, the pavilion had a large circular ground surface for dancing. The music was the only modern thing about the place; as it was Alaska's choice. There were also two large chairs at the far back end of the pavilion that looked exactly like thrones, Alaska and the groom sat on each one.

Mildred and Annabella greeted their main relatives first, including Duchess Mona Beth, who started greeting the rest of the guests with them. The groom's family were also greeting relatives and guests. As soon as everybody was at the wedding, the pop music began playing for five minutes. A wizard of a noble class came to perform the wedding ceremony; for Winter Wonderland had a particular way of performing weddings.

All the guests sat on chairs placed by staff working at the pavilion. While the closest relatives of Alaska and Malcom were sitting in the front. Duchess Mona Beth and Annabella were sure to be sitting at the front isle. Alaska and Malcom were standing below the wedding arch. The wizard performing the ceremony came down to the arch in front of the bride and groom.

To Mildred, it was apparent that Alaska was feeling cold in her antique huge wedding dress. She noticed that Annabella saw that as well and it left her hoping that the wedding spell would go by quick. The wizard begun with a few words before the marriage spell.

"Greetings royals, nobles, lords, and ladies, today I am going to perform the marriage spell on our Princess Alaska of Winter Wonderland and Prince Malcom of Eastern Cataville. Because of conditions set on the marriage contract, I will do the spell five times," the wizard stated.

"With the magick I hast, I embark thee on a wonderful adventureth of marriageth. Keepe thy dignity, loveth yourselves and liveth a lifetimeth of happinesse," the wizard chanted with the movement of his hands five times in very old English. The first time the wizard performed the spell, Alaska and Malcom were still. A soon as the wizard said the words again two ghost-like beings lifted out of both the bride and groom. The third time the incantation was said the two ghost-like beings walked to each other and held each other's hands. When the wizard said the incantation for the fourth time, the beings looked at the audience then the wizard and smiled. The wizard said the spell the final time, the 'ghosts' twirled with each other, until one entered Malcom and the other Alaska.

Alaska and Malcom were no longer still, they looked at each other and walked down to the center of the pavilion, while everyone was cheering and clapping for the officially married couple. Annabella used her snow powers to lower the amount of snow falling from the sky, and raised the temperature slightly, keeping the temperature at a point normal for those in Winter Wonderland.

Everybody began dancing but Mildred couldn't dance and stared at her sister and her new husband in jealousy. She became so jealous that envy became an ocean she was drowning in, yet again. This got worse very quickly.

"Good afternoon, Your Highness, how is the wedding?" a duchess who was a very close relation to the royal family asked Mildred.

"It's good!" Mildred replied with an expression that showed she was trying to hide her disgust.

"When do you think we're going to see you married?" the duchess asked with a smile. The question left Mildred shocked and annoyed, it was a question that she was very afraid of and deeply hated.

"Hopefully soon," she stated with hidden annoyance and she walked away from the duchess, only to have many other people ask the same question, leaving her feeling very anxious and envious that she was about to collapse. She could not take any more questions about her own wedding, especially when most people hated her and would not take her, unlike her sister. The Winter Wonderland society had placed so much pressure on the topic of marriage, it turned many against it. The princess left the main wedding area and went to watch the party from a balcony of the indoor area.

Mildred watched the wedding for a few more hours until she was completely bored. She couldn't wait to leave the party; she picked her stuff up and took off to the nearest train station in that part of Winter Wonderland. The princess was on her way back to the castle.

The rest of the people at the wedding stayed till after midnight and got to witness the New Year fireworks for 1989.

Chapter Twenty-Four
Where Am I Now?

Winter Wonderland, Cataville, March 11th, 1990

IT had been more than a year since Alaska's wedding. Mildred was sixteen by then, but because of her problems with people and the way she looked and the powers she possessed, there was nobody open-minded enough to marry her, even though she should have gotten married according to her society. Alaska and Malcom lived at the palace with Annabella and Mildred, both of them were now homeschooled because they were married, as it was a law in Winter Wonderland that royals and nobles who get married are to be homeschooled, and not attend the academy where other royals and nobles go. Annabella was now preparing Alaska to take over the kingdom once she retired. Many of those things left Mildred envious, especially with having people calling her "spinster" every day.

There was also something that happened that day. That afternoon Mildred was at the waiting room of a hospital, with Annabella next to her. The princess and her mother did not say anything to each other during the entire time. Annabella was panting during the entire time they were waiting. It had been a whole day that the royals were at the hospital patiently waiting. A doctor came to speak to Annabella after the long suspense.

"Greetings, Your Highness," the doctor said to Annabella.

"And to you," Annabella started off quickly then spoke more calmly. "Do you bring any good news?"

"As a matter of fact, I do. I would like to let you know that Alaska and the new princess are well, but Alaska now needs to rest. You can see her in a few hours," the doctor responded with a smile. Annabella was happy. Mildred did not seem to care very much.

Mildred left the hospital for a few hours, she stayed on her own. Receiving a lot of criticism from strangers over being the "unattractively tall princess" or "the fall queen" along with Mildred's least favorite insult "spinster," the idea that hurt the most, that she was sadly famous for.

Mildred tried to spend time having fun, but couldn't, there was still a bit of emotional torture left in her head. She had improved a little bit mentally, but not fully. Her emotions gave her a hard time for some time.

She returned to the hospital. It was a walk; because she was not that far away. Mildred arrived at the hospital, then went to the corridor where her family was. Annabella was about to go into Alaska's room, Mildred followed. She saw the light blue dim room; Alaska was laying down in the hospital bed with Malcom standing next to her and holding her hand. Annabella went to stand next to Alaska on the other side.

"Congratulations, Alaska and Malcom! It's absolutely marvelous to see you guys celebrate the achievement of bringing a new princess to the kingdom," Mildred exclaimed with fake enthusiasm.

"Why, thank you, dear Mildred," Alaska replied to Mildred's comment.

"Doctor, may we see her?" Alaska kindly asked the doctor standing next to Mildred. The doctor nodded, and the nurse went to bring the baby. The nurse was back with a baby girl in a cot. She took the cot to Alaska and placed the baby in Alaska's arms.

As soon as Alaska's daughter was in her arms, she wept tears of joy. Malcom got closer in order to see his daughter, he looked at her and then couldn't stop.

"Can I see her?" Annabella said.

"I'll see her first," Mildred replied while her arm was blocking Annabella. Mildred walked to Alaska and her new niece. The princess saw the newborn and began analyzing her. She thought the child looked absolutely nothing like Alaska, if anything she was the spitting image of her father, Malcom. This scared Mildred for Annabella; she knew Annabella would go crazy; for the baby looked like her father and everyone knew that Malcom looked quite similar to Maximus.

Mildred continued to coo with her sister and Malcom over the baby like doves. Annabella was intrigued. Annabella being Annabella came to her granddaughter and snatched her from everyone else. She took one look at her granddaughter and gasped.

"Mother?" Alaska called out to Annabella who had zoned out.

"Nothing dear, I love her so much!" Annabella said looking back at Alaska. Mildred noticed that what she thought would happen had happened.

"She resembles me very much, doesn't she, Your Highness?" Malcom said to his mother-in-law as if there were no bad feelings in the room.

"She resembles her grandfather, Maximus, my late husband. Extremely!" Annabella said in a tone that was both calm and intimidating. Annabella kissed the baby's forehead, looking almost heartbroken. She placed her granddaughter back in Alaska's arms, then left the room. Mildred followed.

Annabella sat on a chair in the outside hall and began crying. Mildred looked at her mother for a few seconds then went on. As Mildred walked toward the hospital exit, she ran into Alaska's doctor. The doctor asked how everybody was enjoying the baby, Mildred reassured the doctor that all was well. She left the hospital and went to the park for a bit. The princess stayed there until she was bothered by more people asking her when she will be married. These questions stressed her out and made her feel jealous. People always annoyed her with these questions, this had been happening more frequently since her and Alaska's sixteenth birthday.

Mildred couldn't stay calm, she was getting very tired of her closed-minded and backward society. The princess went to the castle, and stayed there for a very long time.

Winter Wonderland, Cataville, June 1990

More time had passed by, Mildred had recently completed the tenth grade. The princess was nearly done with her education, she was constantly criticized over the fact that she still went to the international noble school and was not married and homeschooled. Mildred's state of mind had begun to drift off. Annabella still regularly showed her that she was never good enough, yet she was the one who had to tend to Annabella whenever she broke down, which happened frequently.

The princess continued to suffer. It was a nightmare that never ended. What made her life slightly better, however, was that she stopped having romantic feelings. That fact usually made her pain less.

The pressure to get good grades at school was also intolerable, for years she had barely passed her exams. On top of stress by society to get good grades, Mildred also expected that of herself. Whenever she didn't get good results, she drifted off into thinking how she would be ruined, then thoughts of death snuck into her mind. She had recently gotten the disappointment of her life when it came to academic performance, where she had just received the results of her finals, and she had barely passed.

Mildred was also very much in charge in taking care of her new niece, Evanora when none of the nursemaids were available to provide care for Alaska's daughter. Alaska was too busy with royal duties, so Mildred always did Alaska's babysitting for her, and she did that whenever Malcom couldn't look after his daughter. Mildred was in no shape to take care of the baby, nor was it her job, but she was forced to do it.

It was many things on top of each other that caused Mildred to be exhausted and feel empty all day, every day. There was small hope that she would eventually find an escape, however, her view of an escape now was much more realistic than it had been a few years back. Nevertheless, there was nothing she could do but stay at the castle and live happily, at least for the time being.

Winter Wonderland, Cataville, July 27th, 1991

A year and a half went by, life was still the same. Annabella continued to teach Alaska how to properly rule the kingdom and use her powers. Malcom continued to be in charge of hosting royal balls only, like all prince consorts do in Winter Wonderland. Mildred was still being bullied and abused, societal standards of marriage and academic results were still being pushed upon her to a point she couldn't stand. Mildred was also still in charge of taking care of her niece, not only that, but Alaska and Malcom were expecting a new baby at the end of 1991, who Mildred was also expected to take care of.

Life at the castle had become harder for everybody; the royal family had lost a significant number of servants in a very short time. The reason was Annabella's cruel mistreatment towards the servant, so no new servants could be ordered for the castle because the castle's reputation for treating them was very disappointing.

That day Mildred was fully booked. Mildred's one-month break between her junior year and her senior year was over, she had to study very hard since her academic performance was terrible. She also had to always take care of Alaska because she was sick; and they were running out of servants. The princess had to balance her time between taking care of Alaska, doing chores, studying, and looking after her niece. Sometimes, that day included, she even had to take care of Annabella; who was sometimes completely out of it.

The princess could feel her blood pressure rising, she was grateful that this was the last year she would spend at school. She ended up sleeping at seven p.m. that day, she was mentally, emotionally, and physically exhausted. Mildred went back to being desperate for something to light up her life. She was woken up at six thirty a.m. the next day. She opened her eyes, which were red and looked more tired than they ever had before.

Winter Wonderland, Cataville, May 28th, 1992

Mildred just finished the exams for the final year of school, she was one of the few people her age who still went to the school; the rest were married and homeschooled. By this time, there were only twenty servants left in the castle. She still had the job of a nurse for her family; whenever any of them were sick, she was to tend to them. No matter how busy she was with school work, she was supposed to work on other things as well. The time that she spent studying was strained by the continuous stress of castle chores, the emotional and physical abuse she endured as well as childcare.

Mildred woke up that morning, she went to her bathroom as she always did, and the first thing she saw was the mirror. She looked terrible, she had dark and visible bags under her eyes which were also red. Her hair tied into a messed-up bun. She thought that she was the oldest looking eighteen-year old she ever saw. The princess washed her face, but didn't do much else.

Mildred took a carriage to school; she was to receive her report card from school. The princess was thrilled to finally be done with her education, she had a desperate wish that her studying and effort did not go to waste. She was very apprehensive for what felt like a long time. Once Mildred left the carriage, she saw the school that she had been attending what seemed like a million years. It looked bleak and uninviting to her, she hesitated before walking in.

The princess ran to the school theatre, where the report cards were being passed out. Mildred entered the room gracefully; it was the moment of truth. Did she finally get a good result? Could she leave the castle for university? Many parents of younger noble pupils gasped as they saw Mildred. All they saw was the only princess to complete her education at the school, not the independent and strong woman Mildred had grown up to be.

Mildred tried to ignore everybody in the room. She continued to walk down the aisle till she met with her teacher at the very end of the room.

"Good morning, Your Highness," the teacher greeted Mildred warmly.

"Good morning to you," Mildred replied. The teacher then began looking through his few exam files till he saw Mildred's. He took out Mildred's file then gave it to her. The princess took one look at her file and gasped. "65%" Mildred read; her result let her down once again. Tears filled Mildred's eyes.

Chapter Twenty-Five
Maltreatment

Winter Wonderland, Cataville, June 3rd, 1992

Word got out about the princess receiving a "65%" on her twelfth-grade final, along with being the only non-heir princess who did not attend university. The princess begged her mother to repeat the twelfth grade, so she could get a better result and go to university a year later. The queen couldn't say yes, Annabella thought it was already scandalous that the public knew about Mildred's grades, much less repeating the twelfth grade. Many would think it was unreasonable, but not Annabella.

Mildred found it very unfair that she didn't get a proper education, especially the last year which was completely her mother's fault, for giving her so many tasks when she needed to study, in addition to forcing and abusing her if she refused. It was her mother's fault that all the servants left, leaving her to take care of a huge castle. Mildred got even sadder when she got the idea that even if she repeated her senior year, she would still be obliged look after for the castle more than her education.

Winter Wonderland, Cataville, January 27th, 1993

More than six months had passed since Mildred's schooling ended. Mildred and Alaska had recently had their nineteenth birthday, which appeared in the paper. The newspaper that was most shameful paper ever written about any member of the royal family. It said, "Princess Mildred makes the first princess to be very close to twenty without being married, what a shocker."

This especially was written the day after her birthday, leaving her hurt, but she did not have a say in the matter.

Mildred woke up in her room that morning, and directly went to tend to her nieces, who had increased in number when Alaska had had another daughter that past month. Mildred made sure to feed her older nieces, and begged Alaska to take care of the infant, even if it was just for a little. Mildred stayed with her three nieces most of the day, she made sure to play with Evanora and Angelina, her first two nieces. Alaska cared for the baby a little till she had to begin royal duties. Mildred looked after them for so long, which made them more attached to her than Alaska herself, who was too busy to spend time with them. Malcom would sometimes come to the nursery to help Mildred with his daughters, but that would not last long either.

Alaska and Malcom's daughters would laugh and cry, till Mildred got so tired that she would pass out. The princess was burned out most of the time, tending to duties that were not supposed to be hers, that should be for her sister and brother-in-law. It was six p.m. by the time the young princesses were all asleep. Mildred felt obligated to go out, she freshened up as soon as she got to her bedroom. When she saw that none of her old outfits fit her, she saw in the mirror that she was now extremely tall. The princess went to measure her height, she saw that she was one-hundred ninety-eight centimeters tall. Mildred hadn't gone shopping in more than a year and nine months. This left her to wear some of her grandmother's old dresses that were tailored to fit her specifically.

Mildred left the castle and bought a few new dresses at the royal seamstress in the town square where common people ridiculed and laughed at her. After Mildred bought two dozen dresses, she went to the ice-skating park she had gone to with someone she loved once long ago. The princess sat on the bench, watching those younger than her skate on the lake. Some were on dates, some had playdates, and others were on family outings. Mildred couldn't help but feel envious of the kids younger than her, especially since she was no longer a child in any way.

Suddenly, Mildred heard an old woman giggling. Then an old man. She began hearing voices all over the place.

"It's Princess Mildred, the spinster princess," a voice said.

"Look how tall she's gotten, poor girl," another voice commented.

"I hear she takes care of Alaska's children, and does all the work in the castle now that there are no servants," teenage girls giggled.

Mildred had enough of hearing these comments, she left for the castle. After arriving there, she cried herself to sleep.

Winter Wonderland, Cataville, March 17th, 1993

The past two months had been a pain. Ever since Alaska and Mildred individually went to buy laptops, all Mildred saw on the laptop were pictures of people she knew, younger than her, conforming to the shallow standards of the society and getting married at their young age. She was horrified that she was now at an age when people younger than her were of marrying age. Mildred was supposed to rot with the status "spinster" set by those around her.

Annabella herself had begun to criticize Mildred for not being married. It's not that she did not want to get married, it's that she couldn't find someone she wanted that would want her back. That thought made Mildred miserable.

Mildred was sitting at her bedroom desk chair, reading a few things she needed to. The princess turned her head around and gasped. Annabella was placing her head right next to hers without her noticing; leaving her surprised to see her mother's face next to hers.

"Greetings, Mildred!" Annabella shouted in a scary voice that would have startled anybody.

"Yes, Mother," Mildred responded with her usual disinterest.

"Come down to the ballroom, your presence is requested immediately," Annabella said, suddenly changing her tone to a calm one. Mildred obeyed Annabella, she changed into her most expensive ballgown and styled her hair as requested by Annabella. Once she finished with what she was doing, she and Annabella walked toward the ballroom. Mildred wondered why the queen requested her presence, she knew that no matter what, Annabella's request would not be anything that wasn't shocking and bad.

Annabella and Mildred walked gracefully down the staircase leading down to the ballroom. Mildred saw a middle-aged man, with nine men who looked similar to him in the center of the ballroom. Mildred rolled her eyes, still looking graceful. As Mildred and Annabella continued to walk down the staircase, the atmosphere of the room became was full of suspense.

"Your Majesty, Your Highness!" the man exclaimed as he bowed to Annabella and Mildred.

"Greetings, fair gentleman," Annabella replied calmly to the man.

"Please explain to Princess Mildred why you are here," Annabella asked of the man. The man looked properly at Mildred, who then examined him and the others. He did not seem like royalty, he was not even from the nobility, if anything he was a common man. Mildred thought it was strange of Annabella to have common men over at the castle. The man was of average height and seemed very vulgar, as did the others.

"Your Highness, Princess Mildred, I am Mr. Snifflous of the Black Hamlet. These are my nine sons, your mother invited me to introduce you to my sons. They are looking to court you, please get to know them and choose one of them," the man said. Mildred had a shocked and embarrassed look on her face; this was an example of the strangest things she had ever heard.

"One minute, fair gentleman," Mildred told the man, then took Annabella by the hand and walked her to the very end of the ballroom.

"Mother, what on Cataville do you think you are doing?" Mildred asked mother in a scolding tone.

"Mildred, dear, they're coming to court you, what do you mean when you ask me this?" Annabella replied with fake friendliness.

"Mother, you cannot just invite some common man to the palace and ask me to choose a husband from among his nine sons," Mildred argued with Annabella.

"Yes, I absolutely can, Mildred. You need to get married, you are on thin ice here," Annabella arrogantly said, behaving like the real Annabella.

"You mean you and your dated traditions are on thin ice! Not me!" argued Mildred.

"I will not marry a man I have met for the first time," Mildred continued in disapproval.

"Just speak to the men, you brat!" Annabella whispered, angrily pulling Mildred's ear. Mildred and Annabella stopped arguing, they both walked back to the men.

"I will see them," Mildred told the man as she succumbed.

"Marvelous," Mr. Snifflous replied excitedly.

"Martin, you go first!" Mr. Snifflous ordered his first son. Mildred walked with Martin for a few minutes, talked a little, and came back. Mildred was extremely uninterested in the idea when she came back.

"Next," Mildred ordered with an eyeroll. The second son, Jimmini, walked with Mildred for a few minutes. Then the rest afterwards. The whole process took less than an hour, Mildred ended up hating all nine of them.

"So, who do you choose?" Annabella asked arrogantly.

"None," Mildred said.

"Excuse me while I talk to my daughter for a moment," Annabella said, mortified. Annabella and Mildred walked towards the same place they had gone to the last time they conferred.

"Mildred, what do you mean by choosing none?" Annabella asked like she really didn't understand.

"Mother, have you seen them? Or spoken to them?" Mildred told Annabella, feeling strange.

"There's nothing wrong with them, you're just being difficult!" Annabella replied trying to push Mildred into this.

"Mother, they're very materialistic, they're extremely closed-minded, they're also very vulgar and strange. This is marriage we're talking about, Mother; you can't just make me do this!" Mildred angrily said.

"I do not care; you're marrying one of them! I will not have a spinster daughter anymore!" Annabella responded even more angrily.

"Take one of them!" Annabella then said. Mildred had to succumb, she tried to have a moment to think positively.

"I won't hear of it, Mother, ask the man to leave our castle now!" Mildred shouted. Annabella ended up yielding to her daughter. The men all left. Annabella was more disappointed than ever.

As time went by, Annabella and these men did not stop. Annabella invited them to the castle one more time, Mildred felt the same as before. The princess wanted nothing to do with them, yet Annabella had the audacity to invite them again and pressure her to pick a husband from these nine men. Mildred rejected them one more time and had another big fight with Annabella which gave Mildred a black eye.

Winter Wonderland, Cataville, May 1st, 1993

Annabella's pressure toward Mildred when it came to marriage did not end there. She asked for Mildred's presence in the ballroom one more time, she was honest with Mildred about the fact that it was to see the nine men again. Mildred's attitude was cold when she was told of the nine men seeking her hand in marriage again, especially during their conversation about that in Mildred's bedroom. It was no surprise that Annabella gave her daughter hell, along with another lecture about their society's standards. At the end of the conversation, Mildred received a punch from her mother.

The princess couldn't but give in to her mother's orders, after fighting and getting physically abused over the fact that she wouldn't choose any of those men as a husband. The princess was forced to see them for a third time. Mildred prepared herself, then played with her nieces in the nursery until the nine men arrived.

She immediately began stressing over the fact that she was being forced to see these men for the third time, especially since she hated them. Annabella and Mildred walked down the staircase to the ballroom as usual.

"Greetings Mr. Figgilous, my daughter has made her decision!" Annabella told the men downstairs, leaving Mildred to roll her eyes in obvious discontent.

"It's Snifflous," the man said nicely as she took off his spectacles for a moment.

"Whatever. What's important is that we're discussing marriage," Annabella said in a fake tone. Mildred cringed at how idiotic she thought her mother was behaving. When she and Annabella were at the bottom of the stairs, Mr. Snifflous and his sons walked over toward them.

"So, who did she choose?" Mr. Snifflous asked.

"I would like seven minutes with each of them, please," Mildred said like it was a rehearsed line that Annabella had forced her to say.

"But of course," Mr. Snifflous replied with a smile. The princess got seven minutes to speak to each one of the nine men. Once she had spoken to all of them, the level of stress increased in the room.

"Mildred, make your decision!" Annabella firmly said. Mildred did not want to make that decision like this, she hoped that if she would get married, it would be for love, for someone she actually wanted. But the world she was living in was not suitable for that, much less a perfect one. Even if she wasn't forced to choose between those she didn't like, no one she wanted would reciprocate her feelings, because Mildred was Mildred, and she knew that nobody liked her. That was why she was currently stuck in that position. The princess still, however, wanted to choose between good and better, not mediocre or less mediocre. There went another part of her life ruined by society.

"I choose Coleman," Mildred said, giving in to the repeated cycle, one that wouldn't go away no matter how much she rejected it. So the princess ended up going for the one she hated the least.

"Marvelous!" Annabella and Mr. Snifflous remarked, like kings from a medieval book.

"Let's begin the preparations," Annabella happily exclaimed, making Mr. Snifflous follow her. The eight men that Mildred did not choose from left the castle, some of them showed no emotion and others demonstrated anger after the loss of a financial opportunity.

"So, you chose me?" Coleman said to Mildred in a vulgar way. Mildred walked away covering her nose and mouth, because she found his words dull and his breath smelled. The princess walked back to the nursery and sobbed as she tended to her nieces.

Winter Wonderland, Cataville, May 26th, 1993

As Mildred was planning her wedding, Annabella could not but force herself into the process. Because of Annabella, Mildred did not get any say in her wedding preparations. Mildred wanted her wedding the following January, since in Winter Wonderland,

December and January were the most popular times for weddings, and January was Mildred's favorite and most romantic month. Annabella, however wanted to rid herself of the scandal quickly, so she forced Mildred to have her wedding in June, a month that was not popular for weddings; no one in Winter Wonderland would come to a June wedding.

Annabella also interfered in more choices. Mildred wanted her wedding in the garden where she had celebrated love years ago, but she was forced to have it at the castle. Mildred wanted to choose and buy her wedding gown herself, but Annabella had an ugly 1920s style wedding gown made for her and forced her to wear it. Overall, Annabella forcefully set up the arrangements for Mildred's wedding and left her with no say in the matter; if Mildred did protest, she would receive slaps and hurtful words.

Winter Wonderland, Cataville, June 16th, 1993

The past weeks had passed by without peace, Annabella kept violently forcing her choices upon Mildred. Endless unpleasant encounters took place between Mildred and Annabella, leaving Mildred happy to leave the castle. This was the day Mildred married Coleman Snifflous, she hoped for the best. By then, she wished that this marriage would be good for her.

She woke up that morning at nine a.m. The princess could see a strong blizzard outside her bedroom window. She knew that Alaska and Annabella were hard at work with their winter powers and were creating a huge blizzard that was supposed to last until noon. Mildred went to her fitting room in the west corner of the castle. One of the last few remaining servants was with her, she managed to convince them to restyle her wedding gown; seeing as it was Annabella's choice and was a very ugly dress. The one thing that Mildred was able to do for her wedding was to restyle the gown, but it did not make up for the fact that she wasn't able to choose anything else for her royal wedding ball.

After the princess was done getting dressed, she did not put very much effort into the other parts of her appearance. Despite it being her wedding day, Mildred felt and did nothing like she used to do in 1988. The princess just got on with everything and ended up looking and feeling plain. She left the room and looked down, holding the bannister, she saw her future husband having a conversation with his father.

"I cannot wait until I am royalty, what do you think money would bring me, Father?" Coleman said.

"Keep your eyes on the royal powers, son, it's far more important than their useless fortune. Just be sure to completely attach yourself to this family, be sure their magic enters our family blood," Mr. Snifflous said to encourage his son.

"How are you even sure the right magic will enter our blood? After all, Mildred is the disappointing fall enchantress," Coleman inquired.

"Doesn't matter if any grandchildren you give me have fall powers. Mildred is a part of that family, snow is in her blood, magic will be in our descendants' blood," Mr. Snifflous convinced Coleman. Mildred listened to the conversation, no one noticed her. As she heard their words, she gasped. The princess ran to her bedroom crying. The princess's view of herself was already of being a failure. The repetitive mocking thought of being hated by everyone kept running through her mind. Even though Mildred was not naïve; she expected something similar to this, but she could not help feel hurt. That was because she was tired of people only going to her when they needed something, when there was nobody else, or when it was not for her. What made it more painful was that this was always the case with people's view of her.

The princess angrily walked to Alaska's chambers after a few moments in her room. Once Mildred was close, Alaska could hear her footsteps in the hallway.

"Oh dear, Malcom," Alaska said to her husband, as they were both nearly ready for the wedding.

"You should see what she wants," Malcom sympathetically said. Mildred stomped into the bedroom and dried her tears.

"Mildred, what's wrong, dear sister?" Alaska gracefully asked her sister.

"Stupid Coleman and his brothers only wanted my hand for our magic," Mildred angrily yelled.

"What does Mother see in these people?" Mildred asked.

"Don't be ridiculous!" Alaska responded.

"I'm not, it's true!" Mildred lashed out.

"These people aren't good people, I need to cancel the engagement," the princess continued.

"Mildred, go lie down, dear, you must be very tired after having to deal with wedding preparations all at once. You can lie down on my bed," Alaska warmly answered.

"I am not making things up, Alaska, go tell Mother now!" Mildred continued arguing. Alaska and Malcom stood still and said nothing. Mildred left the room, not bearing to deal with her sister, whose behavior she could not believe.

Mildred stayed in her bedroom for a few hours and redid parts of her appearance that had gotten messed up. The princess would have done more for herself if she was happy, or if it were for happiness, but at the point she didn't care one bit. In a few moments, the door burst open.

"Yes, Mother," Mildred replied dully.

"I'm here to inquire about your revolting behavior!" Annabella heatedly said as if she was in trance.

"Mother, you are out of your mind to call my behavior revolting!" Mildred exclaimed, calm yet enraged. Annabella walked to Mildred and hit her yet one more time, leaving a bright visible scar under her cheekbone.

"I will not have you try to cancel this marriage using delusions!" Annabella loudly screamed.

"I have worked too hard and too long for you to ruin this! I will not tolerate you ruining the reputation of the royal family, Mildred!" Annabella quickly argued. A second later she was out the door, and Mildred was shocked that she was still being forced to marry a man that only wanted power.

The princess was standing with everyone in the ballroom greeting guests. The wedding had started, Mildred wanted this to be over as soon as possible. As soon as a few guests arrived, the marriage ceremony started; because nobody except the immediate family showed up to Mildred's wedding ceremony.

Mildred and Coleman walked down the aisle. It was not as magical as Mildred thought her wedding day would be; an image of shattered dreams. The marriage agreement had already been signed, and by then there was nothing anyone could do to stop the marriage spell from taking place.

The princess was a disaster as soon as they reached the arch. A wizard who performed wedding spells for cheap prices walked in front of Mildred and Coleman. The wizard made a little speech, then he chanted out the wedding spell for the first time. Mildred and Coleman froze like Alaska and her husband. Annabella looked thrilled for her own reputation. The two ghosts came out of Mildred and Coleman as soon as the incantation was repeated as is supposed to.

The wizard repeated the spell for a third time, the two ghosts walked up to each other. However, once the wizard chanted the spell again, the two ghosts couldn't hold hands. Mildred didn't want to hold Coleman's. As the wizard chanted the spell for the last time, the two ghosts just disappeared with no sign. Mildred found herself awake to see her mother, sister, brother-in-law, grandmother Mona Beth, and her new husband's family.

Chapter Twenty-Six
Maltreatment II

Winter Wonderland, Cataville, February 2nd, 1994

A year had passed since the weight of Mildred's marriage had been lifted upon the royal family. Mildred was living in an unhappy marriage that she loathed. The royal newspaper had brought up something new. "Princess Mildred of Winter Wonderland has been married for a year: but will the royal family continue bringing the new generation of their blood?" the paper said. The paper brought up another humiliation Annabella had to worry about.

"Mildred! You need to bring the royal family a new member. It's vital for the standards of society," Annabella stated, sounding very medieval to the ears of everyone around her.

"Mother, you are killing me with the standards of society, couldn't they just stop?" Mildred begged her mother.

"Good grief, no, you must listen to your society," responded Annabella.

"But why? What is listening to these sorts of orders going to give me?" Mildred asked, disappointed.

"Just obey the orders!" Annabella lashed out. But the subject of Mildred bringing a new member to the royal family did not come to an end. Over the next few months, Annabella and Mildred's society continued pressuring Mildred, till she was tired of it and gave in; just to get some peace of mind.

Winter Wonderland, Cataville, June 19th, 1994

After receiving hell and continuous criticism about the way Mildred lived her life, she looked to get society off her back, this all came together on that day, when she had news for everybody. Mildred announced to those around her that she was finally pregnant.

"Congratulations, Mildred!" Alaska shouted, Alaska shrieked loudly, which caused the rest of those in the castle to wonder what was going on. Alaska shouted the news excitedly to everyone around her. This was a relief for everyone, including Annabella. Unlike when this happened for Alaska, Mildred did not get a royal ball. Mildred did not care however, no matter what, she would always live in oppression, even if she was married and regardless of whether or not she was pregnant, her life didn't allow for anything else.

The princess received physical and emotional peace from Annabella and others. No rude words were said to Mildred that day, this was a privilege that continued for some time.

Winter Wonderland, Cataville, August 12th, 1994

The princess was at peace, by then Annabella and Alaska thought to spend more time with Mildred. The princess couldn't believe herself. She used the castle facilities more often, in order to receive the care she needed to ensure she had a healthy baby. What made Mildred panic was that Annabella and everyone else were pushing her to have a daughter, not a son. She did not understand why it was so important that she have a daughter, but she ended up hoping for a girl as well. Mildred was tired of pressure and suffering, she wanted a good life for her future child and herself.

She ate better meals, got better treatment from her family, and relaxed more. Mildred was happy, even though she didn't escape to where she had wanted to, she was able to get a better life here. Mildred's husband went away with the military for five months, leaving her alone. Mildred was left less angry; especially that her husband wasn't there, leaving the castle even more peaceful.

Winter Wonderland, Cataville, December 11th, 1994

Mildred woke up that morning and freshened up and had the large breakfast she needed, then off she went to her spa appointment. Mildred wanted to go on a trip to famous places in Winter Wonderland. Unlike the times she had travelled during her teenage years, Mildred easily got someone to go with her.

Mildred and Alaska left together in the carriage to the mall. The princess managed to buy clothes, furniture, and other items in preparation for her child's arrival. She was more than seven months pregnant by then, it was exhausting to deal with these things herself, but she felt responsible and needed to be in charge of that kind of shopping. Something none of her family members had endured during their lifetime.

The princess ran all her errands, carried the lighter things herself along with Alaska, she had the furniture and the rest of her child's things delivered to the castle. Mildred and Alaska went to sit at the ice-skating park they grew up in. They sat on the benches and had conversations they never had before. Finally, Mildred was enjoying the wind, Winter Wonderland's beautiful areas, the glamorous snowy atmosphere.

Mildred's pregnancy went by smoothly and nobody gave her any trouble whatsoever. The only thing she feared was her old life coming back after she gave birth. This was a mystery that Mildred wondered about, but at the same time did not want resolved, since the previous seven months had passed peacefully.

Winter Wonderland, Cataville, February 2nd, 1995

Mildred found herself awake, in the same light blue dim room she was told she'd been born in. Mildred was very tired, she had just heard her husband, sister, brother-in-law, and mother come into the room.

"Greetings, Mildred," All of them said. The nurse walked in pushing a cot that had a baby laying in it.

"Congratulations, Your Highness," the nurse cheerfully said.

"Here, you have a prince," the nurse said as she placed the baby in Mildred's arms.

"A prince!" Mildred and Annabella exclaimed unimpressed; Annabella in disapproval and Mildred in fear for her new son. The nurse, seeing the royals be that negative, and knowing what they were like, ran out.

"Mildred, you cannot have a boy and expect respect from society," Annabella continued talking in disappointment, with all her true intentions revealing themselves.

"Why not, Mother?" Alaska defensively asked.

"Everyone knows that women are the ones who rule Winter Wonderland, it should never be men," Annabella said truly believing said what she said.

"Mother, you don't believe that!" Alaska responded even more defensively, begging her mother to say otherwise. Annabella left the room in disappointment, making Mildred cry bitterly, without knowing when or if she could stop.

Winter Wonderland, Cataville, April 14th, 1995

The princess spent almost all of her time with her son, along with her nieces whom she was also expected to take care of. Mildred loved her son more than anything, he was the only precious person she ever knew. She went back to having to deal with backlash from Annabella and Coleman. Mildred made a pact with herself to divorce her husband, take her son, and run away from Winter Wonderland.

It was very painful for Mildred to have to deal with the continuous disrespect from her family and her society, but it offended her more considerably to watch them treat the prince that way. Mildred watched the children as usual; she saw how innocent, fragile, and naive they were. It depressed her that when they would grow up some more, the terrible conditions of living in Winter Wonderland would ruin their current happiness, she secretly feared this for them and wished them a different life. Mildred walked from the nursery to the throne room, after she left the only nursemaid strict instructions not to let the baby prince out of her sight; she needed to leave the castle, she couldn't trust her husband, her mother, or even her sister with her child.

The princess put on her coat and left the castle. Mildred took the carriage to the shopping square, where she wanted to buy more milk and diapers for her son. Mildred also wanted to buy him new clothes; as he was outgrowing his, and anything Annabella had bought him was ugly and in bad taste. The princess thought to buy him toys to entertain him when he was a bit older. She also wanted to buy him things that would help with his development.

Mildred arrived at the shopping square, she walked directly to each store she needed to buy things from. Whenever she reached a work of art or a tourist attraction in that area, she took a picture of it and made cards to offer some cultural exposure to her son, so he would remember where he came from. Especially when she took him and ran away.

The princess bought all her things and went home, it was six p.m. when she arrived. Mildred ran up to the nursery, she saw that her son along with his cousins were all sleeping peacefully. Mildred thanked the nursemaid for her time with the kids, she placed her picture cards in her son's pockets, then closed the zippers.

Mildred stayed with the children for a few hours, then she was called to the formal living area. Mildred tucked in her son, she kissed her child's forehead then left the room. When she arrived, she saw Annabella, Alaska, Malcom, and her husband Coleman each sitting on a sofa or a loveseat. They all were drinking hot chocolate, Alaska and Malcom had already drank more than half of it. Coleman had already finished his, and Annabella hadn't had a sip yet.

"Come, have a cup of hot chocolate, we have one for you," Annabella said, which Mildred found suspicious.

"Have a cup, darling," Coleman told her.

"Yes, have a cup…" Alaska told her hesitantly, like she was going to regret it, but she was trying hard to hide it. Mildred chose a seat, then began talking.

"OK mother, what do you want?" Mildred suspiciously asked Annabella.

"What do I want with what?" Annabella deceptively replied.

"Why do you want me to drink hot chocolate?" Mildred further questioned Annabella.

"The four of us decided we were craving hot chocolate, we also asked for a fifth one for you, we didn't want you feeling left out," Annabella said.

Mildred gave in, she wanted to believe them. She saw Alaska appear to be assuring her that everything was alright. Mildred drank the hot chocolate. The five of them talked normally, about normal topics that had nothing to do with hot chocolate. But soon Mildred began feeling tired. The princess decided to go to bed, she walked to her bedroom, and with every second she felt more tired than the previous one. When Mildred changed into her sleepwear, she was exhausted, she began feeling dizzy as well. Mildred went into slumber the second her head hit the pillow, and her body the mattress.

Winter Wonderland, Cataville, April 15th, 1995

Mildred woke up that morning from a very deep sleep. Mildred looked at the grandfather clock in her room, and saw that it was past noon, she had overslept. She began worrying about her son, she ran to the nursery, then ran to his crib. Her son was not there. The princess looked through the entire nursery, she found her nieces, but not her son. There was no sign of him in the nursery. The princess ran out, searched every corner of the castle, yelling and panicking, but she found nothing. Some of the few remaining servants went to help her as she ran around looking for her son, not finding him anywhere. She thought about one place where there would be answers.

Mildred walked to that place, the sound of her heels sounding with every step of the way through the entire castle, especially as she got closer. There were five guards, one at each milestone before Mildred reached where she wanted to go.

"Get out of the way, I want to see my mother!" Mildred angrily told each one of the guards, then moved them aside as they lowered their defenses to let her in. She stomped and stomped, her heels continuing to sound louder and louder in the hallway that led to her mother's chambers. Her stomping heels got louder and louder, more tension filled the hallway as she was almost at the master bedroom.

"Where's Mother!" Mildred violently shouted as she entered the room, and saw her sister and Malcom sitting there.

"I don't know," Alaska replied. Then Mildred saw her mother and Coleman outside the window running through the castle maze.

Mildred jumped, she took off her heels and ran down to the maze as quick as she could. She ran on and on; she went down the staircase that took her faster to the castle courtyard. As soon as she was outside, she ran towards the maze, her long legs much faster than Annabella and Coleman so she was able to catch up with them quickly. She reached out to her mother and husband, pulled both of them back and they both fell to the ground.

"Alright, Mother! Where is my son!" Mildred screeched loud, her voice could be heard from miles.

"Did you check the nursery?" Annabella playing dumb.

"Don't pretend you don't know what's going on!" Mildred lashed out at them.

"My child is gone, and I bet you two are behind this!" Mildred roared at the two of them.

"We put him in an abandoned forest outside of Winter Wonderland," Annabella awkwardly replied.

"What?" gasped Mildred.

"I'll be right back for you two!" Mildred yelled, she began moving her arms, orange dust came out of her hands. Autumn trees were growing behind Coleman and Annabella, trees that moved their branches and talked, they were completely conscious. The trees used their branches to tie Annabella and Coleman's arms and legs. Mildred also used magic that made the trees produce fruit to feed Annabella and Coleman until she got back. Mildred took the fastest car and took off into the afternoon.

Chapter Twenty-Seven
Oppression

Winter Wonderland, Cataville, May 13th, 1995

Nearly a month had gone by, Mildred had still not forgotten what her mother had done. She searched the entire time, she looked for her son in all the forests, all the orphanages, anywhere her child could be. Mildred was gasping, her blood pressure was high. Her heart raced, she was more desperate and heartbroken than ever. The princess barely ate anything all month while she looked for her son all over Cataville. It was apparent that Mildred had once more lost at least fifteen kilograms.

The princess had looked in every corner of Cataville, but there was no sign of her son anywhere. She had suffered enough, she wanted to continue looking for her son, but there was something she needed to do. Mildred rushed back to the castle, because she was very far away, it took her three days to get back. The princess went back to the tree where she cornered Annabella and Coleman.

When Mildred saw her mother and her husband, she saw that they had gotten food from the tree, water from Alaska, and blankets. The two of them looked as pale and damaged as her.

"Mildred, are you going to let us go?" Annabella said with frustration as soon as she saw Mildred.

"I will, but you're still going to explain yourself," Mildred replied in a tone that was angry but calm. She pointed her arms towards the tree, and the tree began to disappear with her magic. Annabella and Coleman were both set free, but both of them were too weak to move.

"Alright, Mother! Speak!" Mildred lashed out at the queen.

"Speak about what?" Annabella said, refusing to cooperate.

"Why did you abandon my son in the middle of nowhere? Why are you so horrible? What did we ever do to you? Why did you have to make my life a living hell?" Mildred began interrogating Annabella, moments away from tearing her mother apart.

"Oh Mildred, I was hoping you would ask me for that story. No one ever asks for my story," Annabella responded.

"It all started when I was born, 1955. I was born to your grandmother Annelise, and my father. Like you and your sister, I also grew up fatherless. Your grandmother Anneliese had to raise me and my siblings all by herself. I was considered a typical scandal, because I was born with red eyes," Annabella started talking, she ended that part of her story by touching her eyes, then removed what turned out to be blue contact lenses. Annabella's real eyes shone bright in the middle of the snow; they were as red as the hatred in her heart.

"My mother was always stressed out, she always focused on my sisters more than me. Like you, I was also bullied as a young girl. This bullying cost me all my hope in people. It got very lonely. I had no friends, all my relatives disliked me, everyone found me to be weird. I received no support from anyone, I was according to the Winter Wonderland standards. I learned to believe in them. Anything out of the ordinary according to the Winter Wonderland standards was frowned upon, this was how your grandmother raised me and my siblings. These standards were forced upon me, until I accepted them," Annabella spoke, continuing to tell her tale.

"I was always spending time with my mother, because there was nobody else to talk to. Even though I was the most beautiful one of my sisters, I was the last to get married. Back then the pressure to get married was stronger and started at even earlier ages. I was expected to find love by the age of thirteen and fourteen. I reached that age, and I still was not married. I got blue contact lenses, then ended up meeting your father by the end of 1969," Annabella continued.

"I remember those days, 1970 and 1971. Our glory days, your father and I were very much in love. I thought I finally had someone who had accepted me for who I was, someone I could confide in. A person I was comfortable spending most of my time with. We got married at the beginning of 1971. My oldest sister was supposed to be crowned queen, but she ran away as soon as she got married. Therefore, I was crowned queen when your father and I were married," Annabella said.

"Your paternal grandparents were no help whatsoever. I will always blame them for ruining my life and destroying the love I and your father had for each other. You see, when I was expected to bring a new generation to the royal family of Winter Wonderland, I struggled. Miscarriages were a big problem; I had many of them. In 1973, I had carried a baby to term, but the baby ended up dying as soon as it was born. My in-laws made it harder, they kept mocking me for not being able to provide them with an heir. A princess that could rule the kingdom and be part of their family. Your grandmother Mona Beth, along with your late grandfather, did not approve of me, they always criticized me. They kept saying bad about me to your father until he fell out of love with me," Annabella spoke, broken hearted.

"In time I grew cold and dark, my view of those around me had changed forever. I was angry, I became rude, and I became more materialistic. Eventually I had you and Alaska, my in-laws finally applauded and respected me after I bore them a family, not one but twin princesses. However, the damage between me and my in-laws was already done, nothing they could ever say or do could ever change what I thought of them. When I saw you as a baby, I knew you'd be as tall as your father, and along with your fall powers, it would be a scandal. My entire life was scandal after scandal, they made me suffer very much, you kept bringing me more of them. Leaving me angrier and more resentful towards you," Annabella talked about this coldly.

"I thought if I belittled you and punished you after every scandal, our royal life would finally be stable, so that was what I started doing. I did not allow your father to see his parents for more than five years. All they did was show me that I wasn't good enough for them. I was then diagnosed with antisocial personality disorder along with PTSD, Maximus had to deal with my continual lashing out, anger, delusions, night terrors, and everything that came with my illnesses which I didn't know I had at the time. Your father got bored, and he stopped wanting to deal with me. When you and Alaska were eight, I received the letter that your grandfather passed away. I hid the letter, but your father found it a few months later, we had a huge fight that day. Your father left the castle, our divorce papers were delivered to me a few weeks later, to which I had no other option but to sign," Annabella said still as cold as ever.

"I sent our divorce papers to the judge, and the judge gave them to the wizard who lifted the marriage spell. It was the hardest thing I have ever done in my life, but I was left with nothing else."

"I lost my mother, I took care of her during the last months of her life. Your grandmother Anneliese was very ill, she wasn't even that old. Your grandmother Anneliese was only fifty years old when she died. It was heartbreaking for all of us, she was the last of my support system. I was left to rot alone, just like you, for years I was mentally suffering every day," Annabella finished telling her story. Annabella looked at Mildred in a way that begged for sympathy.

"I'm very sorry for you, Mother, but I'm even sorrier for myself. You see, Mother, we could've had it all, I could have been part of your support system. No matter that I was never good enough for you, you tortured me! You hurt me! You made me perish! I hate you and my stupid husband with all of my heart!" Mildred lashed out then moved her arms. Annabella and Coleman attempted to run away, but she used her magic to create lightning that struck just a small distance away from her mother and husband.

Annabella and Coleman fell to the floor. Sounds of running came from a different area from the courtyard. A few moments later, a man came right into the area. He was more than two meters tall, he looked handsome yet old, despite being in his early forties. He had a lot of gray hair among his blonde hair. The man looked down at Annabella.

"Maximus…" Annabella breathed in desperation.

"Hello, Annabella…" the man said as he kneeled down to Annabella.

"What are you doing here?" Annabella said weakly.

"Yes, Father, what are you finally doing here?" Mildred yelled at Maximus. He was speechless, he didn't know what to say at the sight of Mildred.

"I've come to collect…" Maximus said but was interrupted by Mildred.

"I don't care why you are here! I don't care about you at all! You are no better than Mother here! You left us long ago, we were all suffering, it was the last thing we needed. I'm finished with you! Every single one of you!" Mildred continued in a rage.

"Now, Mother, I ask you one more time! Where did you take my child? Where can I find him?" Mildred shouted at her mother.

"Mildred, that child is not good enough for Winter Wonderland society, no matter what I won't tell you where he is," Annabella said.

"Mother, that child is everything to the Winter Wonderland society, he is a prince of Winter Wonderland, and my child. For the last time, Mother, which abandoned forest did you take him to? Where can I find him?" Mildred interrogated her mother some more, having absolutely had enough of Annabella.

"I will not be providing you with this information, you're his mother, figure it out for yourself. A boar most probably has swallowed him or something," Annabella answered, which left a death stare on Mildred's face.

Mildred moved her hands, force seemed to be emitted out of her whole body: from her arms, legs, torso, and face. Lightning struck again, hitting Annabella, Coleman, and Maximus. The lightning bolt was powerful, a good deal of damage affected the area. The columns in the courtyard fell apart, some plants died, the stone floor was burned and severely damaged. But most importantly, Annabella, Maximus, and Coleman were all dead.

Alaska immediately came with her husband and Evanora out into the courtyard. There were terrified looks of betrayal on their faces.

"Mildred... What have you done?" Alaska was shocked.

"I brought justice for my son, then for myself. I won't be done till I have my revenge on all of you! I will be back in less than ten years, I will come for all of you!" Mildred yelled, enraged, sounding like a villain. Mildred began laughing, also like villains.

"Guards! Seize her!" Prince Malcom called out to their remaining guards. Mildred laughed out in silliness. She roughly moved her hands from her hips to the sky and with that she was floating on a cloud. Mildred disappeared into the sky.

Chapter Twenty-Eight
War

An Abandoned Forest, Southern Cataville, January 30th, 2004

An abandoned forest, hidden somewhere. The forest was filled with trees with red, yellow, and orange leaves, some of which had fallen. Too much rain was falling from the sky, it was nothing like the rest of Cataville. The area was very exclusive and far away from all the landmarks in Cataville, including Winter Wonderland. That left the area safe and unreachable. In this forest lay a large house made from birch wood, it looked like a mansion belonging to someone from the nobility of Winter Wonderland. A special mansion.

Inside there was a formal dining area connected to a living room, where everything was made of wood. A woman sat on a chair at the dining table. The woman had long red hair that was thin, dead, and damaged. She was dangerously thin, and looked almost starved. Her eyes had lost their twinkle, her cheekbones very prominent, wrinkles covered her forehead, eyes, and cheeks. The woman wore a dress made from red, orange, and yellow leaves. Overall, she looked exhausted and any beauty she had had was completely lost.

The woman was sitting down, daydreaming about a trauma that had been burned into her mind forever. Waves of hatred came out of her heart and surrounded the atmosphere of the entire room. The woman stood up, immediately feeling dizzy and numb. She walked to the stairs and went down several floors, till she was in the deep depths underground of what seemed like a dungeon.

The woman unlocked the steel door that led to a stony area. She continued walking till she reached a large area with barred cells.

"Mildred!! Let me out!" A female prisoner yelled out.

"Shut up you fool!" The woman replied in a demonic voice. Mildred continued walking through the area till she had covered every cell. Each one contained a person that had previously hurt Mildred, be it bullies, former friends, and many more. Many of those people looked at Mildred in disgust, leaving Mildred to look at them with even more disgust. Mildred walked to a specific group of cells, those she had reserved for specific people that had hurt her the most, more than fifteen years ago. Mildred still had a lot anger from her school days. She was also angry at her family.

"Let us go!" one prisoner begged from the other side of the dungeon. Mildred could hear everyone talking, but she ignored them.

"You're the last person to say that! You never let me go from your torture! I lived in the depths of despair for thirty years because of people like you!" Mildred angrily shouted out.

"Mildred, let me go! Let go of your past experiences with us! You don't even take care of yourself!" another prisoner exclaimed.

"But I do take care of myself!" Mildred replied.

"I do not call trapping people in a dungeon, keeping track of others, and eating nothing but autumn leaves taking care of oneself!" the same prisoner yelled.

"Well, you deserve to be locked in there! And if I eat more than four leaves, I'll be ugly again," Mildred said, insulted.

"And don't call me Mildred! I am not a witch! I am Autumn!" Mildred ordered firmly for everyone to hear like she had many times. Autumn left the dungeon underneath her house, and went back up to the main hall.

Autumn walked to the balcony on the ground floor, she decided to go up to the higher floors of the mansion. She walked to the balcony on the highest floor. There she saw Winter Wonderland from very far away. The sight of Winter Wonderland was appalling to her. A normal person would see a winter paradise, while she saw a cursed land of misfortune.

"Oh, how I wish I could replace that snow with acid rain! How I want to give these people what they deserve!" Autumn bitterly said. She went back inside, walked to her bedroom. She went to the night stand next to the bed and took out a notebook.

The notebook was in fact a calendar. She saw that it was nearly time for her to cast terror on Winter Wonderland.

"Excellent…" she exclaimed. "I'll leave first thing tomorrow!" then maliciously added.

She slept that night uncomfortably. Having nightmare after nightmare, one-night terror after the other. Trauma from her past held on to her in her sleep, this was especially because she was nervous about taking on Winter Wonderland and her sister the next day.

An Abandoned Forest, Southern Cataville, January 31st, 2004.

Autumn was sitting in her leafy wooden living room that very morning, she had just freshened up and was now preparing mentally herself. She didn't know how to tackle Winter Wonderland and get her revenge on everyone there. But she did plan to fly there on clouds made by her powers, as well as creating acid rain to fall from the sky when she reached Winter Wonderland.

She left her wooden mansion; taking one last look at it. Autumn built it herself using her powers, it looked like a place she had once known more than fifteen years ago. Somewhere special in her heart, somewhere she used to wish to live in. She began waving her arms, energy bursting out of her hands. A cloud descended down to her until it was at her level, she placed one leg then the other. She stood on the cloud then waved her hands upwards in a curvy motion. The cloud immediately lifted up into the cold sky.

Autumn flew into the higher levels of the sky till there were no changes in the weather. She kept moving forward instead of upward, and kept changing her direction for hours. It was like a boring ride in the carriage, except Autumn's hunger for revenge and ruin was stronger.

After two hours of travelling in the sky on the cloud, she was finally getting into very cold atmosphere. Autumn used her magic to make herself a coat out of fall materials. The cloud started moving downward swiftly; she began landing. She had a view of the entire Winter Wonderland from where she was standing. Winter Wonderland had changed significantly since she had last looked at it properly, nearly ten years ago.

Autumn then started using magic. A monsoon of acid rain fell down from the sky. Down in Winter Wonderland, people were screaming in fear, rocks were breaking along with other things. A flood of acid rain flooded the ground of Winter Wonderland, with most people running for safety.

Autumn began giggling wickedly when she saw that this was happening to those who caused her and her child to suffer. She was now nearer to the ground; the cloud was moving fast. It was moving towards the palace in Winter Wonderland, as the acid monsoon was making all of the buildings crumble. As she moved on, the monsoon was becoming heavier. The castle was right in front of her. The guards began shooting at her, but they missed every shot. Down in the castle, Alaska and Malcom were panicking.

"Alaska what do we do? Your crazy sister is back and she's attacking Winter Wonderland!" Malcom said, panicking like a maniac.

"I've had the guards shoot her with stun guns and the wizards with spells, she has managed to avoid all of them," Alaska replied trying to calm her husband down. Both of them saw that Autumn had landed in front of the castle. She began chanting out a spell as soon as her feet hit the ground.

Alaska did not want to hurt her sister, but she needed to defend herself and her husband. Alaska attempted to at least temporarily stun Autumn; until they could get her out of that state of hatred and anger, instead of killing or hurting her. But this plan failed, and Autumn continued to wreak havoc. Alaska walked out of the castle and went directly to Autumn.

"Mildred… Mildred! Please stop this!" Alaska called to Autumn, trying to reason with her.

"Wonderful, it's my perfect sister coming to save the day! Well, sweet Mildred is gone, my name is now Autumn and I am here to avenge my son and myself!" Autumn stated maliciously.

"Mildred, you are not thinking correctly. Please don't do this! I don't want to have to hurt you!" Alaska replied in search of peace.

"Now you're considering me getting hurt?" Autumn hysterically said, then started laughing as if she had heard something crazy.

"Here's to all the moments of oppression and mistreatment! I'm warning you, my sweet sister, I will not rest till I've destroyed this entire city!" Autumn angrily said. She stepped onto a cloud and standing high up in the sky wreaked more damage onto Winter Wonderland.

The monsoon of acid rain became even stronger, lightning struck in many parts of Winter Wonderland. Lightning lit a few wildfires, although they were put out quickly by the acid rain, still, many iconic and natural places in Winter Wonderland were damaged.

Alaska called for everyone in the entire kingdom to take shelter in the underground shelters that were specifically designed for such disasters. The queen did that by uttering the orders and then using a few spells to ensure her words were heard by everyone who needed to hear them. But nobody knew that the one causing this was none other than their princess Mildred herself.

Within a few hours, people were safely and hidden. Autumn was causing more damage and creating fear upon the land. She, however, left and went to hide somewhere until the start of the following day.

Central Cataville, February 2nd, 2004

Sometime later, somewhere in Center Cataville, a woman with a special connection to Alaska and Autumn was standing in the middle of her mansion looking out the window. The woman was gracefully standing and watching the disasters falling upon Winter Wonderland. The woman had grey hair tied in a Victorian bun, she was wearing an ugly dress, and was eighty-one years old. A man, the woman's most trusted guard, came right behind her.

"This is incredible, she's finally back!" the woman said.

"What's incredible? Who is back Duchess Mona Beth?" the guard asked the woman in front of him. Mona Beth turned around, she had a creepy look of vengeance on her face.

"My granddaughter Mildred has finally come out of hiding. After nine years. Now I can finally get my hands on her," Mona Beth wickedly said.

"Why do you want to get your hands on her? Isn't she your granddaughter?" the guard questioned Mona Beth seriously.

"She killed my son; her own father, after he had disappeared for many years. I hate her and her mother so much for all the pain they have caused. Good riddance, she killed Annabella too, that's one less thing I have to do. I'm going to get rid of her now," Mona Beth said to her guard. The guard did not seem to approve, but her being his master there was nothing he could do.

"Please fetch the carriage and take it to the shelters made for natural disasters. I'm going to Winter Wonderland," ordered Mona Beth. The guard obeyed Mona Beth's orders and called for a carriage to be taken to the emergency shelters. Back in Winter Wonderland, disaster struck.

In the middle of the castle in Winter Wonderland, Alaska and Malcom were discussing something with their own guards.

"Please start a hunting party! Bring back Princess Mildred and ensure that she is brought unconscious to the castle!" Malcom told his guards.

"Also, please have the other guards make sure the citizens of Winter Wonderland are safe and sound in the shelter," Alaska requested from her guards. The guards walked away from the queen and prince consort, ready to obey their orders. Alaska heard loud sounds coming from the shelter beneath the castle. Alaska had a feeling it would be her sister, causing more destruction right in front of her face.

"I have to go somewhere quickly, please stay safe and ensure that everything stays under control," Alaska told her husband, then left quickly not giving him the opportunities to ask questions. Alaska walked down to the deep depths of the castle, then walked further downstairs till she reached the tunnels.

Alaska saw the carriage arrive right in front of her. The carriage, horses and carriage coach seemed like they had been travelling for hours. The carriage stopped as everyone in it saw Alaska. She couldn't see the passenger of the carriage properly, but the passenger came out of the carriage.

"Grandmother! What are you doing here?" Alaska asked shocked as soon as she saw that it was in fact Mona Beth.

"I'm here to help keep Winter Wonderland in order!" Mona Beth replied.

Chapter Twenty-Nine
The Final Death

Winter Wonderland, Cataville, The Rest of 2004

The war between Autumn and the entire nation of Winter Wonderland became more intense. Tragedy struck, many were dying, and others continued hiding underground in unpleasant circumstances. Autumn couldn't be found, but wherever she went, she caused more damage. Alaska and Malcom kept sending out search parties to look for her, while Mona Beth went out with her own search parties. Alaska put in more and more effort into helping her nation and kingdom recover from the disasters that were upon them, but Autumn was bent on destroying all of Alaska's effort.

Whenever Alaska ordered something to be rebuilt, Autumn quickly destroyed their progress. If Alaska found a solution to the flooding in Winter Wonderland, Autumn would make sure that lightning struck and ruined everything, then Autumn would flood the kingdom with acid rain once more. All over Winter Wonderland, the snow was melted.

Winter Wonderland, Cataville, March 24th, 2005

Alaska woke up that morning in her bed, she was restless after barely getting any sleep, and the war was still raging on. Alaska went to the window and saw Autumn outside causing more damage, she saw an opportunity to trap her. She immediately called for the guards.

"Please be as discreet as possible, Mildred is destroying everything. I saw her, we'll catch her." Alaska told her guards. Everybody left the castle. Alaska saw Autumn flooding a village with acid rain, she also caused lightning to keep striking and burning more places in Winter Wonderland.

Alaska knew she had to do this one thing she hadn't done before. She concentrated all her energy for one second, creating a huge ball of snow, she stood on it and flew. Alaska followed Autumn until she was directly in front of her.

"Good morning, dear sister!" Autumn rudely said. Autumn attempted to strike Alaska with lightning, but Alaska avoided it. Alaska tried to stun Autumn with her magic, but Autumn also avoided Alaska's magic.

A fight with magic powers broke out. It went on for hours. Autumn became tired and weak, she turned herself invisible so she could leave. She planned to return the next day to cause more damage, then she would kill Alaska after doing everything she wanted to do.

Autumn soared on her cloud till she was beyond the Winter Wonderland borders, she landed at her destination, where there was nothing but a little cabin some miles away. She used her magic to create wind that would push her quickly to the cabin. Once she reached her hideout, she looked out the window and saw her grandmother Mona Beth on a horse along with her guards, all riding horses. All of them had come out of the tunnels underneath Winter Wonderland. Autumn knew that they were looking for her, and she felt lucky that her grandmother couldn't see her, like she could see her grandmother.

It was still some moments of suspense, but Autumn was smart enough to get through without getting caught. After Mona Beth and her guards left for outer Cataville, Autumn took a deep breath of relief. She took out many pictures of her past from a drawer in the cabin. That night, Autumn cried all the hurt inside her. Still, she thought the damage she was causing was never enough compared to every night she had felt like dying and starving for a better life, every night and day the people in Winter Wonderland made life her hell. Autumn wanted more, nothing was enough. She wanted to cause even more damage the next day. So she went to sleep, sleeping restlessly as usual feeling anxious for the next day.

Winter Wonderland, Cataville, September 23rd, 2005

Crumbled fallen structures, fragments of important places, and a whole society in hiding. Rivers of acid rain pushing through the buildings and roads. The battle between Autumn and Alaska raged on that day. The search continued for the princess, and it only went down from there.

By afternoon Autumn was at the borders of Winter Wonderland. She had murdered all the guards at the border. She was casting magic spells on the castle; she was ready to punish her family.

"Hello, sweet granddaughter," a scary voice sounded from behind Autumn. She quickly turned around to find her grandmother Mona Beth along with her guards behind her.

"Grandmother!" Autumn exclaimed in surprise. "What are you doing here?" she continued.

"Oh, I'm here to avenge what once was mine," Mona Beth exclaimed.

"Guards, seize my granddaughter Mildred!" Mona Beth angrily ordered. Autumn took off on a cloud and went flying before Mona Beth and her guards could get to her.

"Follow that terror on the cloud!" Mona Beth impatiently screamed. Not a second to lose, Autumn was quickly flying on the cloud, while Mona Beth and her guards followed on horses not far behind.

The tension was unbearable, Autumn could feel and hear and see her grandmother following her. She made the cloud go faster; but it was never enough. Mona Beth had nearly caught up with her. She noticed the incredibly long rope that Mona Beth had with her, she flew higher. Mona Beth was extremely disappointed at losing Autumn, but she was also excited about establishing the first step.

Mona Beth went back to the castle and met up with Alaska. Alaska had a concerned look on her face when she saw her grandmother.

"I see you did not find my sister," Alaska said.

"We actually did find her," Mona Beth said with pride.

"Where is she then?" Alaska asked her grandmother expecting an answer.

"We found her at the border casting spells that were making the castle crumble. We could have seized her, but she was too quick on her cloud and we lost her," Mona Beth said, disappointed.

"Well, that's a start," Alaska said.

"Believe me it is," Mona Beth replied.

"Now, Grandmother, remember, we are not going to kill her. We just need to knock her out, then the wizard I ordered can reverse all the damage on Winter Wonderland, undo all her mistakes. With those magic spells cast upon her, she can be the good person she was long ago." Mona Beth nodded in agreement, but unlike Alaska, she wanted to completely get rid of Autumn; she could never forgive her for what she had done.

Winter Wonderland, Cataville, The Year 2006

Autumn was still a fugitive in Winter Wonderland, disasters were still aplenty. But things were looking up for Alaska, Malcom, and Mona Beth. Along with their search parties, they were getting better at tracking Autumn down. They were getting closer to catching her every day, and with each day they made more progress than the day before.

Autumn was devastated, she felt that she needed to come up with a new plan to crush her sister's efforts in catching her. She was already working on a way to overthrow Alaska. One day, she made sure to flood only the castle with acid rain. The flood of acid rain around the castle caused the walls around the castle to be like a dam, barely protecting the rest of the city from more devastation. The land on which the castle was built was getting weaker, it was slowly crumbling, with cracks visible in the ground.

Alaska and Mona Beth were left helpless with the corrosion of the soil. They had been proven wrong in thinking that Autumn was unintelligent, Alaska knew that Autumn did that just to give her something extra to do, which would take up entire time Alaska and Mona Beth would use to stop her.

By March 2006, Alaska had to hire twice the number of guards she had previously, and three times the number of servants. It was no longer enough because there was so much work to do to catch Autumn, as well as helping Winter

Wonderland recover. Autumn had a relapse; she was back to running away from her sister, grandmother, and their guards.

Life got especially harder for Autumn. Her health was failing. She still suffered from the eating disorders she had gotten in 1995. Autumn's weight loss rate was very fast, especially since she did not allow herself to eat more than 5 leaves a day. Autumn thought that if she ate more, her plan would work better. But she still did not allow herself to eat, she was still afraid of gaining weight that the success of her plan was not enough to get her to recover from her eating disorder.

Alaska and Mona Beth caught up to where they were before by July 2006. Alaska had more than a thousand guards, and a thousand servants, along with a couple hundred witches and wizards: some of whom focused on fixing the soil under the castle and all over Winter Wonderland. Others focused on repairing the sights, the economy, and everything else. The rest were working on catching Autumn.

Several months passed, the year 2006 was nearly over. Every few weeks, Autumn would cause damage that was stronger than Alaska and Mona Beth's efforts for reaching their goals. They would catch up quickly and find a way around it, then Autumn would bypass them, and so on. It was an endless loop.

At the beginning of December, Alaska and Mona Beth were losing hope. The war had been going on in Winter Wonderland for close to three years. Alaska had been trying to track down and save her sister for more than eleven years. She began questioning her own worth as a queen. Does the kingdom deserve this? Did she fail Winter Wonderland as a queen? Was Autumn going to win and stay in her terrible evil state?

Alaska and Mona Beth's efforts were deteriorating. Autumn was doing all she could to get revenge on the nation. The castle was nearly completely destroyed and insecure, the economy was close to being dead, and the citizens were still living underground. The important sights broke apart after countless attempts of being repaired. Autumn slowly felt like she was getting somewhere.

Winter Wonderland, Cataville, Early 2007

The year 2006, one of the most tragic years for Winter Wonderland, was finally over. By the time 2007 had started,

Winter Wonderland had hardly anything in it at all. The land was completely barren, all the citizens were living underground where the conditions were getting worse; especially since the soil was also crumbling. Alaska was doing her best not to give up. Mona Beth was getting madder the longer she waited.

Autumn was more physically weak than ever by then; she was sick all the time. Her powers were diminishing, each spell she cast had a weaker effect than the previous one. Autumn feared that her sister and grandmother were getting close to catching her. What Autumn was happy with, was that she had achieved her goals, and had nothing left to do but kill Alaska herself, like she had killed Annabella and Maximus. In early February, Autumn met up with Alaska.

"Greetings, sweet sister!" Autumn said to Alaska.

"I challenge you to a battle, Alaska; if you win, which I doubt, do whatever you want with me. But, if you lose, I will make sure you are as dead as Mother," Autumn replied.

The battle broke out. Autumn and Alaska rose in the sky as each of them fired her powers on the other. Autumn hit Alaska a few times, Alaska continued shielding herself with her own powers, trying her best to get Autumn to surrender. The battle kept going on, Autumn was only keen on killing Alaska; she saw nothing but the pain and anguish she had lived in for more than twenty years as well as the mental strain she had endured for more than ten years. This was something Alaska also saw, which was why she wanted to rescue Autumn from this state of mind, she wanted to finally give her the happiness that she had missed out on all her life by being an understanding and caring sister, by giving her the love and attention their mother deprived Mildred of.

Both Alaska and Autumn were severely wounded after the fight. They both gave up for the evening, and they both used a transportation spell to temporarily part ways.

Winter Wonderland, Cataville, Mid-Year, 2007

Both Alaska and Autumn had been resting for months; they were both wounded after the battle. Whenever they recovered slightly, their bones would go back to being broken; because they would have another battle, they both felt like they were healthier.

This was because Alaska's experience the last few years, and the terrible conditions Autumn had lived in for as long as she could remember, made them too stubborn to think of their own well-beings.

However, with each battle, the result was becoming more inevitable. It was something they both looked forward to. As the month of July approached, the end was near.

Winter Wonderland, Cataville, July 6th, 2007

Autumn woke up that morning in the uncomfortable bed in her cabin. A loud noise sounded right outside, sounds kept coming through the door, sounds of the door breaking down. Autumn knew that the guards had found her. She ran to the window at the back at the house. She had a difficult time leaving the house through the window before the guards caught her. It was vital that Autumn run as fast as she could. The guards were following her on their horses. What caused even more tension was that it was her grandmother Mona Beth who was following her with the guards, not Alaska.

They were catching up with her. The sounds of the horses' hooves galloping and following Autumn raised the tension even higher. She flew onto a cloud, while they all followed her. They all had covered quite a distance, but Autumn's physical state was at its weakest. She was completely losing consciousness, she needed to land. When Autumn landed, her grandmother kept following her. She felt like she was done, she had nothing left. Her grandmother was bent on killing her, along with her sister and getting her revenge for her son and herself.

A cliff was right in front of Autumn, she was cornered between the drop and her grandmother's guards. Her health was failing, she was in severe physical pain, and she had not eaten anything in almost three weeks. There was nowhere she could go, and there was nothing she could do to rescue herself.

Autumn ran to the cliff; her grandmother and guards and horses were very close to her. She made her way and jumped off the cliff. The moment her feet were past the cliff she lost consciousness. Mona Beth had the gun in her hands and pulled the trigger. The bullet hit Autumn in the neck. She fell down the cliff, as good as dead.

Epilogue
Regret

Winter Wonderland, Cataville, January 17th, 2019

A woman stood in one of the biggest rooms of the castle, she was forty-five years old. She was standing in the middle of her bedroom looking at a picture from her early childhood. The woman was blonde, wearing a long blue dress, her hair was braided, and she had freckles on her face, along with a few wrinkles. The woman was none other than Queen Alaska herself.

Alaska was crying with regret, feeling inadequate. It had been so many years, and she couldn't save her family from falling apart. Annabella was dead, Mildred was dead, Maximus was dead, her grandparents except Mona Beth were dead. Speaking of Mona Beth, twelve years ago, Alaska had had no choice but to lock her in the deepest dungeons. Alaska was still in denial that Mona Beth killed her own granddaughter.

Alaska knew she needed to pay her daily visit to her grandmother, it was as much of a chore as much as it wasn't. By 2019, Mona Beth was very ill, being in the dungeon was not helpful either. Alaska walked to a private door hidden through a wall. Technology controlled everything, there was an iris scanner, a fingerprint scanner, and a keyboard for code to be entered.

Alaska had her iris and fingerprint scanned, then entered a nine-digit code on the keyboard. "You can enter, Queen Alaska," a programmed voice said. Alaska placed her hands on a small part of the wall, where a rectangle door which was a hole in the wall became visible and opened. Alaska walked through the door, the door closed behind her. Alaska was in a secret passageway.

The queen walked through the hallway, it was made of cobble stone. Alaska reached a spiral staircase, which went down many floors. Alaska kept walking downstairs till she was in the deepest dungeon. The deepest dungeon was directly above the emergency shelter. It consisted of 5 prison cells, occupied by the most dangerous criminals locked up in the high security. Alaska went through more security, having her face and hand scanned. She went into the room with the five prison cells.

The cells had the most dangerous looking and vulgar occupants. She made her way to the cell which was all the way in the back.

"Alaska…" the old woman said weakly and desperately.

"Good evening, Grandmother," Alaska said as she unlocked the jail door, entered, and locked it again.

"What do you bring me today?" Mona Beth asked her granddaughter.

"I brought you your medication and a cup of water," Alaska replied.

"You never visit me anymore, why is that?" Mona Beth told her granddaughter, like she was the loneliest woman in the world. Upon hearing that question, Alaska knew that Mona Beth's dementia was getting worse. She felt terrible at the physical state her grandmother was in. Mona Beth was frail, she couldn't walk, and her ability to speak had significantly worsened in the past few years.

"Grandmother… I was here with you yesterday, and the day before that, and so on," Alaska said trying to remind and comfort her grandmother.

"Oh but of course, oh dear god," Mona Beth answered.

"Relax Grandmother, you need to rest," Alaska told her, and helped her lay down under her covers.

"Remind me, dear, why am I here?" Mona Beth said under the covers.

"Your conduct at handling my sister was dangerous and horrific," Alaska replied calmly.

"Your sister killed my son. Your mother made him disappear, I hadn't seen him in more than fifteen years. I was so heartbroken, and when he was finally back, your sister killed him. Because of Annabella's foolish choices," Mona Beth weakly said.

"Grandmother, your son was our father. Queen Annabella was our mother, we lived as a dysfunctional family for twenty-two years. You are right when you say that our mother was crazy and foolish. But you don't know your own son's wrongdoings as our father. I'm sorry to tell you but Dad was a coward. He didn't take care of us, he disappeared just when Mother was going through a difficult time," Alaska told her grandmother quickly.

Mona Beth had a blank look on her face, like she couldn't comprehend what was being said to her. Alaska gave her grandmother a kiss on the forehead.

"I have to go dear; I love you. Please promise me you will try to take care of yourself," Alaska said when she was about to leave the area. Mona Beth did not reply, still oblivious, and too surprised to say anything.

Alaska left soon after, no sound came out of that part of the dungeon. She spent the rest of the day caught up in her royal duties and taking care of her children and their children. She looked out the window of her room, admiring Winter Wonderland's recovery after the war ended in July 2007. The snow was back, most of the things had been rebuilt. The economy was growing. The recovery was still not complete, but it was a start. She admired how she had gotten rid of all of Winter Wonderland's old and terrible rules, like the child marriage rules, and the improper societal standards. Nobody in Winter Wonderland now got married under the age of twenty, from the beginning of her reign in 1995.

Alaska spent the rest of the day in peace. By the time she and Malcom went to bed, she had been thinking all day of her grandmother. She thought about visiting her the next day.

Winter Wonderland, Cataville, January 18th, 2019

Alaska found a servant maiden waking her up. These were Malcom's orders.

"My precious Queen, I have terrible news," the servant said. Alaska jumped out of bed.

"What happened?" Alaska panicked.

"Your husband Malcom ordered me to wake you up immediately. I'm very sorry to inform you that your grandmother Mona Beth has passed on," the servant said. Alaska screamed. Without getting dressed she ran out of her chambers and into the dungeon.

Alaska arrived at the dungeon; she went to the cell where her grandmother lay lifeless on the bed. The queen ran over to the bed, hugged her grandmother's body, and attempted to wake her. Mona Beth's body was ice cold, she had no sign of life.

Alaska broke down, all the regrets pouring out. Aside from her husband and children, Mona Beth was the last member of Alaska's family and childhood. Alaska was the only one left. Alaska kept on hugging her grandmother's body, she cried till she thought she would drown in her tears.

Hours later, the entire nobility were invited to the funeral, which had already been organized by noon. Alaska stood at a podium, Mona Beth lay in a closed coffin in front of it. Alaska's husband, children, and grandchildren were in the front row. The rest of the guests sat behind them. A feeling of desolation dominated the entire area. Alaska was to deliver her speech before Mona Beth's burial.

"Greetings women, men, lords, and ladies of Cataville. We are gathered here today for the memorial service of my grandmother Duchess Mona Beth of Central Cataville. Today we celebrate a remarkable woman, who is a testament to the real story of the entire royal family. Mona Beth was the mother of my father, Prince Maximus of Winter Wonderland. Like all of us, she had been through many problems and pains of her own. I would like the story of Mona Beth, just like all our stories, to be considered by all of us. The story of Mona Beth is one where we must all learn something. I speak on behalf of Mona Beth when I say that her final request was that everyone learned to accept and support one another. With my words I ask you to let go of all the principles and standards that harm one's life," Alaska read out her speech with tears in her eyes.

"My grandmother Mona Beth was born in February 1923. She had provided her services and change to the world during her long ninety-five years of life. She was the second longest living woman related to the royal family, after Winter Wonderland's first queen Eliana who lived to be ninety-eight.

Mona Beth was the widow of my grandfather Duke Marcellus of Center Cataville who died in 1982. Mona Beth's story, like many of ours, including my sister Princess Mildred, is a lesson to all of us, that we must not hold on to outdated beliefs and ideas because some of these beliefs might be hurting others or affect theirs and others' situations forever. My grandmother, as a duchess, wrote in her will that investments and awareness is to be raised regarding mental health. Mona Beth also wanted more education on the topic, and that was something my sister Princess Mildred was also desperate for and never received. Kind regards to all of you." Alaska finished her speech peacefully, hoping that her grandmother's last request, also Mildred's last requests as well as Annabella's, be taken into consideration, and that nobody else endures what they endured because of society ever again.

The shadow of regret and resentments inside of Alaska spoke on her behalf during the entire speech. Many of those who were close to Mona Beth went over to the casket to mourn and say their goodbyes.

It was time for the burial. It was peaceful but very depressing. Alaska made sure that Mona Beth was buried with the rest of the family, at the castle cemetery. Alaska accompanied her children and grandchildren, along with the guests, to the memorial dinner. The rest of the funeral went by, and everyone calmed down. There was nothing anyone could do, except honor Mona Beth and learn from her and the rest of the royals.

The funeral was over. The guests had all left, Alaska's children went with their families to their houses or to their parts the castle. Soon there was nobody left but Alaska, Malcom, and those who worked at the castle. It was nine p.m. The night was dark, the stars and moon were shining. That night, a calm mood was felt outside like the snow in Winter Wonderland. Alaska put on her black coat, and a brown cloak over it. The queen walked through the gardens; she couldn't stop moving. She knew about the change she wanted for her kingdom, she had learned from all of her relatives. Alaska was walking to the cemetery, just to say goodbye to those memories forever.

Alaska was soon at a little garden, a little garden that had many white plants as well as gravestones. There were about 15 gravestones, but Alaska focused on five. The first was of her maternal grandmother Anneliese, Alaska knew her grandmother

Anneliese's story, but she barely remembered her, she had died when Alaska was very young. She read the inscription engraved on Anneliese's grave, "A brave and noble queen with a tragic story, raised all of her children alone. July 23rd, 1928 – September 16th, 1978." As Alaska read the writing, she noticed that many of the royal women had lived the same lifestyle, and the one that stood out was even unluckier than the rest of her family.

Alaska turned her attention to the second newest grave in the garden. The grave was for Alaska's twin, Mildred. Even though Alaska read Mildred's inscription many times even though she was the one who had written it. "Princess Mildred felt unloved and was oppressed for long. Mother of a long-lost missing prince. A symbol for Winter Wonderland's judgmental society. January 2nd, 1974 – July 6th, 2007." Alaska read and couldn't help but feel the need to work on her kingdom. Alaska moved her head towards another one of these graves. Annabella's grave. She reread the grave's inscription, and felt that there was absolutely nothing good to say about most of these people's lives. That was something she hoped to change.

"A queen of Winter Wonderland, one of the most graceful women ever. Heavily influenced by unnecessary societal standards. Assassinated along with her ex-husband Maximus on the same day, March 3rd, 1955 – May 13th, 1995." Alaska read and felt great regret. She moved to the last grave, "Duchess Mona Beth of Central Cataville. Mother of Prince Consort Maximus. Lived ninety-five years. A bereaved woman. Early February 1923 – January 18th, 2019." Alaska read and couldn't help but go off to her new mission and create the best life possible for her people.